SO-AJL-923

SLIGHTLY ABOVE TIME

Mark Forti

with Dana Forti
& Camille Miller

Illustrated by Mark Forti

WATCHFUL DRAGON BOOKS
CALIFORNIA, USA

ISBN 978-0-9845099-0-4

Library of Congress Control Number: 2010925531

Printed in the United States of America
on recycled paper.

Visit www.SlightlyAboveTime.com

For Nathan & Daniel,
Sage & Brooke

Vermilion Desert

Thysperia

Loch Fae

Lake District

Scarring

Bramble Thickets

Bridge of Trees

Scarring

Lower Sylph Marshes

Upper Sylph Marshes

Alexa's Journey

Coldwater Camp (Cobbletons)

Faewick Forest

Kendlenook Village

Black Canyon Pass

Great Woblin Plains

Dragontooth Mountains

Birthing grounds

Dryad Bridge

Mangrove Delta

Alexa's Journey

Evernaught Creek

Oth Caves (Evernaught)

Maubulan (Romorian Complex)

Godrenmal Bog

White Mountains

Bristlecone Pines

Sea of Rema

Fool's Point

The Realm Slightly Above Time

Contents

"Life is at its heart a mystery. We can accept the mystery and live in wonder, or reject it and live in doubt and fear."

~Ispirianza, dryad of the Great Oak

Part 1:
The Mystery

ONE

A Day to Remember

*C*ven at the age of thirteen, Alexa remembered well the day she found out that humans don't really exist. Her sister Daria blurted it out when Alexa was just five years old. Alexa was crushed.

She had loved to sit around the evening fires and listen to the wonderful human tales that the dryad fairies told. Of course, most young fairy spritelings are relieved when they learn humans aren't real. Almost all human tales described the humans as a terrible but fantastical race of giant, wingless fairies that love to eat the flesh of chickens and rabbits—and they might just eat a fairy, too, if she didn't listen to her mother!

But the human tales Alexa loved most were those told by one particular old dryad named Ispirianza, the oldest of the Fae Folk in all of Faewick Forest. Ispirianza's stories weren't meant to frighten young ones. They described humans as marvelous and intelligent creatures who could construct great buildings and craft beautiful works of art. Ispirianza even said she'd once visited the human realm of Timefulness.

Alexa had always hoped that one day Ispirianza would take her to Timefulness so she could meet a real-live human and see a skyscraper. So when Daria told Alexa that all of the human tales were simply make-believe, Alexa tried hard not to listen.

"Grandmother," complained five-year-old Alexa. "Daria says that humans don't really exist."

"Daria!" scolded Grandmother. "You know how Alexa loves those stories. You should have let me explain the truth to her when she was ready."

"You mean it's true?" asked Alexa, her little voice cracking. "Humans are just make-believe?"

Grandmother sighed and glared at Daria.

"Well you see, Alexa," said Grandmother, kneeling down to Alexa's level. "There comes a time when a spriteling grows into a young fairy and she finds that some of the tales told to her aren't exactly true. These stories are told in a certain way so that young ones will remember the lessons they teach. Do you understand?"

"But Ispirianza says that humans are real," Alexa insisted. "She knows all about them. She even went to Timefulness once."

"Ha! That batty old dryad?" Daria said. Though only two years older than Alexa, Daria thought she knew everything. "She's told her stories so many times that she can't tell the difference between real and make-believe anymore. Everyone knows that her mind is as weak as her wings."

"Daria, please!" said Grandmother. "Alexa, dear, Ispirianza

is a very old dryad. Some say her tree has roots over 1,500 years old, and dryads are born with the tree they protect. In the old days, some fairies — how should I say this — some fairies used to believe in the old legends simply because they hadn't explored the world as completely as we have. But modern fairies, along with the other forest folk like the Romorians, have now studied the whole world. We now know that those legends are simply myths. So while Ispirianza is a very nice old dryad, we shouldn't believe everything she says. All right?"

"Oh, and one more thing," Daria said. "There's also no Wing Fairy who leaves you gifts after you grow your big wings."

"What?" Alexa cried, looking toward Grandmother.

"Daria, enough!" exclaimed the elder. "Fly to your room!"

Eight years later, Alexa still loved to stare into the fire and dream of unseen realms as Ispirianza told her tales — even if they weren't exactly true.

And while Alexa remembered well the day she lost her belief in humans, she would always remember even more vividly when she suddenly began to believe again. It all started when she brawled with that two-faced snob Tana at Flight School. Alexa had no idea that a schoolyard fight would change her life — and the lives of everyone she knew — forever.

TWO

The Flight Fight

"If you say one more word about my mother, you're gonna regret it," Alexa snapped at Tana, her wings twitching with anger.

"Then tell us why you lie about your age," taunted Tana. A shock tingled down Alexa's spine. Could Tana have found out? "You're not twelve like everyone else in our class, right, Alexa?" The gathering crowd of young fairies began to whisper. Most had finished their lunches and were curious to see how this was going to end. The massive tree branch on which they ate towered high above the forest floor.

"Tell them, Alexa—you're thirteen, aren't you?"

"But that's impossible," objected Tana's friend Lycinda. "No fairy could—"

"Oh, it's possible," said Tana. "My mother said… No, you tell the story, Alexa. It's really quite touching. Tell us why you're too ashamed to admit your real age."

"She's not ashamed of anything," said a new voice. Alexa's best friend, Kandra, pushed through the crowd to Alexa's side.

"Oh, no?" sneered Tana. She crossed her arms at Alexa. "So if I asked your mother how old you are, what would she say?"

"I'm warning you, Tana. No more about my mother," Alexa said, clenching her fingers together to keep from slapping the smirk off Tana's face.

"Okay, then let's talk about my mother," said Tana. "Do you know what birth elements my mother chose to put into my chrysalis when she brought me into the world? It's no accident that I'm the most beautiful and popular fairy in this school. My birth stone was a ruby, my birth flower was a rose and my birth feather was from a swan! Could any mother love her daughter more than to give her such glorious birth elements? So tell us about your birth elements, Alexa." Alexa's eyes darted away from Tana and the class.

"Hey, Tana," Kandra snapped back. "Which birth element made you such a two-faced, back-stabbing brat?" Laughter rippled through the onlookers. Tana's face flushed red.

"Hey, Kandra, how's it feel having a freak of nature as your only friend?" asked Tana. She threw her glare back at Alexa. "So Alexa, tell everyone what birth elements your mother put in your chrysalis again. I'm curious as to what made you so different from your beautiful sisters."

"I told you, not another word about my mother!" shouted Alexa.

"Do you really think you're worth such a sacrifice? I wonder what your sisters, Eva and Daria, think of what your mother did."

"That's it!" yelled Alexa. She flared her wings and darted straight for Tana. The crowd screamed and parted as Alexa grabbed a handful of Tana's hair and swept her off the tree branch. Tana clawed frantically at the air as the two fairies spiraled down toward the forest floor far below. Tana managed to grab Alexa's arm and drummed her wings skyward to avoid slamming into the ground.

Alexa tilted her front left wing and veered toward the stream. She had no trouble pulling the weaker Tana along with her. A good soaking would leave Tana's wings useless for a while. Being stuck on the ground for an hour or so would teach her to keep her mouth shut. Alexa dove for the water.

"Alexa, no!" yelled Kandra. By the time Alexa heard Kandra's screams it was too late. She felt her body shoved backward, and something sticky choked the breath from her neck. A massive spider web wrapped around her wings. Tana squirmed free, fell through the edge of the enormous web, and spun to the ground. Alexa had flown right through the center of a spider's lair and shredded most of its spiral structure.

She told her wings to beat but they could not obey — they were too tangled up in the sticky mats of web. She bounced a few times and dangled upside down by the last few threads, grasping at the strands around her neck.

"Alexa, stay still. Don't struggle!" someone yelled.

"No! Fight to get away! Don't just hang there," another called.

But Alexa could do little more than hang as the blood rushed to her head. The more she fought the webs, the more entangled she became. And her whole class was watching. How embarrassing.

Sweat beaded on her brow as Alexa strained to reach the strands around her feet. The web was simply wrapped too tightly for her to move much. Then a spine-chilling scream rang out from the class.

Alexa looked up in terror at the eight eyes and eight hairy legs of a giant weaver spider creeping toward her across the remains of its web. She flailed her arms and legs in desperation as the empty eyes moved ever closer. As she felt the needle-like grip of the spider's front legs close around her left foot, Alexa could see the spider draw its orange fangs wet with venom.

She quickly shifted her weight and kicked the spider's face with all of the strength she could muster. It swung back and forth on its thread but quickly snatched one of the strands Alexa was hanging from and regained its footing. Suddenly Alexa felt a jolt vibrate through the web. And another. And another.

The shaking wasn't the spider coming toward her but rather the snapping of web threads. Alexa glanced above to see Kandra hovering above them with a twig in her hands that she held like a sword.

"Hang on, Alexa," shouted Kandra above the shrieking students. "Get ready to fall." Kandra frantically hacked through each strand that held Alexa suspended. With one last jolt, Alexa felt the air rush around her as she plummeted to the forest floor. The wind in Alexa's ears grew louder and louder until she smacked into the ground. Her mouth gaped open as she tried desperately to breathe but couldn't. The spider scampered back up the web and took shelter under a tree branch.

After what seemed like forever, Alexa finally forced air into her lungs. No sooner had she drawn in two or three deep breaths than she felt a screaming Tana jump on her and start pulling her hair.

"You could have killed me, you swamprat!" Tana shouted as Alexa slapped back weakly. The students from the tree landed all around the two bedraggled fairies writhing on the ground. Then Alexa felt Tana's weight suddenly disappear. An older Lake Fairy stood holding Tana by the arm.

"A weaver spider that size could easily kill a young fairy!" the Lake Fairy scolded. "Explain yourselves." Alexa saw the special necklace she wore and realized that this must be the new school headmistress.

"Alexa attacked Tana for no reason," Lycinda volunteered.

"But Tana was saying cruel things to Alexa. Horrible things," said Kandra, defending her friend.

"What kind of things?" the headmistress asked.

"Tana just said that Alexa is really thirteen," said Lycinda. Tana glared at her.

"What a ridiculous thing to say," said the headmistress. "No fairy in all of Faewick or Thysperia could be thirteen. Pay more attention in your history lessons, Tana."

"But my mother says it's true," Tana insisted.

"Don't be silly." The headmistress clapped her hands and addressed the crowd of students. "Who can tell me what happened thirteen years ago?"

A small Forest Fairy with golden hair spoke up. "The great fire and drought, mistress. None of the chosen mothers made a chrysalis that year because they couldn't get birth elements."

"Very good."

Another classmate shot up her hand as she spoke up. "The land was barren of all flowers, and the Cobbletons were hoarding the gemstones. Also, a mother cannot protect a chrysalis without rain — it would use up too much of her own spirit."

"Well spoken," the headmistress said.

"But Kandra's mother told my mother that Alexa is thirteen," insisted Tana. "She said her mother put a pine needle in her chrysalis instead of a flower petal."

"A pine needle?" the headmistress laughed. "That's no proper birth element. A fairy couldn't possibly turn out normally with such an element in her chrysalis. Your mother is just telling you stories, Tana." Alexa looked at the ground.

"What does she claim that Alexa's mother used for a gemstone?" the headmistress continued, amused.

"A chunk of granite," said Tana, now sounding a little uncertain.

"Humph," said the headmistress. "Granite is not a gemstone at all — it's just a plain rock. Apologize to Alexa right now. And Alexa, you must learn to control your temper." Kandra put her hand on Alexa's shoulder as Alexa began to cry.

The headmistress must have seen something in Alexa's eyes because her expression changed. She asked wonderingly, "It's not true, is it? Are you really thirteen?"

Alexa tried to run, but the headmistress held on to her.

"Answer me."

Alexa nodded. She was tired of lying. Kandra gasped.

"I just don't understand," said the headmistress, shaking her head. "I remember that year well. Fairies young and old died from lack of water in my home village in Thysperia.

No mother could have even begun a chrysalis under such conditions. But one succeeded? I...I just don't see how she could have survived."

Alexa broke loose and ran into the forest, her flightless wings still covered in spider webs.

"Her mother didn't survive," said Kandra and took off after Alexa.

THREE

The Thing in the Mud

Five long days later, Alexa still couldn't fly even a wingbeat off of the ground. Grandmother had to soak her wings in nettle juice to get the webs off. And wings just don't work right for a while after a nettle soaking, so Alexa was completely grounded—a terrible fate for a fairy as restless and curious as Alexa.

Now curiosity can be particularly dangerous when mixed with boredom. It can make young fairies do dangerous things. Like walk into the forest—yes, walk! But if Alexa hadn't been walking that day, she might never have found that thing on the forest floor that no one had glimpsed for hundreds of years.

The cool moss tickled Alexa's bare feet as she walked. Mud squished up between her toes. The hem of her favorite green dress became soaked and heavy with mud as it dragged behind her on the ground. Grandmother would have been horrified at the sight. A light rain began to fall and the forest came alive with the sound of millions of tiny drops pattering on the leaves.

All Alexa had known her entire life were the trees, moss and water of Faewick Forest, but exploring from the ground was like seeing the world for the first time. So many surprises! Alexa found that if she poked a roly-poly bug, she could make it curl up into a big armored ball. She poked each roly-poly she saw along the way. It worked every time.

Since Alexa had never walked in the forest before, she did not know to watch her step. That's why she nearly broke her big toe when she tripped over something very hard and pointy hidden underneath a thick mat of moss.

"Fricketing swamprats!" She shrieked in pain and hopped around on one foot, never before having felt the pain of a stubbed toe. Then, as she knelt down to try to stop the blood pulsing from her muddy toenail, she discovered it.

Halfway buried in the squishy muck was a strangely shaped rock. Alexa wiped away the mud and moss to reveal a fancy but cracked stone carving. She shoved it aside and discovered another piece lying underneath. The two pieces were clearly part of something bigger. The fairies of Faewick Forest did not carve stone, nor did any other races she knew.

Alexa felt the stone pieces tingle magically in her hands. No, of course not. She must be imagining it.

On her hands and knees, she felt through the muck for more pieces. After several minutes, she ripped loose an enormous mat of moss and revealed something that made her jaw drop. A large ring of stone many times her own height was set into the hillside. Well, nearly a full ring — it was broken. At the top of the ring sat three carvings: a fairy, a dragon and — what was that? A wingless fairy?

She had decided to take the smallest piece to Ispirianza when an inspiration struck her. Alexa hauled the broken pieces over to the ring and fitted them into place to complete the stone circle.

A perfect fit! At that moment, the rain stopped. A warm breeze ruffled Alexa's hair. The very air had changed. It felt heavier. As the wind rustled the leaves on the ground, she could have sworn she heard eerie whispers right in her ear. Very faint, but definitely whispers. The kind of whispers that made the hair on the back of her neck prickle. Alexa looked around but saw no one. She felt the eerie presence of someone or something else near her. Her eyes searched the landscape, and she stilled her breathing so she could hear even the slightest sound. She waited.

CRACK! A loud noise like branches breaking came from the stone circle behind her. Startled, Alexa whipped around, eyes wide and palms sweaty. No more than two wingbeats away from her stood what looked like a gigantic foot, but it was covered with something smooth and white. Massive purple ropes laced and tied it together in a huge bow at the top. What on earth? Coming out of the top of the foot-like thing were what Alexa first thought were two tree trunks covered in a rough blue cloth.

Alexa's eyes traveled up and up until she saw a gigantic face. The creature was nearly the size of a tree! Fear and confusion pressed against the back of Alexa's head. The giant's long hair was not shiny bronze like Alexa's but brown like bark. Its skin was darker and not at all glittery like a fairy's. Despite these differences, the creature looked a lot like a fairy. Alexa sank deeper into the ferns and peeked through the leaves, terrified of being seen. She wondered if the thing could talk. She also cringed at the thought of it stepping on her.

The giant did not see Alexa. It looked confused, even lost. As the giant turned around, Alexa saw something even more amazing—the giant had no wings! Alexa's heart almost stopped. It couldn't be. It had to be.

A human!

FOUR

The Object Left Behind

lexa's mind began to spin. Her entire world was either coming apart or coming together. She couldn't tell which. Even Ispirianza never told of a human coming into the fairy world. According to the stories, humans were all stuck in the realm of Timefulness while fairies lived in the realm Slightly Above Time.

"Run!" she told herself. If the other dryad storytellers were right, the human might want to eat her. At this moment she could be sure of nothing.

But then Alexa looked up at the human's face again. To her surprise, the face appeared kind. It was young, pretty and seemed curious. In a strange way, the human seemed a lot like her.

When she leaned forward to get a better look at the human's clothes, Alexa lost her balance and crunched a dried leaf with her foot. Alexa squeezed her eyes shut and backed farther into the cover of the ferns. "Please don't let the human see me," she thought. But deeper down than thought, she did want the human to see her.

Alexa found the courage to open her eyes again. The human was looking down in the direction of Alexa's hiding place. It began to kneel down! Through the fern leaves, Alexa could see the face getting bigger and bigger. Any desire to let the human see her now fled from Alexa's mind. She grabbed some leaves to hide herself from the massive eyes.

But suddenly, as fast as Alexa could blink, a flash of light filled her eyes and a deafening SCHWOOP filled her ears. And just like that, the human was gone!

But as the human vanished, a very large, very mysterious and very shiny purple thing tumbled from the sky to land on the forest floor with a thud. Naturally, Alexa's curiosity got the best of her. Could the human have left something behind in the fairy realm?

Alexa scanned the landscape for danger. Nothing. She stepped cautiously out of the ferns. Still no one around. So she scrambled toward the purple thing that looked like a giant, shiny gemstone. She poked it with one finger, finding it cool and smooth. Nothing bad happened, so she put her palms against the side and pushed. The gemstone weighed a lot less than such a large stone should have, so Alexa wrestled it into the cover of the nearby ferns. Once she had it safely out of sight of any creature that might pass by, Alexa studied her new treasure.

On top of the gem was a clear square that looked like ice but wasn't cold. Many neatly arranged ovals covered the rest of the gem's surface. Each oval had a different symbol carved on it. Alexa had no idea what this thing could be, but she knew it must be very special, even magical. Perhaps it could cast spells on unsuspecting sisters.

After peeking out of the ferns once more to make sure the human hadn't come back, Alexa studied the gemstone to try to make out what the symbols meant. Losing her balance, she slipped on the slick surface and landed with her bottom slamming onto one of the ovals. Beeeeeeeep! Alexa felt like jumping out of her skin and into the leaves.

What was that sound? Could this be a musical instrument? Alexa couldn't even imagine what powerful magic could have made such a thing. She climbed onto the gem and tiptoed onto a different oval. Another beep. This time Alexa noticed a symbol appear on the ice window that matched the symbol on the oval she pushed. Ooh, fun! She stepped on another one. Another lower-pitched beep, another symbol, and then another. Soon Alexa was dancing all over the gemstone, playing a beepy little melody. What a wonderful, magical music maker!

The gemstone so delighted Alexa that she forgot where she was until she heard a rustling high in the trees. She immediately froze and struggled to listen. She hoped it wasn't a hawk or, worse yet, an Oth. An Oth would certainly capture and kill a grounded fairy. The noise of the music must have attracted someone—or something. She stayed still and quiet for a long time.

Suddenly, "DOO DOO DA DA DUM...!"

With eyes as wide as an owl's, Alexa whipped around to stare at the stone, which was screaming out music—terrible, ghastly music. Bright blue light flashed from the ice window.

The gemstone shook so hard it scooted across the forest floor as though trying to run away. Was it alive?

Afraid the screaming stone might attract things that eat fairies, Alexa sprang onto the gemstone, stomped on the ovals and pleaded, "Stop! Stop!" She happened to jump on the small green one under the window, and the stone fell silent. "Phew, I hope it never does that again," Alexa thought, looking herself over to make sure the thing hadn't jinxed her in some way. Then, quiet as a cat, Alexa crept across the damp leaves and looked out from underneath the ferns to see if anyone had come to investigate the noise.

That's when Alexa heard it. A strange, muffled voice came from right behind her.

"Hello, is anyone there?" asked the distant voice. Alexa spun around but couldn't see anyone. Was it another fairy? An Oth? A Romorian? At first, Alexa thought the voice came from inside the purple gemstone, but that was ridiculous. Then she heard the voice again. Crazy. It was definitely coming from the gemstone. How could anyone fit inside it?

She tried to figure out how to open it to let the voice out. She hit some rectangles on the side, but the voice just got louder. Maybe, just maybe, the gemstone itself was speaking.

A Magical Musical Speaking Stone! Could humans possibly conjure up such spectacular magic?

"I know you're there, because you answered my phone," the gemstone said. "Say something." Alexa looked around again, but no one else was there. Could the stone be speaking to her?

"Um, hello?" Alexa said.

"Oh, thanks a million for finding my phone. I thought for

sure I lost it in the woods," the voice said. It sounded friendly enough, but Alexa didn't trust a voice without a face. "Just tell me where you live," the voice continued, "and I'll come over. You've saved me from getting grounded again."

"You've been grounded, too?" Alexa asked. Maybe it was the voice of a fairy.

"Who hasn't? Now where do you live?"

Alexa felt a little silly talking to a purple gem. "I live in Kendlenook Village in Faewick Forest."

"Faewick, hmm. Is that north of the freeway? Tell me the address and I'll Google it."

"Google the forest?" Maybe the voice wasn't so friendly after all.

"Just tell me the address before my dad kills me." The gemstone started to sound impatient.

"Address? I don't know what you mean." Alexa now knew she wasn't talking to a fairy, since fairies don't have fathers — let alone murderous ones.

"Very funny. Just tell me where you are."

Alexa looked around. "I'm in the same place you are, of course." The voice made an annoyed sigh, so Alexa shrugged and decided to play along. "I'm under a large maple tree with a big knot on the trunk and a black twisted branch that got struck by lightning. There are ferns all around the bottom."

"Hey, I know that tree! That's in the woods behind my house. So I did drop my phone out there. I'll bet it was when I tripped over that crumbly ring of rocks." The voice paused. "Listen, I'm not supposed to go to the woods by myself so it would be great if you didn't tell my dad. Can you stay there while I come and get it? I'm on my brother's cell phone right now. It'll just take me a few minutes to run over."

"Okay, I guess so," said Alexa. She wondered what her grandmother would say if she heard Alexa talking to a Magical Musical Speaking Stone. She had to ask the voice an important question. "You don't happen to be really, really tall, do you?" Alexa asked.

"Tall?" the stone laughed. "No, I'm the second-shortest girl in the seventh grade. I'm twelve. How old are you?"

"I'm thirteen," Alexa replied. "I'm not even allowed to go to the meadow by myself yet. But next year I start my apprenticeship."

"I know how you feel. My dad treats me like a baby," the voice said. "He won't let me ride my bike to school by myself, and I can't even go to the mall without someone's mom tagging along."

Mall? Bike? What was this voice talking about? Alexa could tell by the footsteps in the background that the owner of the voice was now walking over dry, crunchy leaves. Guess she isn't inside the stone after all, Alexa thought. The voice continued, "By the way, I'm Elsie."

"My name is Alexa. I'm of the Meadow. What kind of fairy are you?"

"Fairy? Yeah right," said Elsie. "Okay. I'm at the maple tree now." A pause. "Where are you, crazy fairy girl?"

Alexa looked all around the tree. Nothing. "Well you're not near my tree. Mine has two big boulders next to it."

"Well, I wouldn't exactly call them boulders, but they're the biggest rocks around," said Elsie. "I'm standing right in front of them. There's a centipede crawling on top of the bigger one."

Alexa was confused. "I see it, too. Your Magical Musical Speaking Stone and I are sitting on the ground right next to that centipede."

"Come on, I'm not dumb. As soon as I said centipede, you said centipede. If this is a joke, it's not funny. It's just immature. Are you one of my brother's friends?"

Alexa's brain froze.

"Okay, if you really are right next to the centipede, then take a photo of it and send it to me," challenged Elsie.

"Um, I, well..." said a confused Alexa.

"What, fairies don't know how to use a cell-phone camera?" The voice started talking slowly as if to a very young spriteling. "Turn the back of the phone — I'm sorry, the 'Magical Musical Speaking Stone' — toward the centipede and press the button with the circle in the rectangle twice. Then press the top right button — that's programmed for my brother's phone — and then press the green button to send it. Then when I don't get a picture of the centipede, you'll be busted, Little Miss Meadow Fairy!"

Alexa couldn't begin to imagine where this conversation was going, but she followed Elsie's instructions anyway. She assumed the ovals were what Elsie called "buttons" of the "phone." She shoved at the stone until it flipped over and then struggled to keep it standing up. Once Alexa beeped the "circle-in-the-rectangle" button, the centipede appeared on the screen like magic. Astounding! It was smaller than before, but it was crawling around and looked exactly the same. She pushed the other buttons just like Elsie said, and a big check appeared on the screen. Alexa waited. "Elsie?"

After a few long seconds, a confused and frightened voice

answered her. "What the....? I don't believe it! Okay, you're really freaking me out now. This is not funny. You win, okay? Just stop now. Where are you really? And who are you?" Elsie's voice became serious, and she sounded scared. "You really are here with me, aren't you?"

"I think so, but I can't see you anywhere," replied Alexa. "You're invisible."

"No, I'm not. You're invisible. But you can't be. Are...are you really a...a...fairy?"

"That's what I've been telling you," said Alexa. It was her turn to be annoyed.

FIVE

The Trouble with Dragons

Once they got over not believing in each other, Elsie and Alexa talked excitedly until the sun hung low in the sky. To live side by side in different realms — incredible! Also, Alexa now knew that her new friend would never want to eat her, so any fear she had of this human vanished.

Although Alexa could have talked with Elsie for days, thoughts of Grandmother finally forced her to turn toward home.

After they said goodbye, the stone went to sleep, silent and dark.

The strange and wonderful conversation flew around in Alexa's head. There were so many questions she wanted to ask Elsie now that she'd calmed down and her mind was sort of working again.

She wanted to know so many things. What is a freeway?

A bike? A mall? Did humans tell scary fairy tales to keep their children from wandering in the woods at night? Alexa wondered if Elsie knew a different meaning of the word "google" other than "to spray something with bog goop."

However, Alexa knew one thing for sure: She would get bathroom-cleaning duty for another two weeks if Grandmother found her on foot in the woods. Alexa couldn't even guess the punishment Grandmother would give her if she knew Alexa had seen and talked to a human. Not that Grandmother actually believed in humans.

It was slow going on foot. From the ground, Alexa found it hard to remember the way back home. With every step it seemed she was getting more and more lost. If only she could get some height.

Then a strange warm wind began to rustle the leaves. Alexa heard faint, dark whispers. Or was it just the wind? As the breeze grew louder, so did the whispers. Alexa's blood grew cold.

"Elsie?" she asked the wind. It didn't answer. The leaves rustled once more. The whispers rose with it. Then all of the whispers eerily joined into one voice. Soft but now clear — and frightening.

"Come to me," the whisper spoke right into Alexa's ears. The strange low voice was definitely not Elsie's. It was as deep as the roaring of a distant waterfall. Alexa felt suddenly and helplessly alone in the presence of the faceless voice.

"Who is that?" she cried.

"Give me your hands..." the hollow whisper drifted through Alexa on the wind.

"Where are you?" Alexa asked in a quivering voice.

"I'm waiting for you here," it hissed. "You have awakened my voice...." Alexa frantically looked around. Nothing but trees, rocks and moss. The leaves calmed. As the wind died down, Alexa ran.

She ran as fast as she could and hoped the voice wouldn't follow. She gasped her relief when she caught a glimpse of the Great Oak. And a few hundred wingbeats away from there — home!

As her tree home came into view, Alexa could see the smoke billowing from the chimney atop the steep roofs covered with moss and lichen. Could someone already be home? Then she caught sight of Grandmother and her oldest sister, Eva, flitting toward the front door, their wings glinting in the now blazing sunset. Grandmother's council meeting must be finished. Grandmother was a member of the Intercultural Council of Forest Folk, headed by the High Fairy herself. Eva was always at Grandmother's side these days.

"Grandmother will kill me if she finds out I've been out on foot," Alexa thought, forgetting about the mysterious whispers.

If Alexa could have flown, she would have easily made it through her upstairs bedroom window before the others reached home. Now they would definitely see her returning. She would have to rely on her ability to bend time. She concentrated hard and bent time so that she could move faster, while Grandmother and Eva would seem to fly slower. Had anyone seen her, it would have looked like Alexa was moving twice as fast as usual.

Luckily the thick bark that formed the outside of the house had enough handholds to climb up to her bedroom window without having to fly. Alexa tumbled through the window without even bowing to the tree. It was very rude to go inside any tree without a proper bow — especially the sort of tree in which a fairy lives — but Alexa didn't have time. She could apologize to the tree later. She barely made it. Almost immediately, Grandmother's shrill voice called up to her.

"Alexa! Get down here right away!"

Uh, oh. Did Grandmother know she had gone out? Alexa sprinted for the stairs, then stopped and turned back when she caught sight of herself in the mirror.

"Coming!" she yelled. Alexa splashed water on her mud-streaked face, hands and wings at a washbasin made from a hollow acorn shell. Then she stuffed her dirty dress under the bed and threw on a clean dry one. Alexa tied her sash as she tripped awkwardly down the staircase. She again wondered why fairies bothered to build stairs in their homes. Grandmother had once told her that stairs were a quaint tradition from some historic time. Whatever. They came in handy for grounded fairies, though.

As she entered the sitting room, Alexa lowered her wings as all well-mannered fairies do when greeting elder fairies. Daria and Eva came out of the kitchen. Eva looked at Alexa and shook her head silently.

Grandmother stood with crossed arms and a grimacing face. She was a gray-haired, tough-minded, heavy-handed fairy who didn't think life should be taken lightly. She wore an old-fashioned dress that was spotlessly clean, plain and sensible. Her hair was drawn up in a bun as tight as her spending habits.

Alexa's house (her room is top left)

Alexa began forming her strategy. When had Daria arrived home? Had she told on her? But Daria usually covered for Alexa. Eva must be the snitch.

"Alexa, look at these curtains," Grandmother demanded. Her green eyes flashed. "Burn marks all the way up to the rods! You didn't brush Snarfle's tongue today, did you? I have half a mind to take that flea-bitten dragon back to the breeder if you're going to neglect him like this."

"I thought I had brushed it," Alexa said.

Grandmother lifted a silvery eyebrow. "Putting up with that dragon has grayed my last golden hair." Snarfle lurked in the corner with his long spiky tail between his scaly legs. He seemed to know he was in trouble. "Alexa, you promised when I let you bring that creature home that you would clip his nails every month and brush his tongue every week. Even a tiny dragon with an unbrushed tongue can burn down a house. You know this. I don't care if he is a pure-bred dwarf flitter dragon—fire is fire!"

Alexa complained, "Now that Eva and Daria are always away, I get stuck doing all the work around here. Daria was the one who really wanted Snarfle." Daria gave Alexa a glare and her 'I-could-have-told-Grandmother-on-you' look. Alexa realized that blaming Daria for anything right now was a bad idea. "Why is everything always my fault?" Alexa's wings flared up in frustration.

"Don't you raise your wings at me," Grandmother said. "Eva and Daria have responsibilities much more important than brushing dragon tongues. You'll realize that when you're a little older. Now get that thing out of here." Grandmother shook her head. "I thought I might let you go to the festival tomorrow evening, but now I've gone and changed my mind. That's what I've done."

Alexa's heart broke. Missing the Summer Storytellers' Festival was a punishment much worse than grounding. A choir from Thysperia was going to perform, and Ispirianza would be there. Alexa just had to ask her about humans.

"Grandmother," she began in her most sincere and polite voice, her wings lowered to the floor. "I'm sorry I forgot to brush the dragon's tongue. I promise to remember next time, really. About the festival...."

"Absolutely not. There will be another festival in the fall — if you can manage to stay out of trouble for three whole moon cycles, that is."

"Yes, Grandmother," Alexa sighed. Fall seemed a lifetime away. She took the firepaste and tongue brush from the cabinet. On seeing this, Snarfle bolted for the dragon door. Unfortunately for him, Grandmother had already hooked the door latch, so Snarfle bonked his little horns straight into solid wood. He shrank into the nearest corner and tried to look invisible. Alexa held back a laugh in spite of her anger. Flitter dragons were so cute the way they thought no one could see them if they just hid their heads. Alexa grabbed Snarfle by the scruff of his neck and dragged him out to the back aviary.

"Now hold still," Alexa snapped. Snarfle wriggled his head back and forth as Alexa forced his mouth open. She began to scrape his tongue but paused when she overheard Eva and Grandmother talking in the kitchen.

"Oh, please, Grandmother, you have to let Alexa go," Eva was pleading. "Tomorrow night I will herd sylphs for the first time in front of the entire village. I would love to have my whole family there." Eva had been rehearsing for months with the master sylph herders. Properly herded through the air, a gathering of thousands of tiny sylph sprites created the wind currents that powered the reeds and other wind instruments of the Lake Fairies' orchestra. Tomorrow, they planned to herd three entire gatherings of sylphs.

"Besides," continued Eva, "What would the other council members say if Alexa weren't present to support her own sister?" Alexa began to feel hopeful. No one could get her way with Grandmother like Eva.

Grandmother sighed, "I suppose I'll have to let her go. It just wouldn't look right if she didn't."

Alexa forgot she wasn't supposed to be listening and leaped through the back door. She gave Grandmother a big hug. "Oh thank you, thank you! I promise I won't get into any more trouble." Snarfle followed Alexa inside. He jumped around, huffing minty puffs of smoke in the midst of all of the excitement.

"Yes, yes. Now please let go of me, you're bending my wings," Grandmother snapped, not quite hiding a smile. Alexa skipped outside with Snarfle trailing behind and brushed the little dragon's tongue until it shone.

SIX

Goric the Romorian

A short while later, Alexa heard a pounding on the front door. Grandmother looked at Eva, who shook her head. She then looked at Daria and Alexa, who simply looked at each other. No one knew who might be coming to visit after dark. Proper fairies simply didn't do such things. For some reason, Alexa thought of the dark whisperer.

Grandmother pressed her ear to the wood. "Who is it?" she asked the door. A low muffled voice answered.

"Hello, Gresha. This is Goric. Sorry to disturb you at your home after dark, but we have a matter of life and death to discuss. May we come in?" Grandmother immediately opened the door to reveal Goric the Romorian, a lanky, bearded ground dweller with beady eyes under bushy eyebrows. An untidy pile of scrolls and maps was stuffed under his arm.

"Good evening, Goric," Grandmother said. "Please come in. You'll have to excuse the mess." The room was spotless as usual.

Goric politely lowered his hood as he entered. Two more Romorians with brown, shaggy cloaks followed, nodding respectfully to Grandmother. They carried strange-looking instruments made of wood that Alexa had always imagined could make gold out of sand. She had no clue what they really were.

Romorians were respected as the most intelligent race of the forest and often reminded others of that fact. Alexa had always felt that their oversized noses and goat-like beards made them look more silly than intelligent. They did invent marvelous machines at which all the other forest folk marveled. Goric traveled around in a wooden wagon that seemed to run under its own power. It was months before the fairies and Cobbletons figured out the wagon's secret: rats running inside each of the wagon's six wheels. Alexa wondered with a smile what the Romorians would make of Elsie's Magical Speaking Gemstone.

Grandmother folded her wings and sat on the armchair at the head of the table. "Please begin."

Goric's eyes darted nervously toward Alexa, then Daria and Eva. "It might be best if we could have a word without the young ones around."

"Certainly, Goric. If you feel it's necessary," Grandmother hesitated. "However, I am grooming Eva to take over my seat on the council. She is seventeen now and shows such maturity."

"Eva may stay, Gresha, if you can trust her with a great secret. We don't wish to cause panic among the fairies."

Goric the Romorian

"Of course," said a concerned Grandmother. "Alexa, Daria—could you retire to your rooms please."

"Yes, Grandmother," they said in unison. The two sisters lowered their wings to the visitors and dutifully started up the stairs. Daria stopped and sat on a step just out of sight of the parlor but where she could still hear the conversation. What a sneak. Alexa sat next to her. Daria began to crack her knuckles.

"Daria, stop that," whispered Alexa. "That sounds disgusting."

"Shhh," answered Daria, still cracking her knuckles. "I'm trying to listen."

"Now I don't expect fairies to fully understand our scientific findings," began Goric. Romorians always talked down to all the other races, and they could never explain anything without a long speech. "I know the fairies are simple folk, but bear with me and try to follow."

"I'll do my very best," said Grandmother, doing her very best to hide her anger at the insult. Grandmother was probably the most intelligent fairy on the council.

Goric took a deep breath. "I am just going to come right out and say it. There's no easy way to break this news. A group of my best underlings has just returned from a scientific trip to the Lower Sylph Marshes." Alexa could hear the crinkly unraveling of maps on the table. "Now don't get too emotional, but…it's started again. And it's only getting worse."

"Explain yourself, please," said Grandmother. Goric lowered his voice to a whisper just below Alexa's hearing.

"What did he say?" whispered Alexa to Daria.

"Shhh, I can't hear," Daria whispered back.

"Mercy, no!" Eva exclaimed. "Not the Scarring! Are you certain?" Alexa felt the hairs on her arms stand on end at the sound of that word. She and Daria looked at each other with wide eyes.

"Positive," replied Goric. "It spread to upper Faewick and has destroyed three dryad trees. It's moving toward the village of Coldwater."

"My word, is it as bad as that?" Grandmother gasped. "Do we know any of the dryads who died?" The lives of dryad fairies are tied to their trees; if a dryad tree dies, its dryad perishes as well.

"The names of the dead are Fiorana, Violanza and Rosandria," Goric said grimly.

"I don't recognize those names," said Grandmother. "The Lower Sylph Marshes are quite a distance from here." Grandmother got up from her chair and started pacing. "Do the Romorians have any new ideas on what's behind this terror?"

"Some very interesting theories have just come to light," Goric said. "I needn't go into them now. You ladies wouldn't understand."

"Do you think it destroyed any fairy villages?" whispered Alexa to Daria. "Why has the Scarring started again?"

"How should I know? Quiet," Daria whispered back.

Of course, nobody knew why the earth became Scarred in the first place. The Scarring was a deep and terrible hole that crept across the earth, split the land and left it black, barren and lifeless. It destroyed everything in its path. No trees or plants could ever grow on the Scarred land.

None of the forest creatures could cross over the Scarred

places. Any fairy who tried to fly over was overcome with despair and fell helplessly to the ground. Once a fairy had fallen, the desolate earth would claim the unfortunate soul. No one understood the source of this evil magic.

The holes grew wider and wider with the passing of time, until Faewick Forest became like an island with the Sea of Remal to the west and the black, smoldering Scarring on all other sides. Only the narrow Bridge of Trees connected Faewick Forest to the Lake Lands and Thysperia.

"Could it come to Kendlenook village?" Grandmother asked. "Will it threaten the Bridge of Trees?"

"No, no—look at the map," said an irritated Goric. "It moves toward Coldwater. The Bridge of Trees is safe enough. You fairies worry so much about the Bridge of Trees." Alexa didn't like Goric talking to her grandmother as if she were a spriteling.

"Goric, may I remind you," said Grandmother, "that the very survival of the fairies depends on the Bridge of Trees? We need the brambles that grow on the other side of the bridge." She pointed to the bramble thickets on the map. "Bramble nectar is needed to hatch fairy spritelings. Without it, no fairy babies could ever be born!"

"Fine then, Gresha," Goric shot back, walking his fingers across the bridge on the map. "Just move your village over the bridge near the bramble thickets and be done with it."

"The council has explained this to you before," Grandmother said, slapping her fingers on the village side of the bridge. "We need the birthing grounds just as much as bramble nectar."

Goric pressed a finger to the side of his neck. "I can already feel my blood pressure rising. This always happens when I have to deal with fairies." The long-nosed Romorian took a deep breath. "So you can't birth fairies near the bramble thickets? If you focused your minds on the problem, you could find a way."

"Why do such intelligent creatures find this so difficult to understand?" Grandmother demanded, her voice rising in pitch. "Only the birthing grounds on our side of the bridge have the exact temperature and humidity to birth spritelings. The fairies that live in Thysperia—on the other side of the bridge—come to our side to give birth. The bridge means life itself to the Fae."

"Do you see, Morten?" Goric said to one of the two Romorians who stood silently behind his chair. "I told you they'd get overly emotional." Then he turned toward Grandmother again. "You needn't worry about your precious bridge. All our tests indicate the Scarring won't approach Kendlenook for many, many years."

Grandmother breathed a sigh of relief.

"But we do need your help in convincing the fairy council to help us Romorians stop the Scarring," Goric continued.

"You've found a way to stop it?" Eva asked. Grandmother shushed her.

"We think so, but it will involve a lot of work," said Goric. "That's why we need you to go to the council."

"Tell me," Grandmother said.

"Well, we have applied many scientific tests to the Scarred land and observed its edges," Goric said, making a sweeping gesture over the map. "The soil at the edge loses large amounts of water, crumbles and then falls inward. If we construct a wall to keep the water in the soil, this should contain the Scarring."

"I don't know, Goric," said Grandmother. "There's something spiritually unsettling about the Scarring. It's as if a dark presence forces itself across the land, destroying all in its shadow. I'm not sure a mere wall can stop it."

"Enough superstition," Goric said. "This is science. We've done the tests and it will work. If the fairies had their way they would all hold hands and just sing to the Scarring and hope it goes away."

"That's not a bad idea, Goric," Grandmother said, with a wink at Eva. "I'll send the choir out tomorrow."

"Be serious, please," Goric said. "We need to begin construction on that wall."

"Well, I don't suppose we have any better ideas under consideration," said Grandmother. "And you say we have plenty of time?"

"Years and years," assured Goric. "But we Romorians think it intelligent to begin construction now."

"I agree," said Grandmother. "You'll have my support with the council."

"Thank you," Goric said. "You won't regret it."

SEVEN

Diving Diva

Alexa awoke the next morning with her wings back to normal. After a few test flaps, she leaped out of her bedroom window and felt the freedom of cool wind on her wings. Perfect! Just in time for her advanced aerodynamics class at Flight School. Stunt flying was Alexa's best subject by far. She didn't even have to study.

Today's class was titled "Bi-winged Airflow in Regions of Dynamic Instability." Alexa couldn't believe the way her teacher made a subject as exciting as aerodynamics sound so boring. It seemed to Alexa that the instructor thought almost everything about flying was dangerous. She always told stories of famous flight disasters and made up endless rules beginning with "Never" or "Do not."

Today they were learning about dives caused by a "stall." Alexa knew it by heart: If a fairy's wings tilt too far up in the wind, the wings would stall and make the fairy fall. As

Instructor Thulma told the class, "Crashes caused by wing stalls are the number one cause of flight injuries among fairies. Remember: Dives are dangerous! Don't ever stall your wings on purpose without a trained instructor present." Alexa giggled as she saw Kandra's head nod sleepily. She nudged her friend awake.

The class filed outside to the tree school's main branch to watch the demonstration of how to pull out of a dive caused by a stall. Instructor Thulma flew up several tree heights and stalled her left front wing on purpose. She fell, spinning rapidly downward. She pulled up gracefully about one tree height above the ground and told the class to do the same. As she explained, "If you find yourself in a spin caused by a wing stall, the only way to pull up is to tilt the wings down in the direction of the fall, and only after that, flap your wings to pull up. Never try to tilt your wings up. And never spin faster than necessary."

Alexa raised her hand but didn't wait for the teacher to notice. She blurted out, "But your method makes you fall faster before you pull up, so it's dangerous if you aren't high enough."

Instructor Thulma glared at Alexa. "Oh, child, you have much to learn. I think that you'll find that my way is the only way a fairy can pull out of such a dive."

Once the teacher turned away, Alexa looked at Kandra and rolled her eyes. This was a total waste of time.

The students formed a line and performed the move one by one. Alexa raised her hand again and explained her idea for a better way to pull out of the spin.

Instructor Thulma said that it couldn't work, adding,

"Never take flying advice from a fairy who got herself caught in a weaver spider's web." Alexa's face flushed, and the class laughed.

Once Alexa got to the front of the line, she winked at Kandra and took off. She flew to the right height and stalled a wing. The forest blurred as she dove and spun faster and faster. Then Alexa did the opposite of what Instructor Thulma had done: She tilted her wings further into the spin, making her spin even faster.

The other students gasped as Alexa fell, spinning through a gap in the tree canopy. The wind blasted around her ears, and she was going much too fast to get out of the spin the instructor's way. She couldn't flap her wings strongly enough to break the fall.

Thulma shouted for Alexa to stop and zoomed as fast as she could toward her plummeting student. "No! You'll crash!" she yelled.

Alexa barreled straight toward the school tree. One or two seconds before she hit the branch, she reversed the angles of her wings, so that they were now pointing up, one tilted to the right and one to the left. Her fast spin provided the wings with enough air speed to produce lift. She used all her strength to hold her wings level. It was working! She started to slow down, but it wasn't near enough, and Alexa knew it.

She could barely hear the screams of her classmates over the howling wind in her ears. Alexa tucked her arms to her chest and closed her eyes. She felt her feet touch solid wood and, to everyone's amazement, it wasn't even a hard landing. The class stood silent for a few seconds and then started cheering.

"See, tucking your arms in makes you spin faster," Alexa

explained, trying to keep her voice steady. "And the faster spin created more lift—I call it the Maple Seed Stop." Still dizzy with victory, she half ran, half flew toward her place next to Kandra. Alexa knew she'd get the highest marks for her move, especially since the instructor hadn't ever seen it before. But Instructor Thulma landed forcefully on the branch directly in Alexa's path.

"Young fairy, you've just earned yourself two hours' detention after school. I should clip your wings after that stunt!" Alexa tried to speak, but Instructor Thulma continued yelling. Alexa was in shock at the unfairness of it all.

Later, as she sat quietly in detention at the roots of the school tree, Alexa's thoughts once again flew to Elsie and the Speaking Stone. She couldn't wait to talk to Ispirianza about it tonight at the festival—that is, if Grandmother didn't find out about her detention.

EIGHT

Festival

When Alexa got home, Grandmother was too busy with last-minute preparations for the festival to even notice Alexa, much less hear about her detention. All three sisters spent most of the afternoon fluffing their best dresses and braiding their hair in preparation for the night's festivities. Alexa wore her favorite pearl choker.

Once they looked their very best, Alexa and Daria glided excitedly toward the festival grounds amid the early evening chorus of chirping frogs while Eva soared ahead.

Alexa didn't mean to ask the question, but it blurted from her mouth. "Daria, one of my friends said she saw a human in the woods. That's pretty silly, isn't it?"

"Not at all. I saw one yesterday," said Daria. "It had purple spotted skin and danced on its head while roasting a tasty fairy stew. Then I jumped through the Glass Corridor into Timefulness, where the ferns talk and rabbits make animal sculptures out of ice." Alexa fake-laughed as if she'd meant her question as a joke. Daria didn't look fooled.

Eva seemed to pay no attention as she danced through the air ahead of her sisters, practicing the complicated arm movements of her sylph herding routine. Eva was so beautiful that she made everything around her beautiful as well. If she were to hold a toad in her hand, it would look like the most exquisite creature in the land. Mothers would sometimes ask Eva to kiss their daughters' chrysalises so their spritelings might have some of Eva's beauty. Alexa sighed. Although the entire village said all three sisters looked alike, Alexa knew everyone secretly thought that Eva was the prettiest with Daria a close second. "Cute" was the word used most often to describe Alexa. She hated that word "cute." It seemed just one step above ugly.

Alexa smoothed her hair with her fingers. She thought her hair was her worst feature. She could overlook the fact that her skin wasn't as sparkly as Eva's and that her wings were shorter than Daria's, but she hated that her hair didn't shine as brightly. She also hated that she was the kind of fairy who cared about hair.

Alexa also didn't have a fancy job like her sisters. Daria now worked full time in the forests as a translator to the animals. Eva, of course, had the usual Lake Fairy duties, plus sylph herding and council work. Alexa couldn't even go into the meadow without holding the hands of twenty other fairies, all younger than her.

"Don't you mind Daria," Eva told Alexa. "You can believe in humans for however long you want. I loved those stories too, when I was a spriteling." Alexa ground her teeth. She preferred Daria's insults to Eva's encouragement.

As they approached the amphitheater near the base of the Great Oak, Alexa could see thousands of lights flickering through the tangle of branches. The sounds of chattering fairies and fluttering wings grew louder and louder. Low-pitched Romorian voices broke through the noise. Cobbleton children raced each other on the dirt road below.

The woods opened up into a glorious clearing outlined with torches. Swarms of fireflies lit up the bordering trees. Hundreds and hundreds of viewing boxes surrounded the clearing from the ground almost to the tops of the trees.

"I'm off," chirped Eva. "Wish me luck!" With a quick wave, Eva whooshed behind the stage and out of sight.

A feast of sights, sounds and smells flooded Alexa's senses. Every intelligent race in the forest was present. The Cobbletons and Romorians — the non-flying forest folk — swarmed over the ground like ants. The Fae — all of the flighted forest races including fairies, dryads and sylphs — cluttered the air.

The Romorian professors stood in groups, discussing the latest scientific news, all of them trying to talk at once and no one really listening to the others. The squirrelish Cobbletons had set up booths at the edge of the amphitheater. They sold anything and everything: jewelry, homing charms, wing sleeves, lighting wands, signaling silks, headbands and special lotions to make wings shine. Traders stood in front of their booths, shouting to all passersby. The Romorians looked down on the Cobbleton craftsmen as simple-minded. The Cobbletons, in their humility, agreed with them.

Quint, a Cobbleton of the forest

The largest crowds gathered around the steaming food tents. Cooks stirred fried vegetables in pans of hissing oil. The smells of hot honey cakes and spicy sevenberry cordial filled the crisp evening air. For just eight red beads each, Daria and Alexa bought two little lighting wands that only stayed lit for a night. They weren't good for much more than drawing in the air, but when all the young fairies in the forest lit them on a night like tonight, the trees sparkled with a golden glow.

The entire forest bustled with excitement. The sylphs — tiny wind sprites — gathered by the thousands and swooshed high above the trees, stirring up a cool breeze. Even the owls and the rabbits couldn't resist taking a sniff and a peek from their nests and burrows. Little furry heads popped out of every hole in sight.

Mother fairies flew with their spriteling daughters clutched in their arms. The smallest ones begged to stop at the wing painting booths. Alexa caught the eye of one adorable spriteling in a puffy yellow dress and waved at her. The spriteling smiled shyly and hid her face against her mother's shoulder.

Cobbleton children gathered around the bonfires, trying to catch a glimpse of the Shadow Fairies dancing in the fire glow. They screamed with delight when the shadowy sprites zoomed past.

All of the big festivals took place at the Great Oak because it was close to most of the dryad trees in Kendlenook. As everybody knows, a dryad must always stay in sight of the tree she protects. Seven dryads, including Alexa's beloved Ispirianza, lived close enough to attend the festival. Dryads live as long as their trees — often for hundreds of years — so they always had the most and best stories to tell.

Daria fluttered off and returned with two blackberry sandwiches dripping with sweet sauce. She handed one to Alexa.

"Thanks," said Alexa, biting into it. "And thanks for not telling on me to Grandmother yesterday." Just for fun, Alexa bent time a little so that it looked to Daria as if Alexa ate her entire sandwich in two seconds.

"Show off," said Daria. Alexa laughed hysterically. Of course, all fairies had the ability to bend time as it suited them, but Alexa was particularly good at it. She supposed it was the only useful skill she really had, that and stunt flying.

Soon Alexa felt a rush of air as a young fairy swooped down and made a graceful landing next to her. Alexa turned to see Kandra, in her usual state of overexcitement. She had a torch in one hand and a bag of beads in the other.

"Did you see? Did you see? The new fall sashes are in! Quint the Cobbleton has all the latest in Meadow Fairy colors," Kandra jabbered. Before Alexa could say a word, Kandra pumped her wings and yanked Alexa's arm skyward.

"I don't have any beads," Alexa said. "Grandmother took away my allowance for a month because of the fight."

Then the whiny voice of Tana came from right behind the two fairies. "Hey, Alexa, my sister paid you a nice compliment tonight. She said you're awfully brave to come to a festival without wearing any wing glitter." Tana knew very well Alexa's grandmother believed that young fairies shouldn't wear wing glitter until they were at least sixteen. "But I told my sister that the plain look really works for you."

"Wow, Tana, how nice of you to defend me," Alexa said.

"You know, I would wear wing glitter all the time, too, if my wings were as dull and lifeless as yours." Kandra giggled. Tana just sneered.

"Don't you just love my new golden satchel crafted by Girianna," bragged Tana, changing the subject. It was beautiful, but Alexa refused to love it.

"Kandra, I'm going to see if Ispirianza is in the garden behind the Great Oak," Alexa said. "I'll be right back."

"Okay, but be quick," Kandra said. "The storytelling is about to start."

As Alexa flew alone to the far side of the Great Oak, a warm breeze stirred. A low hiss rose with the wind.

"Come to meeeee…" the dark whisper wafted into her ears. Alexa's neck tingled, and she froze in mid-flight.

"Who is that?" she called out.

"I'm waiting for you here…give me your hands…" the whisper grew louder.

"Where? Where are you waiting for me?" Alexa shouted.

"Uchaf Du Maen…" it hissed.

"What?" Alexa became panicked. "What did you say?"

"Uchaf Du Maen…" the whisper separated into what seemed like hundreds of whispers and drifted away with the dying wind. As the voice quieted, Alexa beat her wings frantically toward the crowded festival once more and straight to Kandra's mother's box seat in the first row.

"Why, Alexa, you look as white as a ghost," Kandra's mother said.

"Uh, well…I'm just excited to hear the storytelling," Alexa stammered.

"Did you find Ispirianza?" asked Kandra.

"No...no, I didn't see anybody," Alexa said, still trying to catch her breath.

Just then, a group of Forest Fairies herded thousands of fireflies overhead, all blinking in unison.

"Ooooooooohhhh..." the crowd murmured. This was the cue to begin the storytelling.

All the fairies glided to their seats in the glittering trees. The horned Cobbletons covered their wares with mats of woven cloth and stashed their beadbags securely inside their tunics. The red glow of Cobbleton pipes soon dotted the ground like dim stars. Silence spread across the clearing. Alexa's spirit lifted.

Ellydia the Ash Dryad took the stage first. She was only two hundred years old or so — rather young for a dryad — so Ellydia could still fly. But instead, she descended into the clearing on the back of a bright orange dragonfly. The insect landed softly within a large ring of flickering torches in the center of the stage. About two-thirds of the fairies and dryads politely lowered their wings to her because of her age.

Ellydia dismounted the dragonfly to loud applause. Her wooden limbs and antlers glowed in the bonfire's light. Ellydia had always been a favorite storyteller because she told such dramatic and animated tales. The crowd grew silent. With a knowing glance and a sweeping gesture, Ellydia began to speak.

"As is my custom on the summer solstice, I will humbly tell a tale of any subject that would please the crowd," she announced.

Alexa immediately shouted, "The humans! Tell us of the humans!" Others joined their voices with hers. Even though the human tales were mostly scary stories told to spritelings, the grown-up fairies and forest folk loved to hear them, too.

"Ah, the dreaded humans!" Ellydia exclaimed, rubbing her hands together. She lifted her eyebrows and swept her gaze over the crowd. Everyone roared with approval, then hushed and waited for her to begin.

NINE

Human Tales

*e*llydia waited. The silence deepened. She began, "A long time ago, a young fairy went out to cut wood. She had lost track of the time and allowed darkness to fall. She thought, 'Oh, no. My mother will worry if I am late coming home.' And she decided — just this once — to take the shorter way through the Human's Woods.

"And just as the name suggests, a human dwelt in those woods. Yes, a human, from that race of giant wingless fairies who chop down entire forests just to build a house. They give birth to live young and devour the flesh of pigs and chickens — they even eat the chickens' eggs, the beasts!"

At this, the young fairies in the audience gasped in delicious terror. Ellydia continued to weave her tale. "As we all know, humans are fat and ugly with terribly smelly breath."

She doesn't know what she's talking about, thought Alexa. Not all humans are ugly and nasty. At least not Elsie.

Ellydia continued. "Our little fairy friend never believed such fantastic stories. But she stayed away from the Human's Woods just in case. However, on just this one night she decided to take the shortcut through the woods. She was about halfway through the deep, dark Human's Woods, when all of a sudden: 'WAHAHAHAHA!'

"A human appeared in front of her. It put a magic invisible cage around her called a jar. A jar has no bars or walls. The fairy could see right through it but couldn't escape, no matter how hard she tried. And the human said in a deep, evil voice:

'You shouldn't have entered the human's den.
If you want to see your family again,
You must answer a question, easy as pie,
And if you don't give the right answer, you'll DIE!'

"The fairy, who was a brave and clever soul, looked the human straight in the eyes and said, 'You clearly have me trapped, and I certainly can't fight you, so I guess I must answer your question.' The human said, 'WAHAHAHAHA!,'

'Count them with your twinkling blue eye,
How many stars can you see in the sky?'

"In their cruelty," explained Ellydia, "humans often ask impossible questions to tease fairies before they kill them. The fairy looked up through the jar. Infinity stretched before her — millions and millions of stars. She couldn't possibly count them all. So she did the only thing she could do. She stayed silent, pondering the stars. The human said, 'Well, hurry up, what's your answer?' And the fairy said she needed some time to think. 'WAHAHAHAHA! Take all the time you like. You'll never find the right answer, you'll never count all the stars in the sky.' But the fairy stayed silent.

"'HURRY UP!' the human cried. And the fairy said 'I need time to think—you said I could have all the time I like.' The human replied 'HAHAHA, yes you can, but you may not move from that jar until you give me your answer—not to eat, not to drink. So you'll still die even if you insist on dying of silence! HAHAHA!'

"And the fairy stayed silent, looking up at the stars. And this went on…and on…and on and on and on and on and on and…dawn! The sun came up. And as soon as the sun came up the fairy looked straight into the human's eyes and said, 'ONE!'

"'AAAAAAAAHHHHHHHH!' With an unearthly scream the human burst into flames and disappeared in a puff of smoke. The jar fell to the ground and broke into a thousand pieces. And the clever fairy, better late than never…flew home!"

The forest erupted in wild applause at the story. The Cobbletons whistled and stomped their approval. The Romorians stood with their backs perfectly straight and clapped their hands calmly. The fairies high in the trees clacked their wings together to bring forth a deafening wave of noise.

Although Alexa liked the new story, it sounded like all of the human tales she had heard before—the simple, clever fairy wins by outsmarting the brutish human oaf. After her experience with Elsie and the Magical Musical Speaking

Stone, Alexa felt that humans must be far more clever and thoughtful than the storytellers said. All except for one special storyteller, that is: the one who now took the stage.

The aged dryad Ispirianza leaned on a walking stick made from the wood of her tree, the Great Oak. Her bent back and trembling hands looked even more fragile than the last time Alexa had seen her. As she hobbled into sight, every single fairy and dryad lowered her wings and bowed her head in respect. Ispirianza had lived so many hundreds of years that no one alive remembered her as a flighted dryad. Her antlers were twisted and gnarled. Her long wooden fingers and toes stuck out from the folds of her simple blue robe. Ispirianza spoke more quietly than Ellydia, but her age and dignity made her words even more impactful than those of her much younger cousin.

Ispirianza lifted her wrinkled face to the crowd and began to speak. Softly.

"You have heard the myths and legends of the humans that have delighted and frightened both young and old. Now let me tell you the true story of the humans." Nervous laughter swept the crowd. Kandra nudged Alexa and grinned. Alexa stretched her neck to get a better view.

A low chatter came from the Romorian corner of the theater. The Romorians did not approve of Ispirianza and the way she distorted their idea of truth. Romorians only believed in things they could see and touch.

Ispirianza waited for silence before she spoke again.

"In an age of Truth and Wonder, long before the Great Shift between the human and fairy realms, magic was everywhere. Under stones and behind all things plain, the most magical

Ispirianza and the Great Oak

gift of all could be found — the gift of hope. That hope became lost. But I tell you the truth, that such hope is not now dead. It can be found right here for those who believe." The listeners were startled by such words.

"In that day, both humans and fairies were united in bringing harmony to the earth. Humans come from the ground, but fairies are born from the breath of the wind, the elements of the forest and the spirits of their mothers. And so while the humans graced the ground, fairies flittered circles of protection around the creatures of the earth and tended to the natural creation.

"Sadly, the time of Truth could not last. Human pride grew, and they became jealous of the fairies' powers. The humans became aggressive toward the fairies. And the fairies responded with something just as dark — a spirit of fear. Afraid for their lives and needing a safe haven, the ancient fairies joined their magic together and bent the fabric of time itself, creating a new realm Slightly Above Time where the humans could no longer feel the fairies' presence. Humans remained below in the realm of Timefulness.

"Fairies and the other forest folk slowly lost their memories of the past, and humans descended into legend. The world tipped out of balance. As time went on, the fairies of old came to rely less on inspiration and more on their own cleverness and Romorian inventions. The fairies lost much of their magical abilities because they no longer used them. Even the mystical passages between the two realms, called the Glass Corridors, were all but forgotten. The twelve carved stone entrances the ancient fairies created were lost to the forest. I myself once visited the human realm before the entrance near my tree vanished."

Many Romorians laughed quietly when she said this.

"They that made the doorways between the realms did so with the hope of bringing the human and fairy realms together again in the future. Maybe future generations shall rediscover a way back into Timefulness and learn to live side by side with the humans. This must be done to restore balance to the earth. And maybe future generations will someday tell stories about us—the inspired ones who brought magic back into the realm and harmony back to the world!"

As Ispirianza spoke, her words burned deeply into Alexa's heart. She felt a conviction to not let her magic die. She also wondered about the fairy magic that had already been lost.

At first the crowd responded with total silence. Then a thunderous round of applause and wing clapping erupted, as if to crown Ispirianza the master of all storytellers. Ispirianza humbly limped off the stage, not noticing the glory the crowd heaped upon her. She looked sad. Alexa knew that Ispirianza told these stories to explain important truths and hated that others thought of them as only fun.

"What would Ispirianza think of Elsie?" Alexa thought. She would ask her that very night.

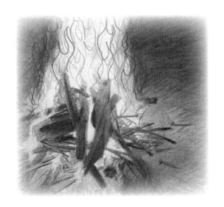

TEN

The Powerful Magic of Humans

The crowd chattered until another formation of fireflies passed overhead. The music was about to begin.

A cool, gentle breeze began high in the trees. The breeze grew stronger and stronger. Tens of thousands of tiny winged sylphs swooshed past Alexa so quickly that she could barely see them. Millions of leaves in countless trees rustled softly. The first gathering of sylphs swirled high around the theater. In the middle of it all soared Eva, her shiny blue dress dancing in the wind as she directed the sylphs using intricate movements of her wand and signaling silks. Alexa felt that the entire audience must have envied Eva at that moment.

Around Eva's neck hung a glowing red homing charm that sent her directions to the lead sylph—known as the caller—who also had a red charm. The caller's charm directed the thousands of sylphs in its gathering. Each sylph had a smaller glowing blue charm around its neck that received the

instructions. The entire swarm waved like a single flowing creature creating a twisting, swirling wind.

Eva herding sylphs

As the audience gazed upward, a second gathering swooped in at ground level and filled the theater with a rushing wind. Every torch in the circle suddenly blew out, but the bonfire burned higher and higher. The third gathering blew in from the north and sounded hundreds of reed flutes planted throughout the forest. A mighty C-note echoed through the audience.

Eva's gathering swirled to the southwest and blew all of the E-note flutes. The third sylph gathering chimed in with a G-note, and the entire forest resonated a mighty C-major chord. The gatherings darted, and the chord changed to A-minor and then to E-minor. The forest vibrated with power.

Next, a new sound soared over the chords. Alexa spotted a group of fairies, each playing the llirhu. Each fairy strummed the first set of the llirhu's strings with her wingtips and the second set with her hands. Then a group of six Cobbletons joined the performance, playing their llirhus by plucking the smaller strings with their nimble fingers and beating the llirhus' lower drum-like chamber with their hooves.

Then a grass curtain fell aside to reveal the Thysperian Fairy Choir. They sang a haunting melody that completed the mood the sylphs and llirhus had created. The Romorians would not have liked the music if they had understood it. All music of the Fae was an act of worship. They were singing in harmony with the Great Song.

As enchanting as the music was, Alexa could not keep her mind off her encounter with Elsie. Ispirianza had retired to her home in the Great Oak. Alexa wanted desperately to talk to her before she went to sleep.

"I'll be back in a bit, Kandra," Alexa said as she picked up her satchel and stood.

"But the music has only just begun!" Kandra objected.

Alexa darted to the edge of the clearing and around the back of the festival gathering. When Alexa landed at Ispirianza's door, she scratched three times at the rough old bark. The door swung open and there stood Ispirianza with a smile. Alexa dipped her wings politely and bowed to the Great Oak.

Inside the dim hollow of Ispirianza's giant tree, a low stone table held a bowl of rosebuds and two cups of elderberry juice.

"Oh, I'm sorry, you have a guest coming," Alexa said, disappointed.

"Yes, and she has just arrived," said Ispirianza. She waved Alexa inside.

"You knew I was coming?" Alexa asked.

"A tree as old as mine whispers many things to its dryad."

Alexa looked around at the inside of the tree. Far above her head she could see the many rings that showed the tree's great age. She knew trees could speak to their dryads through Ring Dreams, but she never expected a tree as important as the Great Oak to speak to Ispirianza about Alexa herself. She gently touched the heartwood wall of the tree.

"I went crazy not being able to fly for five days, and you've spent your whole life in sight of this one tree. How do dryads do it?"

"Sometimes I do envy the freedom of the fairies, old fool that I am," said Ispirianza. "I was born from the Great Oak, but I also must protect and nurture it. In a way, a dryad is both daughter and mother to her tree. I am bound to her, yet she stills my soul and gives me roots. She gives me meaning and love. Life can't offer more than that, child."

The llirhu

Alexa and Ispirianza sank down into feather-stuffed cushions next to the table. Now that the time had come to tell her story, Alexa didn't know how to begin. "Did your tree tell you why I've come?"

"Only in the vague way of trees. You tell me in your own words. And you can sort these termite larvae for me while you talk." Ispirianza pushed a polished wooden bowl of squishy, squirming little worm-like things across the table to Alexa. "My fingers have become too stiff for such delicate work. Mind you don't let any of them loose."

Sorting grubs felt disgusting, but Alexa was glad to have something to do with her nervous hands. She began to separate the termites into three groups according to size. "How is the new woodwork going?" asked Alexa.

"Slowly, of course, but well," said Ispirianza, pointing to a section of the inner tree wall. Circling the inside of the tree were six woodwork drawings made of tiny curving lines carved into the wood. Alexa counted twelve termite larvae already at work on the seventh drawing, chewing steadily along the paths that Ispirianza had traced out for them. The green ink that Ispirianza used softened the wood and tasted like candy to termites. Ispirianza's woodwork art fascinated Alexa and was known throughout the fairy world.

Ispirianza gestured for Alexa to speak.

"Okay, well, I was walking in the forest yesterday," began Alexa. Ispirianza's antlers twitched. "Because of the spider webs. I was grounded," Alexa explained.

Alexa expected another scolding, but Ispirianza just said, "Ah, I see."

"I got lost and tripped over this stone carving thing, so I

put it back where it goes, and then the giant with no wings appeared and dropped a Magical Speaking Gemstone and then disappeared."

At once Ispirianza stopped poking the termites and looked straight at Alexa with her dark, piercing eyes. "Stone carving?"

"Yes, kind of a big ring with a dragon, a fairy and something else at the top," Alexa said. She couldn't quite bring herself to say the word "human" yet.

"Tell me where." Ispirianza spoke in an intense and serious voice.

"West of Kendlenook on a hill near the three clearings," said Alexa.

"How very interesting. I hadn't known the location of that one. I thought all twelve had been destroyed."

Alexa didn't know what that meant, so she pressed on. "Do you think the giant I saw was a real human?" said Alexa.

Ispirianza's gazed up into the hollow of her tree. "I not only think you saw a human, but a very important human at that. But a Speaking Gemstone? How odd."

"Oh, Ispirianza! Elsie looks just like I imagined the humans in the stories you tell. She's pretty and friendly, but she uses all sorts of strange words."

"What did you say her name was?" Ispirianza looked up from the monocle in her hand.

"Elsie," said a perplexed Alexa.

Ispirianza paused, deep in thought. "And you spoke with this Elsie?"

"Elsie didn't speak until after she disappeared," said Alexa. "I was playing with her Speaking Stone and then it started talking to me. But there wasn't anyone inside it, just a voice.

Elsie's voice!"

Ispirianza leaned forward. "Hmmm. That Speaking Stone works like a telephone, but you say it wasn't attached to a wall? All the telephones I saw in Timefulness had wires that connected them to walls. Where is this Speaking Stone now?"

"In a hole under a burst of ferns at a big maple tree. It's pretty near Constanza's dryad tree. It lit up like blue fire and made all kinds of noises."

"How about that. Humans are so fond of making new things, or changing old things so that they make new noises. Such powerful magic the humans have — they call their magic 'technology.' But they can't seem to do the big things. Did you know humans have no control over the weather? It just happens to them, poor helpless creatures." Ispirianza thought for a while.

"Ispirianza, have you really been to Timefulness?" Alexa asked.

"Do you think I just imagine my stories?" Ispirianza asked.

"Well, everyone else does."

"Mercy, child! You're letting the termites out willy-nilly! Pay attention. If any of them get into the live part of this tree I'll never hear the end of it. Termite art is an exacting craft. It's controlled destruction, remember that."

"I'm sorry." Alexa scooped up the grubs creeping across the floor. "Why do you think Elsie's an important human?"

"My tree knows this Elsie well. She often climbs the Great Oak and tells it her secrets."

"Then she does live nearby! Can you show me the way?" cried Alexa.

"Nearby, yes, but farther away than you can imagine. Her

realm and ours are divided by the bending of time. That's why we both live in the same world but do not see each other."

"Like in the story you told tonight?"

"You listen well, young one. If others had listened, we might have halted the spread of the Scarring long ago," sighed Ispirianza.

"Scarring? The Scarring has something to do with humans? That can't be right, the Romorians said–"

"Yes, yes, I know. You'll grow to learn that Romorians have many facts, but not enough truth," said Ispirianza.

"Not enough truth?" Alexa asked.

"Their science can only describe what we see. It cannot tell us true meanings, like why a thing exists. Science cannot tell us about right and wrong. It cannot teach us how to be happy. It cannot even tell us if there is something beyond what we can see — like the realm of Timefulness."

"But the Romorians said we can fix the Scarring if we build a wall to keep the soil moist. Shouldn't we do what they say? After all, they are the most intelligent race in the forest," said Alexa.

"Being smart is not the same as being wise, and being clever is not the same as being inspired," said Ispirianza. "Have you noticed that Romorians never want to teach you what they know? They only want to impress you. They make up big words to explain simple things so others don't understand what they are saying. That doesn't sound very intelligent, does it?"

"I guess not," said Alexa, not quite understanding. "But their ideas have helped us and made our lives easier."

"True, but growth in science without growth in character is

worthless," said Ispirianza. "Fire can either warm a village or destroy it. What good comes from controlling fire if we cannot control ourselves? We may only become better destroyers."

"If you know what causes the Scarring, why haven't you told everyone?" Alexa asked.

"I tried many times, but no one listened. Even if they did, nothing could be done, as the Scarring does not begin in this realm. Strange how no one believes the true stories. They prefer the ones that aren't so fantastic."

Alexa thought for a minute.

"So if humans make the Scarring, aren't they evil like the Oths? But Elsie was friendly to me. I know she would never do something so horrible."

"She doesn't know, child," Ispirianza said with a sigh. "Would you like to know the truth about what causes the Scarring?"

"Of course!"

"Listen closely then," said Ispirianza. "The humans don't understand the effects of what they do in their own world. They knock down trees, scrape the ground smooth and cover it with different kinds of melted rock. They call it concrete and steel. Trees and plants cannot grow in concrete and steel, because the land can no longer breathe." Alexa had no idea what Ispirianza was talking about.

Ispirianza continued. "We fairies can't see or feel anything that humans build on top of the melted rock. All we see is the terrible Scarring that it leaves behind. Don't misunderstand — making buildings isn't bad in itself. It's only bad when humans build without regard for the balance of nature."

Ispirianza set another termite chewing along a new path.

"I'm the only one I know of from our realm who has spoken to a human for many years — that is, until today."

ELEVEN

Termites in the Woodwork

Alexa sat stunned. She had completely forgotten about sorting her termites.

Ispirianza continued. "When the ancient fairies bent time to save our race, they created twelve doorways between the human realm of Timefulness and our realm Slightly Above Time. For two hundred years, fairies slipped through the Glass Corridors to visit the human realm. They kept the peace between our worlds.

"All of the entrances were destroyed one by one. Perhaps the humans destroyed them. Perhaps they crumbled of old age. No one really knows. As the years went by, fairies stopped trying to find and repair the broken entrances. After many more years, fairies even stopped believing in Timefulness, humans and the Glass Corridors."

"Then that's what I found? A lost entrance to the Glass Corridor?"

"Yes, you did," Ispirianza smiled. "It appears whoever destroyed the doorways did not do a very good job on that one. Now, at last, we have a chance to stop the Scarring."

"So we can visit Elsie and tell her about it. She can tell the other humans to stop whatever they are doing wrong, and then everything will be okay. We can go together!"

"I admire your spirit, and I'd love to meet Elsie, but have you considered that I cannot go to the entrance? I am a dryad—a very old one at that—and bound to stay within sight of my tree." Ispirianza's eyes flashed a distant gaze. "I once found an entrance near my tree. I learned the secrets of the corridor and slipped into the human realm before that entrance was destroyed. Such memories I have of my human friend Margaret."

"You had a human friend?" Alexa gasped.

"Indeed I did. I stayed in her world for months," continued Ispirianza. "So long that the fairies of Kendlenook thought me dead. I finally slipped back into our world and told the council of my adventures. The very next day I found the entrance destroyed. Someone did not want the secrets of the corridor discovered. I never saw my beloved Margaret again. Without proof, no one believed my fantastic stories. I blame myself for not guarding the secret. I should have listened to the voice of my tree."

"Do you think I could hear a tree's voice?" Alexa asked.

"No, child, only dryads have that ability," Ispirianza said. "Why do you ask?"

"Ever since I opened the corridor, I've heard a whispering on the wind," said Alexa. "It doesn't sound at all like a fairy's voice. It's deeper and older."

"What did it say to you?"

Alexa's heart grew restless as she repeated it. "It said 'Come to me' and 'I'm waiting here for you.'" Ispirianza studied the carvings on her tree's walls.

"How did your spirit respond to this voice?" she asked.

"I was afraid."

Ispirianza put her hand to her chin in deep thought. "It could be the voice of a tree, but your fear makes me wonder."

"Wonder what?" asked Alexa.

"Most trees speak peace into the spirits of those who listen, but not all trees are — how should I put this — pure," Ispirianza said, lowering her gaze. "Some have become twisted. Did you ask where it wanted you to go?"

"Yes, but I couldn't understand its answer," said Alexa. "Uchaf Du Maen. Do you know what that means?" Ispirianza looked straight into Alexa's eyes in a way that made her heart beat stronger.

"Alexa, promise me you will not speak back to this voice," said Ispirianza in a grave tone.

"Why?"

"I can't be certain, but I believe the words 'Uchaf Du Maen' are from the ancient tongue — a language no fairy, dryad or tree now speaks." Alexa's wings twitched with fright.

"But someone or something spoke it to me," she said.

"Yes. I wish I could consult my elder and dear mentor Zymandria on this matter." Ispirianza's voice cracked with emotion as she spoke Zymandria's name. "She once taught me as I teach you. She studied the old ways and would certainly know much more than myself. We used to speak through our trees often, but we lost contact long ago. I fear she is no longer with us." Alexa thought she saw a tear glisten in Ispirianza's eye as she spoke, but then the old dryad returned to the present.

"Alexa, if it is truly a tree that whispers to you, it is not one that lives."

"You mean, I'm hearing whispers of the dead?" Alexa could barely speak the words. "But why?"

"You have unlocked great power. It should not surprise us that things are happening that we do not yet understand."

"But I don't have any power. I just fell on that stone circle by accident," said Alexa.

"Alexa, can't you see? The Great Song is singing its melody through you. Using one so young is not what I would have expected, but the need is great and you are, after all, your mother's daughter." Alexa could see her reflection in Ispirianza's dark eyes.

"My mother?" asked Alexa, her voice cracking a little. "Please tell me about her. Grandmother never even says her name. I think it makes her too sad."

"I knew Ciriana well. If anyone could protect a daughter's chrysalis through the year of drought, she could." Ispirianza lowered her gaze. "But in the end, your birth proved too much for even her strength."

Alexa's heart sank. "So I did kill her."

"No, no! Send those thoughts far from you, young one," said Ispirianza. "Your mother made her decisions for her own reasons. Great events surrounded the time of your birth. Maybe she knew that this very day would come."

"But I'm not worth dying for," said Alexa. "I'm just a plain little Meadow Fairy who hasn't even discovered her calling yet. Eva is a Fairy of Compassion and Daria a Fairy of Protection, but what am I? Nothing!"

"My tree speaks of you often. It has never spoken of Eva or Daria. Ciriana must have suspected that you might have the gift," said Ispirianza.

"What gift?" asked Alexa. Ispirianza looked concerned except for her eyes — her eyes were smiling.

"The gift that will awaken our world, of course." Ispirianza's voice rose. "Alexa, my mind clears. You must pass through the Glass Corridor into the realm of Timefulness and find Elsie. I do not yet understand how, but my tree believes that Elsie has the power to stop the Scarring."

"Me? Why me? The High Fairy should go, or at least Eva."

"Did Eva meet a human? Did the High Fairy reopen the corridor? No, Alexa, this has been put before you. Eva, your grandmother and the council must not know of your discovery. They would only hinder what needs to be done."

"But anyone could have found the human," Alexa said, ignoring the termites crawling between her fingers.

"Young one, I am not wise enough to know which events come from fate and which come from our own actions. But I have found that it is always wrong to do nothing when it is within our power to do good. The Great Song sings of this."

Ispirianza's words struck terror into Alexa's heart. "I need time to think about it," Alexa lied, edging toward the door. She had no intention of taking responsibility for something so important or going to the humans' world alone, but she didn't want to say that to Ispirianza. Someone older and wiser would certainly step in and take care of the problem.

"Let us hope that enough time remains," said Ispirianza.

TWELVE

Sharks Don't Fly

lexa's mind raced as she laid her head on her dandelion fluff pillow. Hours later, the moon had risen and Alexa still lay awake. The tree house was dark and silent except for Snarfle's snuffly breathing in the corner of Alexa's room.

Alexa wondered if she could just use the Speaking Stone to tell Elsie what needed to be done. Then she remembered Elsie was only twelve, so it wasn't fair to ask her to do the work of adults. Besides, Elsie said that humans didn't believe in fairies any more than fairies believed in humans. Proof would be needed. Proof and a plan.

The moon moved another hand's breadth across the night sky as Alexa thought about all the reasons why she should just stay in bed: Grandmother, her classes in the morning, and hungry night creatures who would love to snack on a lone fairy.

Finally Alexa threw back her blankets and stepped out of bed. She wasn't going to get any sleep, so she might as well give the Speaking Stone a try. With classes all day, night was her only chance to get away. Alexa grabbed a few candlesticks and her lighting wand. If clouds covered the moon, she would have to fly by candlelight. She stole past her snoozing dragon and climbed onto the windowsill. Unfolding her wings, she glided silently to the ground.

The moon gave more than enough light. Alexa glided to the ground and then walked for a few minutes so the flapping of her wings wouldn't wake up Eva, Daria or Grandmother.

Alexa flew to the Speaking Stone without disturbing anything scarier than a tree frog. She shoved the Stone out into the open so she could see the symbols in the moonlight. If she remembered right, Elsie had told her to push the top right button and then the green one in order to send her the photo of the centipede. Alexa took a deep breath and gave it a try. First she jumped on the top right button. The Speaking Stone beeped. The stone's light pierced through the darkness and illuminated Alexa's face and the nearby trees and ferns. Then she knelt down and pressed hard on the green button with her hand. The Speaking Stone beeped again and then made a buzzing noise that repeated.

"Uhhh...hello?" said a sleepy-sounding voice that Alexa did not recognize.

"You're not Elsie," Alexa said, not sure what to do next.

"No, I'm her brother. Who is this? Do you have any idea what time it is?"

Alexa knew by glancing at the moon that it was about three hours past midnight. She told the voice so.

Alexa and the Speaking Stone

"Who are you? No, don't even tell me," the voice said. Alexa heard footsteps, a door opening, and the voice saying, "Elsie, phone." Then a clunk, a rustling sound and a door closing.

"Hello?" Elsie whispered, but she sounded wide-awake and curious. Alexa was relieved to hear Elsie's voice.

"Sorry to Stone you in the middle of the night, but this is so important."

"Alexa, is that you? Don't worry, I wasn't sleeping. How could I sleep when I'm totally losing my mind? You realize it's not normal to believe in fairies, right?"

"Fairies would say the same thing about humans," said Alexa.

"That's crazy," said Elsie. "There are only, like, six billion of us."

"Well, not in my world. And unless you can help me, there might not be much of anything left in my world. We need you to help stop the Scarring."

"The what?"

Alexa continued, hardly taking a breath. "Look, I know you're only twelve and can't stop the Scarring yourself, but Ispirianza thinks you could tell some older humans. Can you get to the High Human—you know, the leader who makes really big decisions?"

"You mean the president? Yeah, right. He only lives like three thousand miles away and has a zillion guys with guns around him all the time," said Elsie. "But back to this Scarring thing. What's that?"

"Maybe you call it something else, but of course you've seen it. You know, the vast empty lands that you can't fly over?"

"I can't fly over anything, remember?" said Elsie.

Alexa found that talking to a human was hard work. All the new words and different meanings for things were starting to make her head ache. "Well, you can't walk over the Scarring either, at least that's what the Cobbletons say. Quint had a friend who got too close and fell in, and it just sucked him under and no one ever saw him again."

"You mean he drowned?" asked Elsie.

"No, it's not water. It's more like sand," said Alexa, now sitting cross-legged on the screen of the phone.

"So it's quicksand."

"No! Look, you can't possibly miss it. It covers almost half the land. What do you see just to the east of our forest?"

"Which way is east?"

"Where the sun rises, dummy." Alexa wondered what humans learned in school. Elsie had brains, but she didn't know some really important things.

"Hmm, just the city," replied Elsie.

"What's a city?"

"You know, skyscrapers, factories, stores, highways…the city, dummy," said Elsie.

"Oh! Are those things made of something called concrete or steel, or whatever?"

"Some of them. Why?"

"We don't have any factories, or any of the other stuff you said. All we see there is a big dark hole. Ispirianza says that humans knock down trees and scrape the ground to cover all the land with concrete and steel. Then you build things on top of that, and the land can't breathe anymore. She says building things isn't always bad — it's only bad if you destroy the land without any thought to nature."

"The land breathes?" asked Elsie. "But it's not even alive."

"It's not like you can talk to it," Alexa said. "My teacher says that every living thing in the whole world is connected to the earth, both plants and animals. The world breathes and its heart beats, like when the seasons change and the ocean tides go in and out. If you destroy one part, then it hurts all the other parts, too."

"Well, it's true there are barely any trees in the city," said Elsie. "It's not very pretty either—all hard and gray. But I've never seen anything like the Scarring you're talking about. Why's this so important anyway?"

"Because it kills fairies, that's why!" exclaimed Alexa. "It gets closer and closer to our homes every year. We only have a thin piece of land called the Bridge of Trees that—I don't suppose you have the Bridge of Trees in your world?"

"Nope, sorry. No bridge. The only trees in that direction are in the park on the way to the lakes."

"That must be it! The Bridge of Trees connects Faewick Forest to the Lake Lands. We won't be able to fly to the Lake Lands if the Bridge of Trees gets covered with Scarring."

Elsie thought about that for a minute. "So just go over the ocean."

"And get eaten by sharks?" Alexa couldn't believe Elsie had suggested something so ridiculous.

"Just fly over the water. You can fly, right?"

"So can the sharks."

Elsie laughed in amazement. "You have flying sharks? Oh my gosh, I have got to see this!"

"Things must work a little differently here," said Alexa.

"Besides, it would take days for a fairy to fly over the ocean. We would get tired and drown. Hey, if you really want to see the sharks, then come back! You came into my realm once already. All you have to do is go back to the same place in the forest and do whatever you did before. I can show you the Scarring and Ispirianza can tell you what to do to stop it."

"I've tried again and again, but I can't get through," Elsie said. "The hole I fell into is all filled with dirt now." Alexa realized how little she knew about the Glass Corridor entrance. Alexa stretched her hand slowly into the opening from her side, but she only felt solid dirt. Secretly she was glad that she couldn't get through. Ispirianza couldn't expect Alexa to do the impossible, could she?

Alexa beat her wings slowly on the flight back home, wondering what to do next.

She wondered if Daria might be right. Maybe Ispirianza was crazy. The old dryad was right about humans being real, but how could it hurt if Alexa showed others the phone? No fairy had that kind of magic. They would have to believe! So Alexa decided to do the only thing she thought was right — she would disobey Ispirianza.

THIRTEEN

Nothing

After school the next day, the front door of the tree house flew open and Alexa rushed in. Grandmother didn't even have time to scold her before Alexa yanked her out of her rocking chair, scattering sewing things across the floor.

"Alexa, what has gotten into you?"

"Grandmother, I know this sounds crazy but I have discovered what causes the Scarring," Alexa stammered. Grandmother's eyes flashed a mixture of shock, confusion and indignation. "Please don't rush to judgment until I show you what I found. The council needs to see this right away."

"Alexa, have you gone quite mad? What—"

"Eva!" screamed Alexa. "Where is she? Eva!" Eva flew in from the back aviary with her gardening tools still in her hands.

"What's all the excitement?" Eva asked.

"Alexa has lost her mind, that's what the excitement is about," said Grandmother.

"Daria!" Alexa yelled.

"Daria's in the forest interpreting Owlish for the Cobbletons," said Eva.

"Well, you two are the ones on the council," continued Alexa. "Come with me!"

"We are not going anywhere, young fairy, until you explain yourself!" said Grandmother.

"You'll see, trust me," Alexa said, pulling Grandmother's arm toward the door. At the base of their tree stood a familiar Romorian with a drop of red sauce on the end of his nose.

"Goric!" Grandmother said nervously, conscious of what a spectacle Alexa was making. "What brings you to our humble home again so soon?"

"Good afternoon to you, Gresha. This young fairy informed me that she has made a very important scientific discovery," Goric said with an air of disbelief.

Grandmother's eyes flew into Alexa's like daggers. Even Eva looked horrified at Alexa's behavior.

"I couldn't get in to see the High Fairy, so I found another elder who could help," Alexa said, flying Grandmother down to Goric.

"The High Fairy! You *have* lost your mind." Grandmother turned away from Goric and whispered harshly at Alexa. "You are making a fool of yourself and of me in front of a very important Romorian!"

"We are so sorry to disturb you," Eva said to the Romorian, floating down from the front door and glancing disapprovingly at Alexa. "My sister seems carried away with one of those childish games young fairies play."

"Indeed, indeed," Grandmother agreed. "Please, won't you stay for some scuttlemint tea? The house is a wreck, but—"

"This is not a game," insisted Alexa. "It's deadly serious."

"So she said to me," Goric said. Eva took Alexa firmly by the arm.

"Good sir," said Eva to Goric with her wings lowered. "If you would excuse us, I'd like to have a word with my baby sister."

"Of course, of course," said Goric. "But if we could please hurry. I have very important matters to attend to." Eva flew Alexa to the back of the tree.

"Alexa, please stop this," scolded Eva. "You are reflecting very poorly on Grandmother."

"I suppose you don't want to stop the Scarring!"

"The Scarring!" Eva said. "Alexa, let the Romorians deal with that. What do you know about it?" Alexa pulled her arm from Eva's grip and flew toward the front of the house.

"I'm going to show the Romorians what I've found," Alexa said. "You don't have to come if you don't want to." When Alexa got to the front of the house, she found Grandmother and Goric laughing together.

"Alexa, dear," Grandmother said, wiping a tear of laughter from her eye. "I've smoothed things over with this fine gentleman, and he's agreed to forget all about this little game."

"Grandmother, you need to see what I've found. No fairy has ever seen the likes of this, I promise."

"Gresha," interrupted Goric. "She seems quite convinced, and I'd like to take a look at this mysterious object. I do not doubt that I can explain it to her."

"Of course, Goric," Grandmother said with a laugh, while shooting a deadly glance at Alexa. "Whatever pleases you." As the group set out for the cell phone's hiding place, Grandmother flew low next to the walking Goric and discussed council politics. Eva and Alexa fluttered slowly behind. Eva whispered sharply in Alexa's ear.

"You should have come to me first before you got Grandmother and Goric involved."

"Don't worry, Eva. Once you see it, no one will have any doubts."

"I hope for your sake you're right," Eva whispered.

When they finally arrived at the maple tree, Alexa prepared them for what they were about to see.

"Okay," she said with authority. She took a deep breath. "I know that humans are supposed to be just legends, but what you are about to see will change your minds. We may even be able to talk with a human this very day."

"Humans?" gasped Grandmother. "Alexa, I have half a mind to clip your wings for wasting our time." Goric just looked down and shook his head.

Alexa smiled.

"Then how do you explain this?" Alexa parted the ferns and lifted the leaves in the hollow where she'd left the phone. Eva's eyes grew bigger.

There, deep in the ferns, sat nothing.

"Alexa, how could you!" Eva scolded.

"But, but I…" Alexa began to cry as her hands searched the ground. She dug further into the leaves, but she found only wood and dirt. Humiliated panic kept her from speaking.

"Goric, you can be assured that my granddaughter will be

well punished for this wild little adventure. We do not need to bother any other council members with talk of this, do we?"

"I've missed an afternoon appointment over this young fairy," Goric said in indignation. "Scientific discovery is simply beyond the ability of fairies. I suggest you stick to pollinating flowers or whatever it is you do."

"But Ispirianza said that—" began Alexa.

"Ispirianza!" Grandmother looked as if she were about to fly to the sun. "I might have known. Filling young fairies' heads with such nonsense. You are never to speak to that senile old dryad again. Do you hear me?"

"Wait, let me show you the stone ring. It's right over there."

"It's not my place to tell you how to raise your grandchildren, Gresha," said Goric. "But when you indulge children in fantasy and foolish imaginary stories, it warps their minds, and they can lose the ability to understand what is real."

Alexa waited in her room without dinner. She hid her head on her pillow and wondered what could have happened to the cell phone. Maybe it somehow wound up back in Timefulness. How would she talk with Elsie again? She heard the muffled voices of Eva and Daria talking about her.

When Grandmother finally came home she flew slowly into Alexa's room. To Alexa's surprise, her voice was calm. Deadly calm. She would have preferred yelling.

"Alexa, I think you understand the seriousness of the situation. You have damaged my reputation in this community. I have patched things up as best as I can with Goric, but more

needs to be done. You will apologize to Goric and the entire Romorian council tomorrow, and then we can discuss your punishment. From now on I need you to act like an adult and let go of these childish fantasies."

Alexa didn't say a word. Grandmother offered her cold bread and jam, but Alexa wasn't hungry. She just wanted to sleep. As soon as she closed her eyes, she drifted into emptiness. The world around her grew quiet. She dreamed of Elsie and her magical phone.

"WAKE UP, ALEXA! NOW!" Grandmother's panicked voice pierced the darkness and snatched Alexa out of a deep sleep like a slap across the face.

"The truth does not care if we believe in it or not. But you surely will not see the truth unless you believe."

~ The Wisdom of the Fae

Part II:
The Tragedy

FOURTEEN

Night Flight

CRACK! A crash like a thousand branches splintering jolted Alexa out of bed. Grandmother called again, "Get up! Fly to the high places! Go now!"

"What is it?" Alexa shouted over the din. A massive tree crashed to the ground somewhere nearby.

"May the Great Song protect us, the Scarring has come to Kendlenook!" cried Grandmother.

A group of fairies flashed by outside, screaming.

"Daria, go with Eva. I will bring Alexa," Grandmother shouted from outside Alexa's window. The next second, Grandmother jammed her arm through the window and yanked Alexa through in one swift motion. Before she could think to flap, Alexa felt her body whizzing through the chilly chaos of deep night.

More trees crashed down, each closer than the last, creating a furious wind that blew the fleeing fairies wildly about. A tower of dust billowed up, and Alexa could no longer see or breathe well. She could only hear the splitting of wood and the cries of countless unseen fairies. Owls and falcons swooped through the chaos, shrieking in terror as they also fled.

Just above her, she heard Grandmother's wings buzz upward and felt herself pulled toward the sky. Alexa gasped for air but only breathed in dust and coughed. After struggling through a fog of billowing dirt, the two fairies popped out of the dust cloud and turned north to join a mass exodus of fleeing fairies, thousands of silvery wings flashing in the moonlight. A monster of smoke and ash chased after them. The trees shook and swayed in a violent frenzy. Some fell into the haze with thunderous fury. It was like the end of the world.

The sight of falling homes and trees was so unthinkable that it dazed Alexa's mind. More fairies than she ever knew existed flew for their lives toward the mountains. Ispirianza always said the caves of the Dragontooth Mountains were the safest place to find shelter in an emergency. Ispirianza! Alexa stopped in midair and turned to look back. As a dryad, Ispirianza couldn't leave the area around her tree. Had the Scarring already taken the Great Oak?

Alexa hovered for a moment. She knew she had to help her friend, but she had no idea what to do. Grandmother took the decision out of Alexa's hands by spinning her around and commanding, "Fly now!" in a voice so forceful that Alexa could not help but obey.

Most of the fairies swarmed toward the distant mountains, but some let their terror rule them. The most fearful ones either flew around and around in small circles or went in the wrong direction.

Alexa glimpsed a lost spriteling flying, confused, around the top of a tree house. "Keep going, Grandmother. I'll be right behind you." In a flash, Alexa drew in her wings and plunged for the spriteling, snatching her by the hem of her dress.

Alexa held the frightened spriteling tightly to her chest and pumped her wings hard. "I've got you. Now fold your wings," Alexa told her. The little one trembled against Alexa and obeyed.

As she flew steadily north among the crowd of fairies, Alexa thanked the Great Song that her wings had fully healed from the effects of the weaver spider's web.

The sheer noise of a thousand clattering wings and piercing screams made Alexa's blood rush. The sharp, deep cracking of tree trunks echoed from behind and followed the panicking group. Each of those cracks might be someone's home.

How could this happen? Goric and the other Romorians said the Scarring wouldn't come close to Kendlenook for years.

Two hours of grueling flight brought Alexa to the first of the dark, mountaintop caves. She planted her feet on the moonlit cliff edge. The earth still rumbled and groaned to the south, but Alexa refused to look that way. Alexa's wings and muscles ached from carrying the spriteling's weight. She now understood why fairies had to compete for the honor of motherhood. Mothers needed so much strength!

Fairies of all sizes and types crowded into the caves and spilled out of the entrance onto the ledge. The sleepy fish eagles that nested in the caves were nervous and restless with all the commotion in their normally peaceful homes. Some flew away into the night.

"Do you see your mother?" Alexa asked the spriteling, who shook her head. "Has anyone lost a daughter?" Alexa yelled, as if anyone could hear her through the chaos. Alexa flapped her exhausted wings and continued to the next cave. It was as crowded as the first, but still no mother. No Eva, Daria or Grandmother either, but Alexa knew they'd be off helping others. That is, if they'd made it through—but of course they did. Alexa refused to think of any other possibility.

By the fifth cave, Alexa was certain her wings wouldn't flap another wingbeat. "We'll look for your mother in the morning," she promised. "Let's rest now." Alexa folded her wings and sank down on a crowded piece of ground near the cave entrance. The spriteling curled up in Alexa's arms and cried herself to sleep, exposed in the chilly predawn air.

FIFTEEN

The Aftermath

Bright sunlight shone on Alexa's eyelids and coaxed her awake. She dared not open her eyes. What happened last night was just a terrible nightmare and not real at all, she told herself. Alexa heard the rustling of a large crowd of fairies, the crackling of a fire nearby and the fussing of young spritelings. She could not fool herself any longer. It had actually happened. Her heart felt like a rock.

A hand gently nudged her shoulder. Alexa surrendered and opened her eyes. Grandmother! Alexa clung to her, relieved that she had at least one family member still alive.

"Eva and Daria are well," whispered Grandmother. "Many forest folk owe their lives to those two. They rest now in the third cave. You did well, too, my granddaughter. This small one would have perished without you. Come, let's find her mother."

As soon as Alexa opened her wings, a dull, aching pain

shot through her shoulder muscles. Soreness from last night's struggle stiffened her movements. Alexa took the sleepy spriteling in her arms again and fluttered painfully after Grandmother above the crowd of fairies strewn about the cave floor.

Alexa noticed that Grandmother's wings drooped slightly, and long strands of her gray hair had fallen out of her hair clasp. For the first time in her life, Alexa thought Grandmother looked frail.

Grandmother led Alexa up the mountainside to the next cave. The face of the gray mountain cliff smoked as candles and hastily built fires burned at the mouth of each cave. It seemed the whole world was smoldering.

A golden- and gray-haired Forest Fairy with a heavily bandaged arm and a torn wing stood outside on a ledge scanning the sky. Her face came to life when she caught sight of Alexa with the precious spriteling cradled in her arms.

Alexa landed softly and handed the spriteling to her mother. The little one clung to her mother's neck and flashed a contented smile. The Forest Fairy held the little one close with her unhurt arm and kissed her soft hair.

"You have no idea..." the Forest Fairy began and then started to cry. "Tavia and I were separated in the darkness. Then the branch fell on my arm and pinned me. I thought..." She broke down again and then took a deep breath to steady her voice. "I am Palina of the Forest. Tavia is my only daughter. I don't know whether the Great Song will ever allow me to have another." She looked into Alexa's eyes. "You have saved... You have no idea." Then the Forest Fairy lowered her wings to Alexa.

A spriteling returned to her mother

The gesture shocked Alexa beyond words. A fairy important enough to be chosen as a mother never showed such respect to a younger fairy without daughters. Alexa lowered her wings also. "I only did what any fairy would have done. I am proud to be of service to you," she said. Grandmother nodded her approval, then led Alexa away.

Alexa felt Grandmother's pride in her and soaked it in. "Now let us collect your sisters," said Grandmother. "The council must turn to the unhappy business of seeing whether our village still stands."

Alexa's wings faltered. What would she find in Kendlenook? Had the Great Oak and its dryad survived last night's Scarring attack? What about her own home?

Alexa flapped steadily along behind a weary Daria just over the treetops. The sharp morning air seemed to quiver with hundreds of fairy wings bound for Kendlenook. Both Daria and Eva had stayed up all night shepherding the wingless forest folk — Romorians and Cobbletons — to safety. Despite a nap after sunrise, they looked merely half alive, but determined and very grown up.

As they approached Kendlenook, Alexa's hands shook with anxiety. If the village had been destroyed, where would she and her family live? If Ispirianza were dead, then would anyone be able to stop the Scarring?

No, she couldn't think about that.

Wisps of smoke curled upward below Alexa. She saw a large number of campfires still burning. Groups of forest folk huddled around each fire in the chilly morning air. They looked like ants when seen from such a height.

"That's where we took the Cobbletons," Eva said, pointing to the camp.

As scary as last night was for the fairies, Alexa realized that those who could not fly were in even more danger. Not only did they travel more slowly, but they also lacked a view from the air, so they wouldn't know which way to go. Without fairies to guide them, the forest folk would have been swallowed by the Scarring. Many probably had been. Alexa shivered.

"This way," said Grandmother, angling off to the west. The three sisters followed. Soon Alexa saw why Grandmother had changed direction. A wide swath of gray and black emptiness lay in their path. It was green forest only yesterday.

Alexa had never seen the Scarring so close. She didn't expect it to be so quiet. She had always imagined it making some kind of noise. Silence was scarier.

"Can't we just fly over it without touching it?" Alexa remembered once asking her teacher.

"Never, ever try that," the teacher commanded. "The air over the Scarring is corrupted. It works against the Fae. Any fairy flying through it will become disoriented and fall into despair. The air sucks her down, and once she touches the ground, well...."

"What? What happens then?" the wide-eyed class of spritelings had asked.

"Once Scarring has a hold on you, it never lets go. You would just disappear under the earth, never to be seen again by the living." Alexa may not have always paid attention in school, but that lesson had stayed with her, sometimes in her nightmares.

The four fairies flared their wings and angled downward. Alexa found it difficult to know where they were, since many familiar landmarks had changed into featureless void.

Down and down they glided. They came to where Alexa thought Ispirianza's Great Oak should be. Smoke and dust shrouded the area. Alexa's breathing became fast and strained. Please still be there. Please still be there. Finally, Alexa caught a glimpse of something in the mist. The familiar form of a mighty oak tree appeared out of the eerie fog. The Great Oak stood whole and undisturbed. She breathed a sigh of relief for the old dryad.

The next moment her spirit darkened again, for she could not find Kandra's house. She flew and flew all around the edge of the Scarring. She knew where her best friend's tree had to be. She could have flown there with her eyes closed. It just wasn't there. The land around it had changed so much that she had to look at the sun to tell which way was east. A panicked grief gripped Alexa's spirit. The Scarring had enveloped the place where she had played hundreds of times with Kandra and her little sister. The leaf hammocks they used to swing in, the tree fort they built from sticks and bromeliad leaves, the kitchen where they would make midnight snacks at Kandra's sleepovers—all gone.

"Kandra?" Alexa asked Grandmother in a trembling voice.

"I don't know," said Grandmother and put a gentle hand on Alexa's shoulder.

A council fairy in a purple dress swooped in next to Grandmother. The two older fairies spoke quietly, but Alexa had good ears.

"Gresha," gasped the new arrival. "The future of the Fae is destroyed!"

"Calm yourself, Hilda," assured Grandmother. "We still have plenty of forest land. We can rebuild what was lost."

"But the Scarring has cut through the Bridge of Trees! We are separated forever from the Lake Lands."

A bolt shot down Alexa's spine. Grandmother looked intently at Hilda. Then, without a word, she dashed off in a new direction, bound for the Bridge. Eva, Daria and Alexa could barely keep up. The forest whizzed by in a blur of green and soon parted into a large clearing of grass.

It was the sound that hit Alexa first. An eerie chorus of wailing and crying rose above the smoldering landscape. Alexa and her family joined a mob of fairies and forest folk at the edge of an enormous chasm. The lush green of the mossy forest abruptly fell off into a burnt wasteland. The Scarring had ripped apart the life-giving trees that led to the lakes.

It was as if someone had drawn a sharp line between life and death.

Weeping fairies wove chrysalises to enshroud the fairies who had lost their lives. If the bodies weren't found, the mourners would place the lost fairy's birth elements into the chrysalis and bury it. Alexa had only seen this done once before, when Lycinda's great-aunt had died. She had asked Grandmother why fairies performed this strange ceremony.

"We come into this world through a chrysalis, therefore it is only right for us to depart in the same manner," Alexa remembered Grandmother saying. "The Fae believe that by weaving a chrysalis around the dead, they close the circle of life and give the soul back to the Great Song. The chrysalis is buried at the roots of the fairy's home tree."

Today the fairies wove many chrysalises and feared that death chrysalises would be the only kind they'd ever weave again.

"This is the end," Eva wept. "What will become of us without the Bridge of Trees?" Daria stayed silent and looked sternly into the Scarring as if trying to work out a solution. She slowly cracked her knuckles as she thought.

Alexa thought hard as well. She had learned enough in botany class to know exactly what this meant. Baby fairies could only emerge from their chrysalises once they had been anointed with bramble nectar. The fairies had to get bramble nectar quickly in order to save this summer's babies, who were already growing inside their chrysalises.

The Romorian council soon arrived with tools to test the Scarring. They did not look anyone in the eye as they gathered dirt samples with their instruments. The fairies and forest folk were too mournful now to be angry at the Romorians' mistake. But that would change.

Grandmother edged her way back to Alexa and held her by both shoulders. The look in her eyes made Alexa's heart stutter.

"What is it?"

"Oh, my dear one, I'm so sorry," said Grandmother. "Kandra did not escape her house in time."

Alexa couldn't breathe. "No, she's probably just sleeping in the back of one of the caves."

Grandmother shook her head and looked Alexa in the eyes. "No, child. Do you see Binda and her two daughters kneeling there? They wove two chrysalises for their dead." Binda was

Kandra's aunt.

"Two?" Alexa dared not look where Grandmother was facing.

"Kandra and her mother."

Numbness blanketed Alexa. Young fairies couldn't die. Only old fairies died. And that was only after a long life full of joys and sorrows. Grandmother must have made a mistake. Or maybe it was just a bad joke and Kandra would soon appear, laughing at her friend's gullibility.

But Kandra did not appear.

Alexa's mind didn't know what to do, so she just stared into the distance as Grandmother held her tightly. She noticed all kinds of strange details, like the tiny rip in the shoulder of a nearby fairy's dress and the lone ant hurrying to catch up with the other ants in the line. The colors around her hurt her eyes. Closing them stung and forced out tears.

The mob divided to make way for seven majestic fairy guards arriving from the west. They carried golden flowing banners with ornate designs. The royal seal of truth was emblazoned at the top. A ripple moved through the crowd as every fairy lowered her wings, and each Cobbleton and Romorian dropped to one knee with head bowed. Alexa felt Daria grasp her hand and squeeze it hard. The Fairy of Truth — the High Fairy herself — approached.

As the High Fairy passed by, Alexa caught a glimpse of the stunning gold train of her dress. The scent of rosemary followed her like a servant. Her knee-length, golden hair was streaked with sparkling silver strands. Alexa had never seen the High Fairy this close. She dared not look at her face. As Her Majesty touched down gracefully at the edge of the void, the mourning crowd waited silently.

As the only Fairy of Truth in Kendlenook, the High Fairy would address the crowd with a lesson from *The Wisdom of the Fae* whenever she appeared in public. This time she did not utter a word. Her back and shoulders straight and strong, she simply stared out to where the Bridge of Trees once stood. Tears ran freely down her cheeks.

Slowly, she pulled a silver dagger from her sash.

Daria and Eva gasped. Alexa looked up.

The crowd rustled as they watched the sparkling blade rise to the sky. Kendlenook fairies rarely used weapons, for they had no need of them. Alexa didn't understand what was happening. The High Fairy lifted a handful of her glowing hair and sliced through it with the freshly sharpened blade, letting the golden locks fall to the ground. Shouts arose from the onlookers. She cut another handful, then another until her hair fell only half way to her shoulders. The crowd wept.

Alexa had heard of this display of deepest grief, but only in stories. She never expected to see any fairy actually cut off her own hair, and especially not the High Fairy herself.

Nor did she ever expect to lose Kandra to the Scarring.

"The Great Song has fallen silent," Alexa heard an elder say. "It has forsaken us."

Alexa wondered if she could have stopped this by obeying Ispirianza right away instead of running from her. Maybe she could have saved Kandra and all the others, so many others. She understood now. It was all up to her.

The huge wooden door of the Great Oak swung open at Alexa's touch. Ispirianza looked up calmly. Alexa stood in the beams of sunlight shooting through the doorway.

"Okay, so how do I travel into Timefulness?"

SIXTEEN

The Key to Timefulness

"You do realize the sacrifices involved, Alexa?" Ispirianza asked in her raspy voice.

"Should I watch Kendlenook's daughters die while still helpless in their chrysalises?" asked a determined Alexa. "Should I turn my back on my own daughters and the daughters of my sisters yet unborn? I must go."

"You will face dangers that you cannot imagine," said Ispirianza.

Alexa couldn't believe Ispirianza was now trying to talk her out of it. "The greater danger is to do nothing."

Ispirianza's silence admitted that truth.

"Help me, Ispirianza. I don't know anything about the Glass Corridor entrance. It's just full of dirt now. And if I do get through, what then?"

Ispirianza smiled peacefully and leaned on her twisted wooden cane. "Fear not, young one. The Great Song lets us know how we must move. Now let us start at the beginning. The entrance will not open unless you have with you an object from the realm you seek."

"You mean Timefulness?" she asked. "So the object is like a key. Does it work the other way around? Does a human need something from our realm to come here?"

"Yes. Your Elsie must be a very exceptional human to have an object from the realm Slightly Above Time."

"But she couldn't..." Alexa stopped to think. "Oh! She must have had the object with her when I first saw her come through. But she didn't know it was important, so she didn't bring it with her when I asked her to come back the other night."

Ispirianza raised a mossy eyebrow. "Inviting Elsie here is an interesting way to try to avoid your own task, but it wouldn't have worked. You must go to her. The answer to our danger lies in her world, not ours."

"The only thing I had from Timefulness was the Speaking Phone. It would have been too heavy for me to carry, anyway."

"No need for that. You forget that I have traveled into Timefulness myself. My human friend Margaret sent me back with many gifts. Come see for yourself." Ispirianza took a lighting wand from a shelf of odds and ends, and, in one flashing motion, lit seven candles on a candelabrum. She then led Alexa down a dark spiral corridor deep into the roots of the Great Oak. At the end of the corridor lay a dark oval chamber filled with a jumble of strange things glowing orange in the candlelight. Ispirianza's long, gnarled fingers waved over the hoard.

"I don't understand," said a stunned Alexa. "These are

from Timefulness? Why don't you show everyone? Then they would have to believe."

"Oh, child, do you think they would accept the truth of another realm simply because I showed them a few trinkets?" asked Ispirianza. "And even if they did, their trust would be based on what they could see and feel. What is needed most among fairies is belief. Hope dies without belief. And hope is what will bring magic back to our realm. Do you understand?"

"A little," said Alexa.

"In the same way, your grandmother and Goric would not have understood if they had seen Elsie's phone. They would have stood in your way."

"You know that I tried to show them?" Alexa felt ashamed.

"Constanza the Maple Dryad sent word to me. Remember you told me the phone was hidden near her tree?"

"I just can't believe the phone is gone. Now I can't speak with Elsie."

"Don't worry, young one," said Ispirianza, her eyes glancing downward. "The phone is right where you left it."

"What do you mean? How could it be back? And how could you know if it were?" Alexa asked. Ispirianza took a long breath and stepped toward Alexa. An uncomfortable silence stood between them. Finally Ispirianza spoke up.

"Because I had Constanza put it back after you tried to show it to Goric."

SEVENTEEN

The Locket

Alexa's shock built into fierce anger. Her hands and wings began to shake. "But... but why?"

"I feared you might show the phone to someone you thought more qualified to travel into Timefulness," said Ispirianza, touching Alexa on the shoulder.

"How could you do this? I thought you were my friend!" Alexa yelled, yanking her shoulder from Ispirianza's hand. "Grandmother was so angry she wouldn't even speak to me!"

"I'm sorry you had to go through that," Ispirianza said, staying calm. "I know it's hard for you to understand, but my tree felt an urgency about the Scarring. Though I had no idea that it would come so near so soon." Ispirianza raised an eyebrow. "Tell me, Alexa, what would the Romorians have done with the phone had you given it to Goric?" Alexa tried to think through her anger.

Ispirianza quickly answered her own question. "They

would have taken it apart to study it and made it useless to you, that's what. And they would have taken the pieces of the corridor to Maubulan to try to find out how they work, wouldn't they?"

"I guess so," Alexa said quietly.

"And what would the fairy council have done, hmm? I'll tell you: They would have wasted valuable time arguing about whether or not the human realm exists and would certainly have failed to get through."

"But I…no, you brought shame to Grandmother's name! She says her reputation is ruined," Alexa insisted through a tear. Ispirianza's face grew stern.

"What fairy in Kendlenook is thinking about her reputation after last night?" Ispirianza snapped, pointing her cane at Alexa.

Ashamed, Alexa said nothing.

"I have trust in you, young one," Ispirianza's scratchy voice rose. "I trust that you will think outside yourself. Remember the daughters of Kendlenook, for the Great Song's sake!" The room fell silent. Alexa studied the floor.

"You're right, Ispirianza," Alexa whispered. "Of course you're right."

"Even if the lives of the youngest ones weren't in danger, something even bigger is happening." Ispirianza's voice was no longer raspy but strong. "There is something we need even more than bramble nectar. We need faith restored to our spirits and magic back in our realm. And not the kind of faith that comes from showing off some human gadget, but rather the kind that even Scarring cannot destroy." Alexa began to pace back and forth across the room.

"I'm sorry, Ispirianza," Alexa fought back her tears. "I shouldn't have questioned you. Please show me what I need to do." Ispirianza put her gnarled wooden hand on Alexa's shoulder and stopped her from pacing.

"I know you can do this task, but you don't know it yet." Alexa tried to calm her spirit, but her wings still quivered a little. Ispirianza's face brightened again. She could see that Alexa was regaining her focus.

Ispirianza's twisted fingers waved once more at the pile of magical human items. "You must choose your entrance key carefully. Be sure that the object feels right in your hands and sparks your imagination. Remember, a fairy's magic dwells in her imagination. Touch these things, study them. Whichever object chooses you will prove vital to your success."

Peering inside the dim chamber, Alexa felt she was gazing into an unknown world of bizarre and magical creations. Objects of every shape, size and color stared back at her. She picked up a silver-colored twist of thin metal about the size of her arm.

"Humans call that a paperclip," said Ispirianza, "but I can't for the life of me recall its use." Alexa closed her eyes to feel it. Nothing.

Alexa put back the paperclip and took up a heavy disk of coppery metal the same color as her own hair. It had a relief carving of a bearded face and strange symbols on it.

"Humans use those to buy things in the same way that we use beads. It's called a penny." It fascinated Alexa but had no special attraction for her. Another strange object looked like a cozy white sleeping bag with a bend in the middle.

"That's a sock to keep a human's foot warm. It has a twin

that I left in Timefulness." Interesting, but it didn't speak to Alexa at all.

The instant Alexa touched the next object, she knew it was her key. She didn't know how she knew, but she did. A long chain held an old and tarnished silver oval the size of Alexa's head. The oval had a curly design around the edges and a dusty but gleaming stone set in the middle. The stone looked white at first, but when Alexa looked closer she could see ripples of pink, green, yellow and blue. It must be a gemstone, but Alexa had never seen this kind before. She wished she'd had one of these in her chrysalis instead of that horrible lump of granite. Alexa released the tarnished clasp on one side, and the oval opened to show a realistic drawing of a young face.

"This is the one," said Alexa.

"My, my," said Ispirianza. "It's strange you should pick that locket out of all the objects. Wonderful, but strange."

"Who is the fairy in the drawing?"

"Not a fairy and not a drawing," said Ispirianza. "That is a photo of my friend Margaret."

"I know what a photo is!" said Alexa. "I made one of a centipede for Elsie."

Ispirianza smiled. "Margaret gave this to me so that I would remember her, as if I could forget such a friend. This is the smallest human necklace Margaret could find, but it weighs far too much for me to actually wear it."

Alexa put the necklace back in the basket. "No, it's too special to you. Maybe the paperclip—."

"Alexa, this is your key. It is not mine to keep." Ispirianza put the necklace back in Alexa's arms. Then the old dryad took a deep breath and sighed. "Unfortunately, the second thing you need will prove as difficult to catch as it is to see. Listen carefully, for the lives of the fairy daughters may depend on how well you remember what I am about to say." Alexa arranged the oval with its chain carefully on her lap and locked her mind on every word Ispirianza said.

"Fairies cannot fly by themselves in the realm of Timefulness. The very weight of time there makes a fairy sink to the earth. You'd struggle even to walk."

"Like the Scarring?" gasped Alexa.

"No. The Scarring pulls you down and consumes everything. Timefulness is different. In Timefulness, the air simply cannot hold you up. Since time is bent slower there, your wings beat slower as well. You will need long strands of pixie silk in order to fly. The pixie silk keeps you connected to our realm above time and allows you to return."

"Where can I find this pixie silk?" Alexa asked.

"You have, of course, seen the Shadow Fairies dancing in the firelight?"

Alexa nodded.

Ispirianza continued, "Do you know that each silent Shadow Fairy is the image of a fairy like you? When you see Shadow Fairies in the light, each one belongs in a way to one of the fairies nearby. You have a Shadow Fairy, each of your sisters has a Shadow Fairy, your Grandmother has one, and so does the High Fairy.

"Your own—and only your own—Shadow Fairy can spin pixie silk for you from her own spirit. After you catch her, you must convince her of your worth, for it is a great sacrifice for a Shadow Fairy to give up part of her spirit and her freedom. But she will make this sacrifice if she believes your task worthy."

"She loses her freedom?" asked Alexa.

"To fly in Timefulness, you must be tethered to your Shadow Fairy, who remains above time. It's almost like you fly in the human realm but cast a shadow here. In fact, if someone could see your Shadow Fairy above time while you were tethered to it with pixie silk, they could locate you in the other realm."

"But everyone knows you can't catch a Shadow Fairy. All of my friends have tried. They fly faster than lightning, and they hide in the shadows of the trees and mountains. And how would I even know which one is mine?"

"You will have to think of a way to recognize her. Sometimes it's the subtle shape of your wings, or the way you move your body."

"But how can you make them stay still long enough to get a good look at them?" asked Alexa.

Ispirianza fingered the wooden beads on her necklace. "The only way I know to hold a Shadow Fairy still long enough to speak to her is to trap her in a circle of candledark."

Alexa had heard the word before but never knew what it meant. "Candledark?"

"Candledark. You well know that if a fairy needs to travel at night, she uses candlelight to see her way?"

"Of course."

"Candledark is the opposite of candlelight. It creates an area of darkness within light."

"Who would want to do that?" Alexa asked.

Ispirianza's expression grew darker. "Oths."

Alexa had never seen an evil Oth fairy before, but just hearing the word made her panic. "Why can't we just bring Elsie here?" she pleaded.

EIGHTEEN

The Truth about Liars

I spirianza grasped Alexa's arms in an encouraging gesture. "The Oths dwell in caves and seek the cover of darkness. They use candledark to travel in the noonday sun because the bright sunlight damages their eyes. The sun can even blind them if they stay in it too long without the protection of candledark.

"Candledark is not simply a shadow but a source of darkness itself. It casts blackness on everything nearby. The magic of the Oths reverses much of what is natural—truths become lies, and light becomes darkness. Their darkness is not just the absence of light, it's something you can feel—it radiates coldness and emptiness."

Alexa shivered. "So where do I get it?" she asked, already dreading the answer.

"The distant caves of Evernaught," Ispirianza answered. "The dark lair of the Oths, which lies hundreds of thousands of wingbeats to the northeast of Kendlenook."

"Let me make sure I understand. You want me to steal candledark from the Oths? But won't they, um, kill me?"

"They will try," said Ispirianza. "So you must take great care not to be seen. Remember, though, that the Oths are not gods, but merely fairies who have allowed lies to twist them into something else."

Alexa felt as if someone were squeezing her lungs. "I'm no match for even one Oth, and you want me to sneak past an entire brood of them in their own homes?"

"I would gladly go in your place to seek candledark, but you know that I cannot. I offer you all the protection that I can give: that of my sister dryads. The Great Oak will spread news of your quest to the other trees. The trees will pass the information to their dryads through Ring Dreams. You may call upon any dryad for help along the way."

"But what if I need help and there is no dryad tree nearby?" Alexa wondered. "Can I take another fairy with me? What about Daria and Eva?"

Ispirianza studied the swirling pattern in the heartwood of her tree. She ran her hand lovingly over its smooth surface. "Not your sisters," she finally answered. "But do not worry. The Great Song will move others into your path. It always provides everything you need to complete the harmony you must play."

Alexa waited for her to explain, but she did not. "Ispirianza, why can't my sisters come with me? They know so much more than I do. You're not telling me everything."

Ispirianza said nothing, but gazed upward into the tree's inner rings.

Chapter 18

"Your tree has told you something," Alexa said. "You've had another Ring Dream!"

"You have guessed correctly," sighed Ispirianza. "I have wrestled in my mind over whether or not to tell you."

"It has something to do with my sisters, doesn't it?"

Ispirianza sighed. "If anything should happen to Eva or Daria, you may not have the will to complete your task. Alexa, I'm sorry, but the Great Oak has foreseen that someone on your journey will die."

"Die?" gasped Alexa.

Ispirianza looked apologetic. "I know that's not what you want to hear."

"But I've chosen to put myself in danger," said Alexa. "I won't make that decision for anyone else. I'll go alone."

"You may go alone, but you won't be alone. Others will help along the way, my tree has seen this. But the Great Oak also warns of one other danger."

"Just one?"

Ispirianza nodded. "The Great Oak says to beware of the one with an hourglass-shaped mark on her ankle. She will prove the greatest obstacle to your success. Do not trust her motives."

"What kind of mark? Like a birthmark?" Alexa asked.

"My tree could not say. Only be careful of anyone with a mark shaped like an hourglass. Its wearer may undermine your entire mission. Promise me you will remember."

"I will remember."

Ispirianza talked on until the late hours of the night, explaining what she knew of Elsie and the Scarring. Alexa realized that she must not only stop the Scarring from spreading but also repair the Bridge of Trees.

"Ispirianza, how long before the daughter chrysalises will die without bramble nectar?" asked Alexa.

"You well know that most fairies are born soon after the summer solstice, but that will not happen this year. A chrysalis may survive for up to four more weeks without opening. That's all the time you have."

"Four weeks then. Maybe less," said Alexa. Her heart fluttered.

Ispirianza stood and laid her gnarled arm around Alexa's shoulders. "May the granite in your spirit strengthen you," she said. "May the eagle make you soar, and may the pine keep you close to your roots. And may you always move with the Great Song."

NINETEEN

A Secret Revealed

lexa awoke later than usual. Classes were cancelled due to all the damage the Scarring had caused in and around Kendlenook. Alexa felt grateful that her own home still stood. Thoughts of Kandra hovered at the edges of her mind, but she forced them away. Too painful. She bounced back and forth between terror and excitement.

Alexa began preparing for the journey to Evernaught while alone at home. All that day, Alexa gathered bits of food and extra clothing into a single cloth satchel that she could carry around her neck.

Alexa wrapped Ispirianza's big, heavy human locket carefully in an extra dress and added it to the bag. Snarfle followed her around the house, watching curiously. An audience of Alexa's stuffed dragon dolls also watched from her bed like adoring fans. She added acorn containers of yucca soap, her hair comb and toothbrush carved from pine wood, extra sashes and towels—everything she could think of that she might need on a long journey.

Grandmother swooped through the front door early in the afternoon. After greeting Alexa wearily, she went straight to bed, not having slept in more than a day.

Eva and Daria were nowhere to be seen. Now was Alexa's chance to talk to Elsie once more and tell her the plan. She quietly closed the front door as she left.

Sure enough, the phone sat right where Alexa had left it. Ispirianza was much more cunning than Alexa had expected. Alexa landed on top and stepped on the first button. The phone beeped and a blue light flashed. A fairy's voice shot out from behind her.

"Alexa! What in Kendlenook are you doing?"

Alexa jumped into the ferns. She recognized the voice as Daria's.

"Daria! Did you follow me, you sneak?"

"I suspected you were up to something when I saw you leave the house," Daria snapped. "Get away from that thing, it could hurt you." Daria's golden eyebrows rose as she leaned in to study the amazing object.

"No, it won't, I promise. Elsie taught me how to use it."

"Elsie? What kind of a name is that?" Daria asked, not taking her eyes off the phone. Alexa took a deep breath and started to explain. She had no choice.

"Well, you know how I tried to tell Grandmother and Goric that the humans cause the Scarring?"

"Uh, huh," Daria prompted, her eyes illuminated by the brilliant light of the phone.

"Well, this is what I wanted to show them, but it got, um, misplaced. Elsie's a human. I saw her with my own eyes."

"You actually know what this thing is?" asked Daria.

"It's called a phone. Humans use it to talk to each other over long distances," said Alexa.

"Don't be silly," Daria said.

"Fine, watch this." Alexa stepped on the buttons in the correct order to call Elsie on her brother's phone.

"No, Alexa! Don't," Daria pleaded.

"It's okay," said Alexa. "Just wait." The phone started to buzz.

"Alexa!" said Elsie's voice.

"Elsie? How did you know it's me?" asked Alexa. "Can you see me? I can't see you."

"Caller I.D.," said Elsie. "No, wait, don't tell me: You don't know what caller I.D. is."

"No idea," said Alexa. "Anyway, my sister Daria came with me. She doesn't believe that humans exist. She thinks I'm lying."

"Hi, Daria," said Elsie.

Daria's wings twitched nervously. She opened and closed her mouth as though to speak, but she kept quiet. Alexa was enjoying shocking her sister. Daria reached out and gently poked the shiny purple stone like it might bite her.

"So do you flitter around the meadows like Alexa?" Elsie asked.

"No," said Daria, still not sure whether she should speak to the alien gemstone. "I'm of the Forest. Are...are you really a human?"

"Last time I checked," said Elsie.

"I'm, uh…I find that hard to believe."

"You think it's easy for a seventh grader to believe in fairies?" Elsie's voice said. "Hey, Alexa, I have an idea. Will you use my phone to take a photo of yourself like you did with the centipede? Daria can push the button for you."

Alexa did as she was told and sent the photo to Elsie's brother's phone. Daria was now completely confused but did whatever Alexa said without question.

"Oh, my gosh!" Elsie's voice said in awe. "You do have wings—they are so beautiful! Oh, you've just got to come into Timefulness now. No one will ever believe me with just a picture. Wait a second, I'll send one of me."

Soon, a perfect image appeared on the screen of the Speaking Stone. Alexa immediately recognized the magical giant she had seen. The photo showed Elsie from the waist up looking back over her shoulder. "I turned like that to prove that I don't have any wings," said Elsie. Alexa and Daria traded looks of amazement.

"But how do you know my sister?" asked Daria.

Elsie explained the whole story to Daria, who now sounded less confused and more like a big sister.

Daria said, "Elsie, Alexa thinks she can come to your world, and she wants to try it. We have a big problem here that she thinks you can help solve."

"Yeah, I know. Scarring, right? I'm up for anything."

In grave tones, Alexa explained that she needed to do a few things before she could journey to Timefulness.

"Okay," said Elsie. "I'll be waiting."

As they flew home, Alexa outlined Ispirianza's plan. Daria thought for a long time before she said anything. She had an excellent mind for making plans and finding the flaws in others' plans.

"Okay, little sister, there are certainly some crazy things going on here—I'll give you that," she finally said as she began to crack her knuckles. Alexa grimaced at the sound. "Even if Elsie isn't human, that Speaking Stone thingy makes the Romorians look like woblins. And I don't think the Oths could be behind this. If they could make such a thing, they certainly wouldn't use it to talk to us."

"Hmm, we definitely can't tell Grandmother. She doesn't believe in humans and would never let you go," Daria continued, forgetting that she herself had only believed in humans for an hour or so. "We should talk to Eva, though."

"Eva?" cried Alexa. "Miss 'Follow-the-Rules'? She would tell Grandmother faster than a sylph's wingbeat. Or worse yet, go to the council. Ispirianza said that would only lead to disaster."

"I don't think she'll tell Grandmother," said Daria. "Not once she knows that I'll be going with you."

Alexa stopped in midair and thought her heart would stop, too. "No, Daria, you can't! Ispirianza said I have to do this alone. That's exactly what she said." That wasn't exactly what Ispirianza had said, but Alexa couldn't think of any other way to keep Daria from going with her.

Daria swooped in front of Alexa and hovered right in her face. "Listen, even that crazy old dryad wouldn't send a twelve-year-old to the caves of Evernaught alone."

"I'm thirteen," Alexa said.

"Well, whatever," said Daria. "You need a Fairy of Protection, and guess what? I am one! So I'm going with you, and no arguing."

Alexa didn't know what to say. A squirrel scampered up a nearby tree trunk, chirping to itself. A mosquito buzzed in the silence. She knew that it wouldn't help to tell Daria that someone was destined to die on the journey. Daria had such a strong will and a fierce protective instinct that even the threat of death wouldn't deter her.

"Okay, you can come," Alexa lied. She had no intention of letting Daria go with her.

"Good, that's settled," said Daria, and the sisters fluttered on toward home at treetop height.

As they descended into Kendlenook Village, something dove down on them. Eva swooped in, buzzing like a dragonfly. She must have been watching for them.

Eva held up Alexa's satchel. "What is this?" she demanded. "Where in Kendlenook do you think you're going?"

Nowhere in Kendlenook, Alexa thought, but she said nothing. Daria came to her rescue. "Calm down, Eva. I know all about it. Let's go inside and talk. Grandmother isn't home, is she?"

"No, the council went to settle a dispute with the Cobbletons. They're trying to profit from the destruction by overcharging the Romorians for the tools they need to build their wall," said Eva. "Come on. You had better have a good story."

The three fairies flew into the tree house together. Snarfle waddled up to Alexa and rubbed his blunt horns on her leg.

For dinner, Eva had prepared a beautiful meal of broiled mustard flowers and sow thistle leaves accented by a lemon and sunflower-seed sauce poured on top in an ornate design. As they ate, Daria told Eva everything she knew. On the way home, Alexa and Daria had agreed that Eva would accept the wild story better from Daria.

"So you actually spoke to this human?" Eva sounded uncertain.

"I said so, didn't I?" shot Daria. She always got impatient whenever anyone doubted her. "And Alexa saw her." Alexa felt better having Daria on her side.

"There must be another way," said Eva. "Even if the Great Song has chosen Alexa to visit the human world—which I'm not at all sure about—then someone else could go for the candledark. Alexa has no experience with Oths. She has no idea how much power their lies can hold. Even if you go with her, Daria, I don't know…maybe Grandmother and the council—."

"No!" cried Alexa and Daria together.

"You can't tell her," said Alexa without taking a breath. "She wouldn't believe me, and she would watch me so closely that I'd never be able to slip away. I have to go now if I'm to have any chance of saving the daughters of Kendlenook."

"Don't worry, Eva. I'll be with her. I don't want to brag but you know I'm the toughest fairy in this forest," Daria bragged.

"Well, we do need to move quickly, and the Romorians have all the help they need here. I suppose we should fly down this path as well in case what Ispirianza says is right," said Eva, though she looked unhappy. "When will you leave?"

"Tomorrow morning, early," said Alexa. Daria nodded.

"When will you come back?" Eva started to tear up.

"I have to pass through Kendlenook on the way back from

the Oth caves to the Glass Corridor entrance," said Alexa.

"You mean 'we,'" said Daria.

"Yes, of course, we."

"You be careful, little sisters," Eva sniffed. "I just couldn't go on if anything happened to you two." Tears flowed from her eyes.

"Oh, Eva, you're such a sap," said Daria, now sobbing herself.

The three sisters held each other tightly, crying and then laughing at each other for crying.

Night came. The evening chorus of frogs drifted on the air. Did Timefulness hold such sounds? Alexa wondered.

"Tomorrow morning, then," said Daria with determination. She sent Alexa to bed, saying that she would stay up to map their course and pack her own things.

Once the light in Daria's room went out, Alexa waited awhile just to be safe. She then grabbed her bag and Daria's map and slipped out her open window into the ink-black night. She reached back in and picked up Poof, her favorite stuffed dragon, from the crowd of dolls on her bed. She started to stuff him into her now heavy satchel, but then she looked at Poof, stroked his fluffy horns and then set him back on the bed. Alexa decided to leave all childish things behind. It was time to go. Alone. She closed the shutters to her bedroom window so Poof couldn't see her leave.

She fluttered outside each of her sisters' bedroom windows for a moment, watching them sleep so peacefully. Tears clouded Alexa's vision.

Taking one last look at her childhood home, she whispered goodbye and glided into the still and vast darkness.

"One traveler passes through the forest and experiences awe and wonder. Another sees only rocks, trees and dirt. Both are reality. Which will you choose?"

~Zymandria,
dryad of the White Mountains

Part III:
The Journey

TWENTY

A Friend to the Friendless

Alexa awoke the next morning to a racket of chattering birds. She felt damp and chilled all over. She'd slept for only a few hours, curled up under a thicket of blackberry bushes. The morning dew had soaked not only the bottom of her satchel, which she'd used as a pillow, but also one whole side of her dress. The clammy fabric clung to her leg. She squinted and looked around to figure out where exactly she was.

The night before, Alexa had tried to get as far from Kendlenook as she could, but after three hours of hard flapping, her shoulder muscles began to ache and her eyes refused to stay open. She'd never slept on the ground before, but she was too tired to search for a suitable tree. Now she sat in the sun trying to dry her dress and wings. She gently opened and closed her wings in the warming rays. Then she rummaged through her satchel and took out a piece of hard buckwheat bread for her breakfast. Alexa gazed off toward the high and barren Dragontooth Mountains that lay north and west of her. The Oth caves were somewhere past those forbidding slopes. She unfolded Daria's map and studied it.

By noon, Alexa came to the Cobbleton town of Wallowbriar. It bustled with the sounds of Cobbleton wagons crunching through the streets and craftsmen making their wares. She traded some shells for twine and a gourd of flowerseed oil to flavor wild plants.

She finally came to a familiar meadow. It was the farthest she had ever been from Kendlenook. Last year when she'd visited here on a school field trip, it had seemed like the edge of the world. Today, it was merely a starting point.

Alexa gently perched on top of a lifeless tree and looked back toward home one more time. "No tears," she said to herself. "I will succeed. I will come back."

The forest soon grew thinner and gave way to a vast expanse of grasslands. To the east in the distance rose the smoke of the cooking fires from Coldwater Camp, the largest Cobbleton outpost in the region.

Feeling exposed, Alexa caught a thermal air current and rose high above the trade road so that no one could sneak up on her. The farther she traveled, the more she felt like a stranger to the land—a tiny dot drifting in a vast, featureless sea.

The sun crept higher and higher as Alexa flew on. A fish eagle circled high above in the wind currents. A rabbit scampered across the field below. A little bird sat perched at the roadside far below, singing a sad little song Alexa had never heard before.

No, not a bird. Her curiosity aroused, Alexa went down and hovered in front of it. She stared at the tiny winged creature huddled miserably at the edge of the grass. It hid its face in its unusually large ears, moaning something about how much it had suffered.

"Birds definitely don't talk," thought Alexa. "At least not in any language I can understand." She had certainly never known a bird to feel sorry for itself. Alexa crept up on the strange little sprite. She poked the creature with one finger. It startled, but didn't even look up.

"Hello, there," said Alexa in her friendliest voice. Alexa jumped back when, in a flash, it zipped farther into the long grass and hid its head again. Fast little thing.

"I won't hurt you," said Alexa. "What's the matter?" She looked closer at it. "And what are you?"

"Who, us?" it asked nervously. Alexa didn't see anyone else.

"Yes, you."

"We're just someone d-d-doomed to die," said the creature without looking at Alexa. It began to wail.

"Doomed? I'm not so sure about that. Are you hurt?"

"N-not in body, but very m-m-much in my spirit." It flopped down face first on the ground. "You really don't know what we are, d-do you?" it asked.

Alexa examined the little creature. It had big sad eyes, long tufted ears coming straight out of the sides of its head, thin wings and no legs. Beneath its waist was a long thin tail that came together at the end in something that looked like a flowy fish's tail. Under its navel sat a round pot belly. "I really haven't got a clue what you are," she finally said.

"We're a f-f-freak of nature," it said. "A singer without a s-s-song. A shark that c-can't fly. A homebody without a home. A weasel without—"

"I get it," Alexa interrupted. "You're down on yourself." She looked harder. "But I still have no idea what you are." The creature sighed, then reluctantly leaped into the air and darted and swooshed around and around Alexa's head. A slight breeze began to blow.

"A sylph! You're a sylph!" Alexa exclaimed. "Huh. I didn't recognize you because I've never seen a sylph sitting still, or alone for that matter. Where is your gathering?" Sylphs always moved in groups of thousands or more.

The sylph shrugged and began to cry again.

"Don't worry, little sylph. Go see my sister Eva. She will know just what to do. She's a sylph herder." The sylph gave Alexa a terrified look, so she tried a different approach. "I don't know much about your kind, but I can help you look for your gathering. Come along with me." Alexa just couldn't leave the poor little thing alone.

"Oh, n-n-no," it said. "You won't want us with you once y-you know our story. Just leave us here to die like we deserve."

"Come now, you couldn't have done anything that terrible," said Alexa. "My name is Alexa. What's yours?"

"What do you mean?" asked the sylph.

"What do your friends call you?"

"You mean you want t-to know the name of our gathering?"

"No, just yours."

"Us?"

"Just you. Singular you...what do they call you?"

"What does the caller call? The caller calls signals to us... wait...what?"

"No, no." Alexa was getting frustrated. "Look, if someone wanted to talk to just you, what would they say?"

"W-why should anyone want to talk to me over anyone else? Talking to all others in my gathering will do. The g-gathering is one."

"You don't have a name? What kind of mother doesn't name her children? How do you know who you are?" The sylph looked at Alexa blankly. "Well, I shall have to think of a proper name for you then."

Alexa craned her neck to inspect its tail. "What are you l-looking at?" it asked, twisting around to look.

"Just seeing if you have an hourglass-shaped mark."

"W-why?"

"Long story. But you don't really have ankles, let alone a mark, so I can probably trust you."

The sylph just looked at her. "What a strange f-fairy you are." Its voice sounded a little stronger. "Why is a Meadow Fairy f-flying all alone out here anyway?"

"Oh, you know I'm a Meadow Fairy. I'm on a journey to... to do something important," she said. "Now what's this about being doomed to die?"

The sylph timidly circled Alexa and told his story. Alexa didn't know why, but she had come to think of the sylph as male, maybe because he was so different from her. He talked faster than fast and was very excitable, as if he expected to get eaten at any second so he had better get his thoughts out quickly. Alexa welcomed the distraction from her own worries. Comforting another can be quite comforting.

"Our gathering l-lives in the Lower Sylph Marshes. You probably don't know of that place. Fairies r-rarely go there. We only have one thing to do, b-b-but we do it really, really well. Absolutely. Or not. Our job is to blow the winds from the northeast so that the r-rains come to the southern forests at the r-right times. Our caller is one of the best, sort of amazing. We won last year's Monsoon Award for s-speed and accuracy."

"Such a noble task, little sylph," said Alexa, trying to make the sylph feel better. "Why, without the hard work of sylph gatherings, the weather would just happen without rhyme or reason." The sylph seemed to grow a little taller at the compliment.

"But sylphs have no p-purpose without the gathering. Alone, a sylph does not have enough p-power to guide the winds. And, well..." The sylph bowed his head and circled a wing-length behind Alexa. "We no longer have a g-gathering. The caller took our homing charm and sent us into the grasslands to d-die. Alone."

Alexa gasped. "Why would your caller do such a terrible thing?"

"The others say we have done a great wrong and brought sh-sh-shame on ourselves."

"Just tell me what happened. And stop referring to yourself in the plural — it's annoying. You're not with your gathering anymore," said Alexa.

"We're...I mean, I'm sorry. I just knew I would annoy you with who I are, or am... I am here because I disobeyed the c-c-caller of my gathering. We blew the winds north of the m-marshes three sunsets ago. A sylph of our gathering f-f-fell behind. Its homing charm became, how do you say, stubborn… or sour? No, I mean sick! It didn't follow the caller's c-calls — some of them, or not. And the sylph could not follow the motion of us. We…I disobeyed the caller's signal, flew out of formation and pulled this sylph b-back to the gathering. So you see, I deserve to be b-banished. Absolutely. All sylph-minded know, a sylph can't live long outside of its gathering. They send me to die, but at least they do not send me to that t-t-terrible place."

"Terrible place?"

"They call it the Asylum. It's like a j-jail for crazy and twisted sylphs. I would rather d-die than go to th-that yucky place."

"You get punished for helping a friend?" Alexa was outraged.

"To have a friend is to favor one over another. We must treat all of our g-gathering alike. Death is too good for us…I mean me. I need to suffer before we die. I'm a bad, t-terrible sylph." He began hitting himself over the head with his stick-like hands. Alexa grabbed his arms. They felt like she could break them with a squeeze. She let go.

"Stop it! You are not a bad sylph. You did what anyone with a heart would have done. What happened to your friend?"

"Oh, the friend sylph is still w-with the gathering. Friend did not disobey."

"That hardly seems fair. You should get a reward!"

"Oh, no! No, no, no. That is not the way of the g-gathering. Our fairy herder tells us if one sylph starts to th-think for ourself, the entire fabric of the gathering could unravel… absolutely. Or not," said the lowly creature.

Alexa reached out to comfort him. "Don't touch me! I'm a sick, sorry sylph. I just want to p-p-perish like the caller wishes. I deserve the darkness of d-death," he said rather dramatically.

"Well, I don't care what your caller says. I think you're a hero. In fact, I just thought of the perfect name for you." Alexa stopped and hovered in front of the sylph. "You shall from now on be called 'Arthur the Valiant' after the hero in one of Ispirianza's human stories. Arthur was a great king who liked camels a lot. He and his council had dinner at a round table at knight," said Alexa.

"Arthur," repeated the lone sylph quietly. He seemed to like it — kind of. "I guess you could c-c-call me Arthur."

"Now, Arthur, listen to me. Among fairies you would be punished for not helping a friend in need. I am your friend and I need your help. I will be your gathering from now on, and I will take care of you. Do you know the way to the caves of Evernaught?"

"Oh hey! Sure! Absolutely. Evernaught. Flown over it lots of times. It's just past the Great Woblin Plains. I can take you th — I'm sorry, y-you said Evernaught, right? Um…just so you know, those are the c-caves where an icky brood of evil f-fairies dwell. Only a deranged snifflenymph would want to g-go there…of course."

"Just call me a snifflenymph then," smiled Alexa. "So you do know where it is?"

"A bit. Kind of. But just so you know, if we go there, we'll p-probably die. Absolutely will die." Arthur said.

Arthur the lone sylph

"Oh, so now you want to live, do you?" It was kind of fun teasing this little guy. "Will you help me?" Alexa looked straight into the watery eyes of the sylph and waited for an answer. Arthur bobbed from side to side, wringing his hands, but said nothing. "How far from here are the caves, anyway?" Alexa asked. Arthur's nose wrinkled in concentration as his mind went to work on a flight plan.

"Well, we f-f-figure a young fairy like y-yourself probably averages...maybe... 32,000 wingbeats in a nine-hour f-flying day—including stops for food and w-water...we'd say four days if the wind stays at our b-back." Arthur smirked a little and continued: "We—I mean Arthur—can d-d-do a 240,000-wingbeat day without m-much trouble, in case you were wondering."

"Wow," Alexa tried to sound encouraging.

"But just s-so you know," said Arthur. "Oths are v-very bad—and mean. They're not nice. At all."

"Well, I have to steal candledark from their caves. The fate of the world kind of depends on it." Alexa glanced at Arthur to see if he was impressed. He just looked frightened.

TWENTY-ONE

The Magic of Time

O ver the next two days, Alexa and her new friend Arthur traveled over woods and meadows, leaving the trading road far behind. The cliffs of the upper Dragontooth Mountain chain crept up slowly before them. Dark clouds moved shadows across the land. A warm wind blew through the grass. With it, a dark whisper rose:

"Come to where I wait for you...."

Alexa's skin began to crawl. She whipped around to see where the voice came from.

"Did you hear that, Arthur?"

"Hear w-w-w-what?" Arthur began to shake.

"Come to Uchaf Du Maen...." the whisper spoke.

"That! Did you hear that weird whisper?"

"A w-w-weird whisper? I don't like weird whispers," said Arthur.

"Who are you?" cried Alexa, ignoring Ispirianza's warning.

"Show me your face!"

"That's okay, Alexa. I don't n-n-need to see the face," Arthur said while shaking back and forth.

"I'm waiting…" the voice echoed away.

"If you can't make any sense, then leave me alone!" Alexa yelled at the wind.

"Okay, now you're r-r-really freaking me out," said Arthur.

"Let's get out of here," said Alexa. Arthur was already gone.

She caught up to him an hour later, where he had started making a camp.

"Do me a f-f-avor," said Arthur. "Please d-d-don't tell me if you hear any more whispers."

At night, Alexa's mind would fret and worry over the task she had agreed to do. But with the long stretches of silence, her mind also became still and her thinking unclouded. A feeling welled up within her that chased away her fear. She remembered Ispirianza saying: "Whether we realize it or not, each of us is spending her life away. How are you spending yours?" For the first time in her life, Alexa's spirit was filled with a sense of purpose. She was spending her life on something worth a life.

Alexa spent part of each morning collecting wild foods with Arthur tagging along, not wanting to be left alone even for a moment. Arthur did not eat plants. As he flew, he would chomp gnats and other tiny insects without even interrupting his sentence. In one instant she would see a bug flying by and in the next—whoosh! It was gone.

Alexa liked Arthur's company, even though he tended to dart into the nearest hiding place every time a frog croaked or a squirrel chirped. But Arthur definitely had his good points. Sylphs almost never run out of energy, and Arthur always stood guard at night because sylphs never sleep. As Alexa studied how Arthur flew, she realized he steered by tilting his ears in the wind. Though it looked kind of silly, it allowed his wings to focus on one thing: speed. He flew so quickly that he had to fly in circles just to stay back with Alexa. He simply did not know how to fly slowly.

He also didn't know when to keep quiet. The constant, maddening chatter sometimes made Alexa wonder if his help was really worth it. After his ninth explanation of how to change a cumulus cloud into a nimbus cloud, Alexa snapped.

"Yes, yes. You've told me how weather patterns work," she said. "And I already know an awful lot about airflow, thermals and barometric pressure. I am a fairy, you know. I get top marks in Advanced Aerodynamics even though the instructor doesn't like me."

"I'm s-sorry. I'm annoying you, aren't I?" asked a deflated Arthur.

"No, no, you're fine."

"You really d-don't have to pretend you want to talk to me. I can take it."

"Arthur, no. I'm glad you're with me."

"Just let me know if we ever do anything that m-makes you feel frustrated, sad or depressed. We just couldn't bear it if I thought I caused that." Arthur waited for a reply. Alexa stayed silent. Arthur hovered close in front of Alexa like a bumblebee and looked her in the eyes, stopping her in mid-flight. "I'm not frustrating you, am I?"

"I'll let you know, okay?" said Alexa.

"Okay, good. Just p-putting it out there."

"Let's just change the subject."

"Okay. So t-tell me again about this whole time b-bending thing," Arthur said.

"It's kind of complicated."

"We're a really s-smart sylph. I can understand."

"Well, you know about the two types of time, right?"

"Of course…k-kind of. Not really. No. How could there be d-different kinds of time?"

"If you really think about it, there have to be two types. The first we call solid time; it always moves at the same speed for everyone everywhere. The other is liquid time, which we experience in our minds. Liquid time can move faster or slower for each of us, get it?"

"Yes, of course. Well, n-not exactly. I really have n-n-no idea what you're talking about. Absolutely. No. Time can't change speed."

"Hmm. I told you it was tricky. You're partly right. Time can't change speed, at least solid time can't. Think about it this way: You know how sometimes it seems like time is flying?"

"Yeah, like when you're having fun!"

"Exactly. And sometimes it seems like time just creeps along, almost like it's standing still?"

"Oh y-yes. Like when I'm in cloud-shunting class and the sylph master keeps on talking and talking—s-so boring."

"Okay, so think about it. How could time travel faster if time can't change speed? And, in fact, solid time doesn't change speed. It's the same for everyone. But liquid time— your own personal time—can move faster or slower within solid time. If all time were the same kind, how could time be moving faster in time? There have to be two kinds, get it?"

"Um. I think s-so."

"Well, we fairies are really good at making liquid time go faster and slower. We call it 'bending' time."

"Can other creatures f-feel time moving faster or slower?"

"Sure. Ispirianza says even humans feel like time is moving slowly or quickly sometimes, but they can't control it. It just happens to them."

"But no fairies really believe in h-h-humans."

"Most don't. Only a few of us know about humans and their realm."

Arthur looked impressed. "W-wow," he said.

"Time can be very heavy for humans," Alexa continued. "One event slowly follows another in a straight line. They can never feel the freedom we fairies have to flit and fly through liquid time. It's a totally different experience, but in the same world."

Arthur looked around nervously, as if he expected a human to jump out of the ground and eat him. "Where do the humans live? Why haven't I ever s-s-seen one before?"

"They live on this earth, too, but they can't see or touch us."

"Why n-n-not?"

"That's even hard for me to understand." Alexa soaked up Arthur's admiration and plunged right into her new teacher role. "At the time of the Great Shift, the fairies fled from the humans. The fairies joined their magic together and bent liquid time for themselves and all the other intelligent creatures in the world. They bent time just a little faster than humans could experience it. No matter how fast time flies for a human, it's never fast enough to catch our liquid time. And no matter how slowly time may seem to creep along for us, it's always just a little faster than humans can feel it. That's why our realm is called Slightly Above Time."

"So it's like we're always a f-few seconds ahead of the humans."

"Not exactly, but that's a good way to think about it. Remember, solid time always stays the same."

"So the humans can't s-s-see any animals at all?"

"They can see lots of animals, just not the intelligent races like fairies or Romorians. Or sylphs, of course. Time bending only affects animals that can understand time. Rabbits and ravens and centipedes have no concept of time, so they don't feel it bending—we see the same animals that the humans do."

"Okay, that is c-confusing," said Arthur.

"All fairy magic is based on bending time. Here, watch this!" Alexa pulled a piece of buckwheat bread from her satchel and put it in Arthur's hand."

"No, thank you. Sylphs don't eat b-bread," said Arthur.

"Just watch it," said Alexa, looking intently at the bread. All of a sudden, the bread vanished from Arthur's hand.

"Wow! Fairies c-c-can make things disappear? That's amazing!"

"It didn't disappear. It only looked like it to you," said Alexa, opening her hand and showing him the bread. "I bent my liquid time so fast that you didn't even see my hand reach out and take the bread from yours. By bending my time faster, I could grab and hide the bread so quickly that you didn't even see me move. To me, it looks like you're moving extra slowly."

"You should j-j-just move fast like that all the time. No one could catch you, and you would always be safe."

"I wish I could do that, but bending time takes a lot of concentration and energy. I can only do it for a few seconds of solid time, and it makes me so tired. Ispirianza said we modern fairies have lost a lot of our magic because we don't use it. The fairies of old were much better at bending time. She said her teacher Zymandria, the Bristlecone Pine Dryad, could bend time for days. Zymandria used to make her tree grow faster than all the other trees in the White Mountains."

"The White Mountains aren't n-n-near Kendlenook," said Arthur. "I thought dryads had to stay close to their trees. How could Ispirianza talk to a dryad thousands of wingbeats away?"

"Through their trees, of course."

"Of course! No...not r-r-really getting it."

"Tree magic is really cool. But that's a whole different story. Better just get the time-bending idea down. Do you understand now?"

"Um, it kind of makes our mind hurt. But I think I had it for a second there."

"A second of solid time or liquid time?" joked Alexa.

Arthur just whimpered.

Evening came, and the sun set in so many violent colors that it pierced Alexa's heart with its beauty. The wilderness made Alexa feel afraid but alive. The moon followed them through the forest as they looked for a place to sleep. They found a cozy, hollow log and curled up inside it.

The next day Arthur and Alexa flew into a dark canyon full of strange trees, the likes of which she had never before seen. Despite Daria's well-drawn (and now well-worn) map, Alexa soon became lost. Arthur could have flown straight over the Dragontooth Mountains to Evernaught, but Alexa knew her wings wouldn't hold her up in the thin air above the massive mountains. So she found the nearest dryad tree to ask for directions.

"Hello?" she called to the sycamore tree. A wooden head with antlers poked out of a hole in a knot of the tree. The dryad had an amazed look on her face. Alexa lowered her wings. "Hello, my name is…"

"Yes, yes, child, I know. You're Alexa of the Meadow!"

TWENTY-TWO

Evil in the Distance

"Nataliana, come quickly! It's the Bright One," the dryad yelled.

"Bright One?" Alexa said. Arthur started to bob up and down with excitement.

"Will you show us the locket? Please?" Three more dryads flew from their trees and gathered around, peppering Alexa with questions.

"O Bright One, could you bless my child?" said Nataliana, holding a dryad spriteling up to her.

"Bless? How do you bless a child?" Alexa asked.

"Place your hand on her head and say something nice, please, could you?"

"Remember yourself, Nataliana," the first dryad said. "The Bright One has enough to worry her without dryads shoving spritelings into her face. Is that the human's locket in your satchel? Could I hold it, please? Oh, where are my manners?

161

My name is Floristina. How is Ispirianza? Is she still moving around in her old age?" Alexa wondered at the dryads' strange behavior. She knew that dryad trees could speak to each other, but she had no idea news could spread so quickly.

"She's fine. I...I just need some help finding my way," Alexa said.

"Yes, yes, of course. Directions to Evernaught," said Floristina. "Keep flying until you reach those slate cliffs up yonder. You'll find a great canyon pointing north. That's Black Canyon Pass. Fly through it and turn west at the Great Woblin Plains."

"I hope we don't have to fly through 'Uchaf Du Maen,'" Alexa joked to Arthur.

"What did you just say?" asked Floristina. "Do you know the ancient tongue?"

"Oh, no," Alexa said. "I just heard someone say those words."

"Well, if I remember my lessons correctly..."

"You speak the ancient tongue?" she asked.

"No one alive really speaks it," said Floristina. "But I learned a few words as a child. Let's see...this was so long ago...'Maen' means 'stone,' 'du' or 'ddu' means 'black' or 'darkness,' and 'Uchaf, means 'highest' or 'great.'" Alexa stared at the dryad's wooden face in shock.

"Is there a place called 'Uchaf Du Maen'?"

"A place? A place called 'Highest Stone of Darkness'? No, that would be a very strange name for a place, wouldn't it?"

Alexa was disappointed and relieved at the same time. She didn't really want to know about Uchaf Du Maen.

"Thank you for your help," Alexa called as she and Arthur

continued on their way.

"Go with the Great Song!" the dryads shouted after Alexa.

"So where d-do you want to camp t-tonight, O Bright One?" Arthur asked. Alexa laughed.

On the third night, the two mismatched friends camped in a forest clearing. The silvery moon sailed high into the crystal sky. After washing her dress, Alexa stretched the twine she'd bought in Wallowbriar between two trees and hung her dress to dry. She then carefully unraveled spider webs with sticks and wound them around the camp. She attached the ends of the webs to dry leaves so if anyone flew into camp in the middle of the night it would slow them down and make enough noise to awaken her. Arthur made a good lookout, but it didn't hurt to have a backup.

At dawn, Alexa awoke with a sleepy halo of hair sticking out around her head. She didn't bother to comb it—the wind would just mess it up again. Arthur flew above the treetops to look around. As usual, the little sylph said he saw something scary, but it turned out to be nothing more than a group of sparrows rooting for worms. As they traveled, he flew nervously around Alexa studying her face.

"What are you worried about?" Alexa asked.

"I'm worried that you th-think I worry too much," Arthur said. Alexa laughed. Arthur frowned. "Which I d-don't, you know. I worry the exact amount that the situation requires."

"Well, stop it," Alexa said. "Not everything is out to get you."

Just then Alexa noticed that all the birds had gone silent. She listened. Then she flew up to the top of the tallest tree and peeked out from between its highest branches. She waited and watched. Arthur crept up next to her, trembling.

"I thought I saw something," Alexa said, "but now it's gone. See, now you're making me jumpy."

Suddenly Arthur squeaked and bolted for cover in a nearby hollow tree. A few seconds later, Alexa saw what had scared Arthur. An eerie smudge of darkness moved against the pale blue sky like a tiny storm cloud. As the mysterious form changed direction, it separated into three separate shadows. Alexa's wings shivered. The things seemed to hover near the place that Alexa and Arthur had camped the night before.

"Arthur, what is that?" Alexa asked, her heart beating wildly.

"Nothing good. Not g-good things!" stammered Arthur, now hiding his face.

"Arthur, tell me."

Muffled through the hollow tree, Arthur finally brought himself to say the word: "Oths!"

"Oths?" said Alexa. The word flew back down her throat and she choked on it. "How could that be? We can't be close enough to Evernaught for them to find us by accident, and they couldn't know anything about us and our journey."

"Yes, they could know...kind of," said Arthur. "Sylphs speak of the Oths' g-great magical powers." He ducked down lower into a group of leaves. "Oh, no. Okay, bad. Here they come. They're c-c-coming closer. It's definite now. Absolutely." Arthur pointed a shaking finger at the three black specters. Alexa and Arthur shrank deeper into their perch. Alexa pushed away some leaves and peeked out.

The Oths had flown close enough for Alexa to get a good look at them, but they were still quite far away. The center Oth was tall and menacing and had dark streaks like claw marks below each eye. Her dress looked like torn black lace over a shiny dark purple fabric. She called orders to the other two. They were definitely looking for something—or someone. The other two Oths at her side wore strange masks like the faces of some kind of unnatural birds. One of them stopped in mid-flight and turned her face toward Alexa.

"D-d-do they see us?" Arthur quietly squealed.

"No, they couldn't possibly—"

Then the Oth slowly pulled down her mask to reveal two dark but beautiful eyes that seemed to look straight into Alexa's. Alexa slowed her breathing and her heart, hoping to somehow disappear. Then the Oth raised her mask again and kept following the other two. They turned and flew in the other direction.

"Let's get out of here quickly," said Alexa, "but turn more to the west."

"Okay, we go." Arthur was gone in a flash.

Alexa and Arthur flew hard for several hours, not daring to look above the treetops again. When they stopped to rest and eat in the early afternoon, they could find no sign of their pursuers. "Maybe they aren't really following us," Alexa hoped. The birds and bugs here sang their normal songs.

Alexa alighted on the forest floor to search for edible plants. She pulled up a licorice plant by it roots—the stems were great to chew on while flying—and then squealed in delight.

"Arthur," she called. "Come look at this!"

"What's wrong? Are y-y-you hurt?"

"No, just come here."

Arthur obediently buzzed over to peek over Alexa's shoulder. "A roly-poly bug? What's so s-special about that?" Arthur backed away from the armored insect.

"Watch this." Alexa poked the roly-poly with her finger, and it promptly curled up into a ball. She gave the ball a flick, rolling it toward Arthur, who sprang out of the way.

"Isn't that great?" said Alexa, smiling.

"Wonderful," said Arthur. "Now it can s-s-smoosh me instead of just eat me."

"Oh, Arthur, you really need to relax." Alexa looked up, but Arthur was gone. Scaredy-cat. Alexa knelt down and poked another one. She studied the stripes on the little bug's back.

WHACK! A bare foot with purple toenails kicked the poor bug out of sight. Alexa looked up and then jumped backward. Her throat went dry. The black eyes of the middle Oth looked down at Alexa. The skirt of her flowing black robe left one leg bare. A dark band spiraled up her lower leg like a snake. Purple streaks flowed down her ink-black hair, and her eye makeup snaked down her cheeks like purple blood. She looked a lot older than Alexa but much younger than Grandmother.

The Oth pulled a silver dagger from her sash and studied the jagged blade, as though she thought it the most beautiful thing. She then looked down at Alexa and smiled.

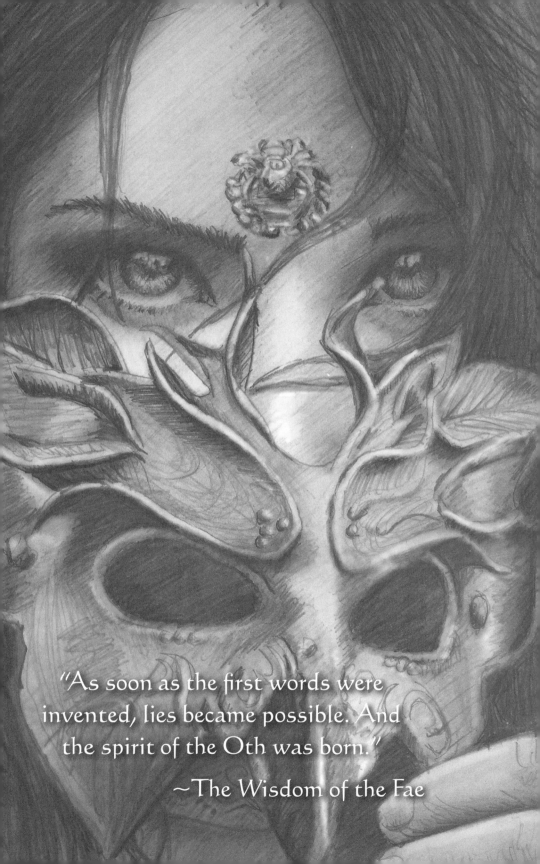

"As soon as the first words were
invented, lies became possible. And
the spirit of the Oth was born."

~The Wisdom of the Fae

Part IV:
The Enemy

TWENTY-THREE

In the Grip of an Oth

"Well, look what I found," the Oth said in gentle and motherly tones. "A little Meadow Fairy who appears to have strayed quite a long way from home. Lost, are we?"

Her speech was strange—the accent definitely not Faewickian.

Alexa shook her head slightly but said nothing.

"She certainly can't be up to any good way out here. Didn't you have a mother to teach you that monsters lurk in the wilderness? Or maybe an old dryad?"

Alexa wondered whether the Oth made a lucky guess or if she actually knew something about her. "I...I'm not alone," Alexa said, struggling to hold her head high. "I'm with a group of Lake Fairies traveling to the Upper Sylph Marshes."

"Dear, sweet child. Lies do not suit you. Have you not heard what happens to a fairy who lies?" The Oth smiled.

She leaned into Alexa until she was uncomfortably close. "They turn ugly, that's what happens. Luckily, I found you before one of those twisted souls did. You would not consider me ugly, would you?" Indeed, Alexa found her strikingly beautiful, but she didn't say so.

The Oth polished the dagger on the hem of her dress. "Still, it wasn't a complete lie. You do travel with one other. I wonder where it hides now. What a loyal companion you have chosen for yourself."

"I'm not out to hurt anyone," Alexa said. "I'm just a nobody Meadow Fairy." She grasped the end of a stick lying next to her on the ground.

"You are absolutely right, my dear," said the Oth. "You are a nobody. I appreciate your truthfulness, really I do. But I can also see that you need help, and so my heart fills with compassion. Just tell me what you seek, and I can help you."

"Thank you, but I think I can manage for now," quivered Alexa. The Oth casually scraped her dagger across the bark of a tree, making a grating noise that chilled Alexa's blood.

"It must be a terribly important task for you to risk your life out here all alone."

Alexa concentrated as hard as she could to bend time so she could escape in a flash. She bent it a little faster for herself, threw the stick at the Oth and bolted for the sky.

The Oth pulled Alexa to the ground in a blur of movement and twisted Alexa's arm behind her. She smelled of rose petals and something musky that Alexa couldn't identify. Either the Oth was very quick or she could bend time even better than Alexa could.

The Oth bearing a lumastone

"I think you will find me very helpful," the Oth said through her teeth. "I can see to it that you find what you want." Alexa felt the point of the dagger at her waist. She whimpered but did not speak or move.

Then Alexa heard the faint whirring of wings, an unearthly screech from the Oth, and suddenly she was free. Alexa jumped for the treetops, wings pumping hard. She smacked her leg hard against an outthrust branch. The wound sent pain streaking through Alexa's body, and she could see blood dripping beneath her. Arthur appeared flittering to her right, spitting and grimacing.

"She t-t-tastes terrible," he explained and sped ahead.

Arthur actually bit the Oth! Alexa couldn't believe he had summoned such courage.

Arthur looked back as the Oth advanced. "Okay, well, g-glad to help. I'll be g-going now," said Arthur as he disappeared into a hole on the side of a hill.

The dark fairy buzzed her wings and closed in on Alexa. The young Meadow Fairy flew hard until she felt a familiar warm updraft of wind. A thermal current! She began to fly in tight circles and spiraled upward into the bright sunlight. Her only chance lay in staying in the light. Ispirianza said that Oths could not stand bright light for very long.

Alexa risked a quick look down at her pursuer. The Oth pulled an object from her robe and bent it. Suddenly a cloud of darkness swirled around both Alexa and the Oth. The air grew cold and damp. The darkness came from a purple and black stick in the Oth's hand. The stick was like no lighting wand Alexa had ever seen. Candledark! Alexa looked into the heart of the candledark cloud and saw not just darkness but nothingness itself. What terrible magic the Oths could weave.

Alexa's heart sank. With the help of candledark, the Oth's skin and eyes were protected from the harsh sunlight. She could now follow Alexa for as long as she liked.

Alexa tried to bend time but couldn't focus. She trimmed her wings and darted out of the cloud, but the Oth closed in on her. Now Alexa could clearly see the crooked dagger sticking out of the eerie dark mass of the candledark cloud. The sky around Alexa grew darker and darker until Alexa could only see a few wingbeats in front of her. A hand reached out of the darkness to grab Alexa's injured leg.

Suddenly a flash of red and orange shot out of the forest below. The Oth turned toward the newcomer, who she clearly considered more of a threat than Alexa.

The brightly colored fairy — for it was indeed a fairy — pulled out a long golden sword, swished it around and engaged the Oth. Alexa flew for cover in the trees. The Oth's crooked dagger clanged against the sword over and over. Alexa had never seen such strength and courage, but it wasn't enough. The fairy was losing.

Alexa's shame overshadowed her fear. Even Arthur had found courage enough to help earlier, but now Alexa was hiding while a stranger fought her battle.

So Alexa flew straight at the candledark cloud, trying to distract the Oth enough to give the other fairy a chance.

Yes! The fairy's sword sliced through the candledark cloud and separated it, leaving the Oth exposed. Out in the bright sunlight of midday, the Oth's eyes weakened and she started to fly erratically. With a frustrated wail that echoed through the hollows and canyons, the Oth turned and fled.

The reddish fairy did not follow, nor did Alexa. Instead they stared at each other in mid-air, struggling to catch their breath. Something about the new fairy unsettled Alexa. Maybe it was the sword.

Then Alexa noticed the blood dripping down her leg from where she had slashed it on the tree branch. The wound began to throb as if someone was pounding it with a wooden club.

"Ya know, you should tend to that, Meadow Fairy," the new fairy said. She accented her words a little differently than the fairies of Kendlenook—harsher and faster somehow. Her orange and hot-pink dress and flaming red hair stood out against the background of green and brown forest. Red paint in the shape of flames swirled across her temples and down to her cheekbones. The fairy looked about Daria's age and carried herself with a confident swagger. The hilt of her now-sheathed sword glinted and swirled like golden fire.

"And we should rest," continued the red fairy. "Somewhere else, in case that Oth comes back with more of her friends." Alexa felt nervous following this strange and wild fairy, but she definitely preferred her company to that of Oths.

The two fairies landed beneath the cover of trees. "I didn't need your help, ya know," said the colorful fairy as she licked her finger to wipe a spot of blood from her shoulder.

"But I sure needed yours," replied Alexa. "So, thank you." She sat next to the other fairy to nurse her own, larger wound. She tore a strip of cloth from the bottom of her dress and wrapped her bleeding leg with it. "I'm Alexa of the Meadow," she said.

"Pleased to meet ya. I'm Mara of the Fire."

"Fire? You're a Fire Fairy? I've only heard of Fire Fairies

from Kandra's...from a friend's mother who met one once north of Thysperia. What are you doing out here?"

"Nothin' really. Been kinda bored. We Fire Fairies don't have much ta do 'til the brushfires start in late summer. Long way from home, aren't ya?" asked Mara, swinging her legs back and forth under the branch on which the fairies sat. Alexa craned her neck to look at Mara's ankles but couldn't see them well enough.

"Mm, hm," nodded Alexa. Then on to a more urgent topic: "Who in Kendlenook was that Oth? I've never been so scared in my life. She's so elegant and terrible at the same time."

"I dunno many of them by name, but I sure know that one. That was Aerioth. You certainly picked a fine Oth to get ta know," said Mara.

"Oh, great!" said Alexa. "The Oth coming after me would be the worst one."

"Hey, we're alive, and she's gone." Mara grinned with the pride of victory — or at least survival.

"But how could she have known about me?"

"Prob'ly just followed your trail. You're awfully sweet smelling. And I hope you don't mind my sayin', but you're not so great at sneakin' around."

"No, I don't mind, you're probably right. But she knew things about me, so I don't think she found me by accident."

"Well, who else knows where you are?" asked Mara.

"No one except my sisters and Ispirianza back in Kendlenook, and they would never tell the Oths."

"Have you talked near any ground squirrels? Ya never know whose side those little buggers are on," said Mara. "Where ya going anyway?"

Mara and her sword

Alexa decided to trust her new friend, at least a little. "Evernaught," she said, watching to see how Mara would react. Mara looked Alexa up and down.

"Um...you do know what Evernaught is, right? No one wants ta go there," said Mara.

"I'd rather go anywhere else, but I need candledark—at least ten or fifteen sticks," said Alexa, still trying to get a peek at Mara's ankles.

"What for? Plannin' to turn Oth?"

Alexa laughed nervously. "Of course not. I need it to catch my Shadow Fairy."

"That'll be a trick. Again, what for?"

"I need her to spin pixie silk for me."

"Uh, same question."

Alexa was pretty sure she shouldn't reveal Ispirianza's whole plan to an almost total stranger, so she said, "That part's kind of a secret."

"If that Aerioth knows, it's not much of a secret anymore."

"Well, I don't think she knows that part. At least I hope not."

The Fire Fairy crossed her legs, looking completely relaxed. "So you've just been flitting around by yourself, hoping ta swipe some candledark?"

"Well...when you say it like that, I guess it doesn't sound like a great plan." Alexa wondered where Arthur had gone and whether he would return.

Mara pulled up the hem of her bright orange skirt to examine a small tear from the scuffle with Aerioth, and Alexa again searched Mara's ankles.

"What are ya looking at?" Mara asked.

"Oh, sorry. I need to know if you have an hourglass mark on your ankle."

Mara's eyebrows lowered as she studied Alexa's face. "That's an odd thing ta say to a stranger."

"Ispirianza told me not to trust someone who has an hourglass mark on her ankle, that this fairy — or whatever — would get in my way. Her tree knows things about the future." Again, looking back on what she'd just said, Alexa thought she might be giving away too much information. But it felt good confiding in someone who could help.

"Dryads, huh? Don't know many myself. Knowin' the future would seem to come in handy, though," said Mara with a look like she didn't know whether to believe Alexa or not. But Mara stuck out both of her ankles to give Alexa a good look at them. "See? No hourglass."

"Did you see Aerioth's ankles?" asked Alexa.

"Not really. That dagger kept my attention."

"There was a band of some kind wrapped around one of her legs, right where the mark might be. I bet she's the greatest obstacle to my journey."

"Ya think? How long did it take you to come up with that?" asked Mara. She kept searching Alexa's face. "You do know that Oths keep their stores of candledark deep in their caves, right?"

"Of course they do," Alexa sighed.

"Let me get this straight," said Mara. "You know the Evernaught caves are home to the most dangerous swarm of murderous killers known to the Fae, and you intend to…"

"Fly right into them," said Alexa.

"Hmm. How many fairies did ya say were in your army?"

asked Mara.

"Well, I thought I had it all figured out, but now that I'm out here…"

"Okay, Miss Meadow Flowers, if I were to come with ya, what could you do for me?"

"Why would you want to come with me?" Alexa said. She knew she could use the help, but this Mara seemed like the type who would draw attention to herself and anyone with her.

"Because ya need me. But I expect to be paid."

"With what?"

"I figure by the way you're dressed, you prob'ly have a rich family. And whatever you're doing must matter ta somebody."

"Actually, it's important to everyone this side of the Bridge of Trees. If we succeed, I'm sure the council in Kendlenook will give you tons of beads."

"Beads, huh? Do I look like I need beads out here in the middle of nowhere? What else ya got?"

"Shells, maybe? Or a new — wait, I didn't even ask for your help."

Mara laughed. "I'm just kidding. I'll go along just ta see a sweet little Meadow Fairy like you get torn apart by a cave full of Oths. That sounds like high entertainment ta me." Alexa laughed nervously back, flashing a concerned look at Mara.

"Look, I really don't need your help," Alexa insisted.

"You've obviously never seen Evernaught. Believe me, Flowers, ya need serious help. I can get you as far as Evernaught, but after that, you're on your own. I may be good in a fight — but a cave full of Oths? That's just suicide."

"But that's just it," Alexa replied. "You're a great fighter, but I don't want to fight for the candledark. I just want to sneak in and take it."

Mara sat back down. "Uh huh, with your great plan."

"Okay, so I don't have much of a plan." Alexa scanned the sky for Arthur. She didn't want to be alone. And the Great Oak did say there would be others. Of course it also said…but Alexa banished that thought for now.

Alexa sighed and said to Mara, "Do you want to help me work on it?"

Mara grinned.

TWENTY-FOUR

Fairies Without Callings

ara certainly did not blend into the landscape. The Oths could probably see her bright red hair from hundreds of wingbeats away.

As the two fairies flew off in search of a hiding place, Alexa felt more relaxed. It was nice to give up some of the responsibility to someone else.

Just after Alexa and Mara crawled into a small cave that Mara had found, Arthur poked his head around the cave's mouth. He must have been following them from a safe distance the whole time.

Not even looking, and as quick as lightning, Mara grabbed him around the chest with both of her hands and squeezed. "Explain yourself, sylph! Why are you spying on us? Where has your gathering gone?"

Arthur squeaked several times, too afraid and too short of breath to make any real words come out of his mouth.

"Let him go, Mara," said Alexa, grabbing Mara's arm. "This is my friend Arthur. Arthur, this is Mara. She saved me from that Oth, and she's going to help us get candledark from the Oth caves."

"P-pleased to meet you. You s-seem really nice…kind of. Or not," stammered Arthur. Mara let him go, and Arthur flew behind Alexa and hid in her dress.

"A sylph with a name? That's ridiculous," said Mara. Alexa told Mara the story of how she had met Arthur and named him. Mara just said, "Uh, huh," and then ignored Arthur.

"Okay, about that plan," said Mara. "I'd say we got about two days of hard flyin' to get ta Evernaught. Then we need to watch the caves and figure out how ta get in. Not even I've tried anything as reckless as that. Maybe one of us can create a diversion — ya know, get the Oths mad enough that they come pouring outside to see what's up. But we'll have ta distract those fricketing bumbleflies." She glanced at Arthur and raised an eyebrow.

"N-n-not me!" said Arthur.

"You're too small to carry the candledark, so we need you to take care of the bumbleflies. Just get them ta chase ya — that shouldn't be hard."

Arthur cowered behind Alexa.

"Bumbleflies?" asked Alexa.

"Ya don't know about the bumbleflies? This gets better by the minute. They guard the Oth caves. Nasty little beasties. Actually, not so little — several times the size of a normal wasp and way meaner. And they don't die when they sting someone neither."

"How can we possibly get past the Oths and a swarm of

their pet bumbleflies?" Alexa felt her hope slipping away.

"Little harder than you thought, huh, Meadow? Our only chance is ta sneak in at night. Most of the Oths stay out all night doing…whatever it is that Oths do. The bumbleflies stay on guard no matter what time it is, though."

"Wait a second," said Alexa. "The bumbleflies certainly wouldn't attack an Oth, would they?"

"No, the Oths hand-feed the bumbleflies as larvae," said Mara. "They aren't dumb enough to attack the hand that feeds 'em, which is a good thing since each one has enough venom ta kill a hundred fairies. The Oths feed them the pollen of poison hemlock plants ta keep 'em really wicked."

"So maybe I could disguise myself as an Oth and fly right past them!" Alexa felt proud of the idea. Mara's eyes lit up.

"You're more devious than I thought. I'm ashamed I didn't think of it myself," said Mara, smiling. Then, quite suddenly, "Gotta go. I need to take care of something." And just like that, Mara was gone.

When she had not returned an hour later, Alexa began to worry. She forgot her concern, though, when Mara swooped in, turned her bag upside down and dumped out a huge pile of mustard flowers, watercress leaves and several plants Alexa didn't recognize. "Dinner," she announced.

"What in the world are those?" Alexa asked, pointing to some leaves she had never seen before.

"See the leaves with square stems? Called lambs quarter. Grows everywhere out here."

Alexa studied another leaf. "Is that stinging nettle? You've got to be kidding! Those sting like blazes when you barely touch them!"

"Not if you know how ta cook 'em." Mara pulled out a wand and sparked a clump of dried mugwort leaves. It flared into a roaring flame in an instant. "Really helps ta be a Fire Fairy out here," said Mara. She threw four stones into the blaze and pulled out a wooden bowl and bladder of water from her satchel. After pouring the water into the bowl, she used two sticks to move the red-hot stones into the bowl. The water quickly came to a frantic boil.

Mara tossed the stinging nettle in, careful to touch the raw leaves with only her red-painted fingernails. Then she threw in bits of mustard and watercress and added liquid from a small vial from her satchel. Alexa couldn't believe how well Mara could take care of herself out in the wilderness. An appetizing aroma soon filled the cave. Alexa had not had a hot meal since she left Kendlenook, and her stomach rumbled.

A few minutes later, Mara poured some stew into a bowl and gave it to Alexa.

"It's delicious," Alexa said with her mouth full, spooning the stew in as fast as she could cool it by blowing.

"My mother says it's packed full of vitamins that make your hair shine and your wings strong," said Mara. "Not that you need anything for your hair, Alexa."

Alexa couldn't believe someone actually complimented her hair. She crammed a handful of miner's lettuce into her mouth. "Thanks, but you should see my sister Eva. She's a Lake Fairy with this gorgeous silver hair that you wouldn't believe."

"Let me guess, one of those perfect older sisters that you spend your whole life trying ta live up to?" said Mara.

"I don't even try," said Alexa. "I could never do anything

as well as Eva. She's a scribe for the council, she herds sylphs in the orchestra, and dirt wouldn't even dare to come near her. Even my middle sister, Daria, makes me look bad. She's a Forest Fairy who wins all the top wreaths at the Thysperian Games every spring and manages to come out looking like a heroine no matter what she does."

"What are their callings?" asked Mara.

"Compassion for Eva and Protection for Daria. Eva helps me get out of trouble sometimes, but Daria just bosses me around all the time and says it's for my own good."

"How about you?"

"What about me?"

"What's your calling?"

Alexa's eyes darted downward. "I don't know it yet. What's yours?"

Mara smiled. "I don't know yet either."

"What? I thought my calling was taking its time to reveal itself, but you must be at least fifteen!"

"I'm twelve," said Mara.

"You are not!" exclaimed Alexa. "I'm thirteen, and there's no way you're younger than me."

Mara just shrugged.

"But that thing you did to the Oth and how you act and everything. How did you learn all that?"

"You gotta know what you're doin' out here."

"And your mother lets you wear face paint?" Alexa looked at the red swirls on Mara's face. She couldn't imagine what Grandmother would say if Alexa showed up at home wearing that.

"My mother's not really around much. I've been pretty

much on my own for a while," Mara said while staring into the fire. She threw a mustard flower petal high in the air and caught it in her open mouth. Alexa felt a little sorry for her.

"Wow, I can't imagine that. My grandmother makes enough rules for five mothers."

"Who's this Ispirianza you keep talking about?" asked Mara.

"Only the most amazing dryad ever! She tells the best stories and lets me visit her inside the Great Oak and sort her termites. She's the oldest dryad in the world—except for maybe her mentor. Zymandria lived in the White Mountains and they used to talk to each other through their trees."

"Used to?"

"She hasn't heard from Zymandria in eons. She thinks Zymandria's tree either died or got cut off by the Scarring."

"Ispirianza sounds pretty cool," said Mara.

"Definitely," said Alexa. "But she actually believes in humans." Alexa expected Mara to roll her eyes or laugh, but she didn't.

Alexa worked up the courage to ask, "You don't believe in them, do you?"

"Listen, after ya seen some of the stuff I have out here, you'll believe in anything. You ever seen a hawk pick a full-grown woblin out of its hole?"

"Oh…oh…I have!" said Arthur raising his hand.

"I'm not talking to you, sylpho," Mara snapped. Arthur frowned and then flew outside to either sulk or stand guard. "Never seen a human myself, though. As long as they don't bother me, I won't bother them," said Mara. "Hey, I have an idea!" She reached back and pulled a tiny wooden box and a brush out of her bag.

"Face paint!" said Alexa. Mara lit a blazing fire on a makeshift torch.

"Come over here where the light is better," said Mara, opening the box.

Alexa wavered for a second and then decided that Grandmother couldn't be upset by something she would never know about.

"Look up," said Mara as she brushed red face paint under Alexa's lower eyelid. "Stop blinking. You want paint in your eyes?"

"It's hard not to blink," said Alexa as her eyes watered. "You're about to stick that brush in my eye. I don't know how you do this without poking out your eyes."

"It's much easier ta do it on yourself."

Alexa let Mara brush designs around her eyes and down her cheeks.

"Okay, done. Go find a still pool and look at yourself," said Mara. "Red's not really your best color—I'd say you were more of a lavender fairy—but not bad if I do say so myself."

Alexa slipped out of the little cave. She couldn't wait to see how grown-up the designs made her look. Behind her, Mara's voice called, "Look out for Oths!"

Alexa stopped and looked back, but Mara laughed and motioned for her to go on. "How can she laugh about Oths?" Alexa thought. "She must be the bravest fairy I've ever met."

Then she caught her own reflection in the water and gasped. Alexa felt a little guilty for disobeying Grandmother, but it only lasted a second. She did look older, maybe even fifteen or sixteen.

TWENTY-FIVE

A Devil of Dust

Alexa felt much more secure with Mara around. But the encounter with Aerioth had planted a seed of terror in her heart. The seed sent down roots into Alexa's dreams. While it kept her awake, she soon learned to use her fear. It kept her sharp. It made her stronger.

The fairies slept for several hours in the cave. Arthur woke them once the sun had set, and the trio traveled on together. Arthur began to get used to Mara's presence and even started chattering again. Mara just ignored him.

Then Mara began boasting to Alexa that she could outrun anything in the sky, including a peregrine falcon. Arthur perked up and said he would gladly race her anytime. Alexa certainly knew who would win that race. Not letting it go, Arthur began to zoom and zip right in front of Mara's face so fast that she could barely see him. Alexa and Mara's hair blew in the breeze he caused. He even started to blow Mara backward. This clearly annoyed Mara, but she still said nothing.

"Your being a Fire F-Fairy and all, you might be interested in knowing our g-gathering used to put out forest f-f-fires with rain," Arthur bragged.

"You'll have to excuse me," said Mara. "I'm sufferin' from an acute case of not caring."

"We've put out sooo many forest f-fires that you Flameys have accidentally started over the years, let me tell you." Arthur was no longer in control of his tongue. Alexa smiled and knew Arthur was in for it.

"There's an old dryad proverb: 'Don't taunt a dragon unless you can face the fire.' So try not to use the word 'Flamey' to a Fire Fairy's face," said Mara. "It's not a smart move."

"It's dumb for the smart to want to look smart to the dumb," said Arthur. Alexa was shocked at his boldness. Maybe it was because he knew he could easily outfly Mara in the open air.

"You callin' me dumb?" asked Mara.

"I'm just quoting an old d-dryad proverb," Arthur replied. "See, I may be dumb, but I'm smart enough to know it. You're not even that smart."

"Look sylpho," Mara snapped. "One more word and I'll…"

"W-what? Fly so slowly that you'll bore me to death?"

"Right!" Mara unsheathed her sword and took a swipe at Arthur.

He zipped out of the way any time the sword came near. Frustrated, Mara put her sword away and kept flying.

"Keep that swamprat away from me," she said to Alexa. Arthur continued to fly in circles around Mara, just out of sword reach. The more time he spent with Alexa, the more confidence he seemed to gain. She was becoming his gathering.

"Hey, Mara," Arthur said. Mara closed her eyes and took a deep breath. "Did you know th-that there is no word in the fairy language for 'faffleblatus'? In fact, there is no known language that does have a word for it." Mara gritted her teeth together and looked like she wanted to scream.

After they flew through the rocky cliffs of Black Canyon Pass, the sun rose and the canyon opened up into an expansive valley. To the west, they could see a vast chasm of Scarring. Alexa looked away. She was afraid she might lose all her courage if she thought too much about what the Scarring had done to much of her village. She also thought of Kandra. No, she couldn't think of Kandra.

"Get down!" shouted Arthur. Alexa and Mara both bolted toward a tree for cover. Something about the sylph's voice told the two fairies that he had spotted a real danger this time. Arthur had already burrowed into a hole in the trunk by the time Alexa and Mara got to the tree.

"What is it?" Mara asked.

"Look—look out at the Scarring!" Arthur pointed in the direction of the dead expanse. Alexa strained her eyes and searched the dark landscape. About two thousand wingbeats away, she saw several figures walking slowly through the Scarring in a line. She counted seven of them.

"Who in Kendlenook could that be?" asked Alexa. "No one can survive in the Scarring. Why doesn't it consume them?"

"Apparently, there are some who can get through," said

Mara. "They're not flyin'. Maybe it's Cobbletons."

"No way. The Cobbletons lost hundreds to the Scarring," said Alexa. Then an idea popped into her head and her heart soared with hope. "Maybe we could get whoever they are to bring us bramble nectar from the other side of the Bridge of Trees!"

"That'd certainly make your life easier," said Mara.

"Arthur, do you think you can go higher and get a good look at them?" asked Alexa.

"I can see them just f-f-fine from inside this hole, thank you," Arthur said.

"Come on," said Alexa, her heart beating faster. "I need you to be Arthur the Valiant now. Please! This could save my whole village and more!"

Arthur turned to Alexa with a sad face and shook his head. "Th-th-they certainly won't help you, b-b-believe me."

"Well, what are they?"

"I'll give you a hint. What's b-b-black and purple and smelly all over?" said Arthur.

"No!" Alexa was stunned. "Not more Oths! But how?"

"Maybe they don't despair in the Scarring like fairies do," Mara thought aloud. They watched as the line moved out of the Scarring and disappeared into the forests of Thysperia.

"Why don't they fly?" Alexa asked. "Maybe they know something we fairies don't."

"Just because the Oths can travel in the Scarring doesn't mean we can. Oths are completely different from us," Mara said.

"Not that different," said Alexa. "They used to be fairies."

"O-O-Oths were once like you?" asked Arthur. "How does

that work?"

"Ispirianza says that a fairy becomes an Oth when she decides to live her life through lies instead of truth. She takes an oath to obey the High Oth. Even spritelings born to the Oths must pledge allegiance to the High Oth and complete a test of loyalty when they're old enough. When a fairy becomes an Oth, her wings change shape. They become sharper and sleeker. And when the process is complete, her hair, fingernails and even her heart turn black. Soon her very soul fills with darkness and she is forever an Oth."

"Is it f-f-forever and ever?" asked Arthur. "Can an Oth ever turn back into a fairy?"

"Ispirianza has never heard of an Oth changing back—and she should know. Zymandria once told her the only thing that could possibly turn an Oth back is the power of forgiveness. The problem is that no one has ever known an Oth to ask for forgiveness. It's not in their nature. They're never sorry for the evil they do."

"But I've heard l-l-lots of fairies lie without turning into Oths," said Arthur. "And Oths must t-t-tell the truth sometimes."

"They do. In fact the Oths usually start their lies with the truth," Alexa said. "There's an old fairy saying: 'May your lies always be awkward, for the Oths tell wonderful, beautiful lies.' My grandmother says, 'Fairies are honest sprites who sometimes lie, but Oths are liars who sometimes tell the truth.' Once you find it natural to lie, lies become your nature."

"Well, at least that's s-s-seven fewer Oths in Evernaught right now," said Arthur, still looking deep into the Scarring. "Let's g-get away from here. This place depresses me."

"And you're normally so cheery," muttered Mara.

Alexa agreed with Arthur. She could feel the emptiness of the nearby Scarring poking at the edges of her mind.

As they traveled on, a driving headwind slowed their progress to the point where they were almost moving backward. Even under a clear blue sky, the wind blew right through Alexa's dress and chilled her to the bones. The swirling tube of a dust devil rose high in the distance, danced around and then disappeared into nothing.

"This is miserable. What are the sylphs thinking?" asked Alexa.

"That's no sylph wind," said Mara. "Out here the weather does what it does, unless the sylphs are called to change it." Suddenly the gale shifted.

"What's happening?" Alexa cried. Another dust devil was forming right in front of them, and the spiraling breeze engulfed the three travelers. A loud howling filled Alexa's ears. The dust devil carried them higher and higher in the updraft. Alexa strained to fly toward the ground but kept rising.

"Don't fly d-d-down," yelled Arthur. "You'll just get tired. Let it carry you up and then f-f-fly out. Watch!" Arthur buzzed his wings so fast they seemed to disappear. He gained terrific speed as he flew straight up to the small circle of blue sky above them. Once he was moving fast enough, he took a hard right turn and zipped out of the updraft.

The last thing Alexa wanted to do was fly upward since she was already higher than a fairy can safely fly. But if Arthur could do it...

Alexa beat her wings and immediately shot up with so

much speed that it terrified her. She veered right, but the swirling wind just pushed her violently back into the dust devil. It was like running into a wall. Mara zipped by like a flaming arrow, and Alexa could see her darting back and forth into the walls of the wind tube just as she herself had tried to do before she'd followed Arthur's lead and flown upward. Arthur must have escaped because he could fly faster than the fairies.

Alexa felt they were running out of time. The air grew colder and thinner as they rose on the current. Soon they would reach an altitude where fairies wouldn't be able to breathe, but Alexa did not panic. She slowed her breathing and concentrated. The wind around her seemed to slow as she bent time. Then with all of her strength she flew straight up. She jetted past Mara and beat her wings with all of her might. When Alexa turned hard this time, she felt a strong side wind and then popped right out of the top of the dust devil. She spotted Arthur far below and angled down to him.

"N-n-nice flying," Arthur congratulated.

"Glad to be out of that nasty thing," said Alexa. "Let's take cover until this breeze dies down. No use tiring ourselves out."

"Where's Mara?" asked Arthur. Alexa looked back toward the dust devil that traveled slowly away to the west.

"She's still trapped!" Alexa exclaimed.

"She s-s-saw how you got out. She'll follow, right?"

"I don't think she can. I had to bend time to get out. She probably can't bend time as well as I can—even Eva and Daria wouldn't be able to do it."

"Oh, look," said Arthur, pointing at the drifting dust. "It's

slowing down and shrinking. See?" Alexa could see Mara's red dress and golden wings spinning high in the blue sky and floating slowly downward as the swirl weakened.

"No, Arthur, look!" screamed Alexa in horror. "The wind has blown her over the Scarring!"

TWENTY-SIX

The Face of Fear

Arthur whimpered as they watched Mara struggle high above the gaping Scarring. The dust devil had now completely disappeared. Without some hard flapping, Alexa knew Mara would land on the Scarring's surface in just over a minute. She could also tell that Mara would touch the Scarring far beyond Alexa and Arthur's reach.

"Flap, Mara, f-f-flap!" Arthur yelled.

"She can't," cried Alexa, her matted hair blowing in the wind. "The Scarring has sucked the life from her wings!" Mara's distant cries rang in their ears. Her wings were spread, but her body merely floated downward in a slow, pitiful spiral.

"W-w-w-w-what do we do?" Arthur stammered.

Alexa looked around. A few trees grew at the edge of the Scarring, but none with long enough branches to catch Mara.

"Arthur, follow me! I have an idea," said Alexa, and she folded her wings and dove to the ground.

"Why are we flying down when Mara is up there?" Arthur squeaked, but he followed Alexa's dive down to the cliff at the edge of the Scarring. Alexa dumped out the contents of her satchel onto the ground. She threw aside food, her extra dress and even Margaret's locket. The wind quickly filled Alexa's empty bag and nearly took it sailing away. Thankfully, Arthur snatched it before it blew into the Scarring. Alexa pulled the coil of laundry twine she'd bought in Wallowbriar from her pile of belongings and unraveled it.

"There's no way you can throw the twine out that far," said Arthur.

"I don't think I'll have to," said Alexa. "The wind has been our enemy, but maybe we can make it our friend." She tied one end of the twine to the straps of the satchel. When she lifted the empty bag, it filled with wind just as she had hoped.

Alexa looked up to see Mara sinking ever faster toward the abyss. Then Alexa grabbed the loose end of the string and bolted skyward with the empty satchel trailing below. Once she had climbed about sixty wingbeats, the satchel lifted off the ground and filled with air. The wind pushed it diagonally out over the Scarring and into Mara's path. It took all of Alexa's strength to both fly into the wind and hold onto the twine. Mara was now close enough for Alexa to see the expression of sheer terror and despair on her face.

"Grab the twine!" yelled Alexa. Mara just screamed.

"Arthur, get up here!" Alexa called out. She looped her end of the string several times around her wrist. "I won't be able to hold this alone once Mara grabs on." Arthur buzzed up to

Alexa and held the twine with all of his might. They watched as Mara fell below their line of sight and braced themselves.

Mara reached the twine and frantically latched on. Her speed pulled Alexa and Arthur down toward the Scarring. Mara struggled for a better grip as her hands slipped down the twine toward the satchel at its end.

"We're not strong enough, Arthur," cried Alexa. "We'll be pulled in with her. Quick, dive to that tree!" Alexa and Arthur dove to a tall pine tree several wingbeats from the edge of the dropoff. Just as Mara reached the end of the string, she jammed her left foot into the satchel and held the line above it with her two hands, violently yanking Alexa and Arthur toward her and away from the safety of the treetop. Alexa and Arthur pulled against Mara's weight, while their bodies draped over the top of the upper pine boughs. Their hold was not tight enough.

Alexa let out a cry as they crashed into the branches and the breath was forced from her lungs. Her body and Arthur's scraped against the rough bark and pine needles, while Mara's right foot dangled just above the surface of the Scarring. Mara's weight almost jerked Alexa's arms out of their sockets. To lock the line in place, Alexa whipped the twine around a thick branch. But the tree branch bent as Mara swung like a pendulum below. The bough bent further, and Mara's body dipped lower until her fate seemed unavoidable.

Mara's right foot touched the surface of the Scarring. She let out a blood-curdling scream.

"Pull, Arthur," yelled Alexa, her face blood red. "Pull!" To their relief, Mara's foot did not sink into the void. "We've got her for now, but this won't last long. Pull!"

Mara falls toward the Scarring

Alexa wedged her foot into a cleft between branches and pulled until her arm muscles burned. The twine dug into her now bloody hands. Mara edged upward, but Alexa simply couldn't pull against the will of the Scarring for much longer. Arthur helped as much as he could.

"Help me!" Mara cried. "Everything is turning black!"

"She's d-d-doomed," said Arthur. Alexa took a deep breath and pulled once more. Mara budged an arm's length off the Scarred ground and then plopped back down. Alexa's raw hands were losing their grip.

Suddenly an unfamiliar pair of spry wooden hands grabbed onto the line. Mara surged upward from the smoldering earth. Another tug and Mara shot up higher off the ground. Alexa caught a glimpse of the new arrival and nearly dropped the twine. Two piercing eyes shone through the tangle of twisted wood that was the face of Alexa's helper. The dryad blended into the tree so well that Alexa would not have seen her if it weren't for her eyes and the strings of wooden beads around her neck. Bark and lichen covered parts of her body. She both frightened and awed Alexa.

The young and wild dryad smiled between grunts. "I'm glad my tree can be of service to you, Bright One," she gasped. The green and pliable arms of the dryad lifted Mara's weight steadily. As Mara's limp body cleared the cliff, they lowered her to the safety of the unscarred earth between the tree and the cliff. Alexa, Arthur and the dryad crowded around the pitiful form crumpled at the base of the tree. Alexa gently turned Mara over. Mara's hands still grasped the twine, and her eyes were only half open.

Sendrya, the wild dryad

Mara licked her parched lips and coughed. She spoke in a soft, raspy voice: "I really didn't need your help, Flowers," she said between coughs. "I had it all under control."

Alexa managed a slight laugh and collapsed in relief. Arthur didn't find it funny at all.

Alexa and Mara slept in the shade of the dryad's tree, each holding the other's rope-burned hand. The dryad and a dazed Arthur stood watch. The two fairies slept the day and most of the night away. When they awoke, the dryad, who introduced herself as Sendrya, made them a hot meal.

"You have saved our lives, Sendrya," Alexa said as they prepared to continue their journey. "You have risked your own life to save strangers, and I am forever in your debt."

"You are no stranger, Bright One," said Sendrya in a proud voice. "And it is I who shall be forever in your debt when you stop the Scarring. We dryads do not have the luxury of flying away from danger. For years I have lived at the edge of death. Every day I dread the Scarring's advance, and I wonder each evening whether I will see the next sunrise."

Sendrya's voice cracked. "Allow me to bestow this blessing on you, Alexa: May you remain strong in the face of fear, may you stay determined in the face of obstacles, may you see your task to the end, for the sake of all daughters of the Fae." Sendrya lowered her wings. "It is my honor to have met you!" Mara and Arthur glanced at each other in amazement.

As the trio left to continue their journey, Mara nudged Alexa and whispered, "I think that dryad mistook you for someone else." Alexa laughed.

TWENTY-SEVEN

Furry Heads in Holes

The three travelers flew northwest, staying well away from the Scarring. The trees thinned, and a great grassy plain spread out before them. The world became only waving grass and enormous blue sky. To the north, the Upper Sylph Marshes coated the earth like a vast green sea.

Excited to see his homeland, Arthur jabbered on proudly about the epic gatherings and month-long feasts the sylphs would have when the gnat swarms rose above the marsh in late summer. Alexa paid little attention, and Mara seemed to pay none.

At Mara's suggestion, they started flying all night and sleeping during the day. Mara said they would be safer if no one could see them.

Alexa could feel her body changing day by day. She grew leaner, stronger and more aware of her surroundings. She constantly felt hungry, but thought less and less about food.

Back in Kendlenook, she'd thought she was starving to death if she missed one meal. She was learning to push through pain and hunger, ignoring it and even enjoying it.

Alexa's leg wound still throbbed and began to itch. Every time she scratched it, it would reopen and ooze fresh blood onto the bandage. Mara threatened to tie Alexa's hands behind her back if she didn't stop scratching.

As the sun rose, Alexa thought she saw something moving out of the corner of her eye. But when she turned, she only saw grass and rocks and a few holes in the ground. Was she seeing danger in every shadow now, like Arthur? Then she spotted the glint of two eyes in the blackness of one of the holes.

"Wait, Mara," called Alexa. "Look at this." Mara sighed and flew back to take a look.

A little furry head peeked out of the hole, spied the two fairies and ducked back underground. Arthur yelped. Another head popped up from a nearby hole and pulled back as soon as the fairies spotted it. Then another farther away. And another.

The entire field for thousands of wingbeats was pocked with little holes. The creatures living in them had brown and black fur that looked as soft as dandelion fluff. They had alert, piercing eyes and twitching whiskers under their fairy-like noses. The graspy hands on their front paws were big and dirty from digging. Alexa thought they looked grumpy, nervous and sneaky all at once. Puffs of dust and a musky odor rose up from a few holes. The slightest hint of a shadow from above sent any visible head diving for cover.

Alexa peeked into a hole, but she couldn't see anything

except a dark tunnel curving off to her left. Hoping the animal would come out again, Alexa backed away from the hole and waited quietly.

"Ground woblins," said Mara, landing with a swoosh of wings. "The plains are full of 'em. I hear you can travel for thousands of wingbeats in their tunnels without ever seein' the sun or moon. Ugly buggers, aren't they."

"I don't know," Alexa said, still peering into the hole. "They're so ugly they're almost cute."

"No, they're so ugly they're ugly," said Arthur, looking everywhere but at the holes. "And they stink."

"I learned about woblins in school," said Alexa. "Aren't they sort of intelligent? Not like fairies or dryads, of course. Or sylphs," she added, glancing up at Arthur. Arthur nodded back politely. "But my zoology mistress said they have their own language."

"Never heard them say anything but 'chirp' and 'squeak.' Come on, let's go," said Mara.

"They g-give me the heebie-jeebies," said Arthur, still hovering in the air.

"Everything g-g-gives you the h-h-heebie-jeebies," Mara shot back. "I bet butterflies give you the heebie-jeebies."

"You g-gotta admit, all those skinny legs make them look kind of creepy," Arthur said with a little shiver.

"Have you looked at yourself lately?" Mara said, disgusted.

"It's just n-not natural, wallowing in the g-g-ground like that," moaned Arthur with a shiver.

Another woblin stuck its head out again. Alexa tried to talk to it, using her gentlest voice. "You can come out now. We won't hurt you. We just want to look at you and talk to you."

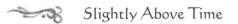

A woblin peeks from its hole

Chapter 27

"Zhep keek, shirp!" said the woblin and disappeared back down the hole.

"How rude!" said Arthur.

"Hmm," Alexa said, a little disappointed. "'Zhep keek, shirp?' I wonder what that could mean. 'Zhep keek, shirp.'" Mara and Arthur had already taken to the air, waiting impatiently, so Alexa gave up and took wing herself. As they flew over the Great Woblin Plain, a chatter of strange calls rose from the ground, often pausing as the fairies and sylph passed overhead. The woblins were definitely talking to each other, Alexa thought, but she couldn't understand a word.

As the sun rose higher, the fairies sent Arthur ahead to search for a place to hide during the daytime. The flat meadowlands offered little shelter, though. Mara began to act more and more nervous. She kept twisting the bracelet on her wrist and looking back and to the sides, as if she thought someone were following them. Alexa could see several flocks of birds in the distance, but nothing at all dangerous.

"Don't be such an Arthur," Alexa chided Mara.

"We're total Oth bait out here," Mara responded. "Anyone can see us from hundreds of wingbeats away."

"Let's try that island of trees over there," said Alexa.

The trio landed in the tiny oasis, a still pool of water surrounded by young trees and green grass. Mara didn't like it—still too exposed, she said—but Arthur insisted that no better cover existed anywhere nearby.

Mara looked tired, but they were all hungry, so she announced she would go look for food.

"I can do it, Mara," said Alexa. "You've taught me some of the plants that grow here."

"But some good plants look a lot like poisonous ones." Mara threw the strap of her bag around her neck and jumped into the air. Alexa thought Mara had more endurance than any fairy she had ever met.

Alexa rested her head on her spare dress and closed her eyes. She dreamed of the dark whisperer. The whisper grew louder and then changed into the voice of Eva calling Alexa's name. In her dream, Alexa searched and searched but couldn't find her sister. Then a closer, louder shout startled her awake. A heavy breeze blew in from the south. It grew so violent that it almost blew Alexa into the little pool.

"Arthur?" Alexa cried. Sand and dust blew into her hair and face. As usual, Arthur had disappeared at the first sign of trouble.

"Where are you?" a fairy's voice called through the wind, but the voice was not Mara's. "Alexa?"

"Alexa, there you are!" the voice shouted. A gathering of thousands of sylphs swooped into the little oasis, their movements perfectly coordinated and their tiny purple homing charms glowing.

Alexa held her hand over her eyes and squinted to see through the glare of the midday sun. Riding the wind and herding the gathering was Eva in a flowing blue dress. And in the midst of the wind soared Daria.

TWENTY-EIGHT

The Home for Ungathered Sylphs

lexa sprang into the air and hugged her sisters tightly. Then she pulled back, remembering Ispirianza's warning.

Eva tapped the homing charm around her neck with her wand. At a signal from the caller sylph, the sylphs of the gathering flew to the nearest cloud, nudging it toward the mountains.

"While we're here, the Dragontooth range could use some rain," Eva told them. Her hair and dress were spotless. "Alexa, you could use a bath and a hairbrush. You look frightful!"

"Nice to see you, too, Eva. How did you find me?" asked Alexa, still in a state of shock at the sight of her beloved sisters in this remote wilderness. "We—I—have been flying really fast. How did you catch up with me?"

"Are you kidding? Sylphs can create hurricane-force winds if you herd them correctly," said Eva. "I convinced the head of the weather society to give me an assignment in Black Canyon Pass. Sister, you are really out in the middle of nowhere." Eva looked around at the vast and unfamiliar landscape.

Daria couldn't keep quiet any longer. "That was a dirty trick, sneaking out on me in the middle of the night, you swamprat!" she said. "Now, more than ever, you need a Fairy of Protection! If we could find you so easily, an Oth could, too."

"Well, it wasn't exactly easy," said Eva. "I am a pretty good sylph herder."

Daria rolled her eyes and opened her mouth, but Eva spoke first.

"What is that on your face? Are you wearing face paint? Wait 'til Grandmother—"

Alexa started to answer, but Daria threw another question at her.

"What in the name of Faewick is that?" asked Daria, pointing at a bush behind Alexa. Arthur had stayed hidden while the sisters talked, hoping to avoid the attention of the new fairies, especially the sylph herder. He poked his head out from behind the scraggly bush.

"Oh," smiled Alexa. "This is—"

"A sylph!" cried Eva. "And it's not part of my gathering. It...it doesn't even have a homing charm!"

Arthur looked down.

"Alexa, where did you get a lone sylph?" demanded Eva. "And why would you keep it with you?"

Alexa explained how she'd met the despairing sylph and why the gathering had exiled him. "He's been really helpful and, well, Arthur is my friend."

Chapter 28

"Arthur?" said Eva. "You named it? Like a — a pet!"

"Not a pet, Eva, a friend. You won't believe this, but Arthur didn't even have a name before I helped him choose one."

Eva just stared at Alexa with wide eyes. Daria smirked and shook her head.

"Alexa," Eva scolded. "I know you thought you were doing the right thing, but you really should have left that sylph alone in the forest." Arthur hid his head in the bush again.

"But he would have died!"

"Maybe," Eva agreed. "Or he could have gone to the Home for Ungathered Sylphs."

"You mean the Asylum? No! Arthur told me all about that horrid place." Alexa searched Eva's eyes. "I don't understand you, Eva. You're supposed to be a Fairy of Compassion — and a sylph herder!"

"Do not judge what you don't understand. Your idea of compassion has only one side," said Eva.

"You don't think he deserves to live freely?" asked Alexa, astonished.

"Deserving has nothing to do with it," said Eva. "Have you no compassion for the Fae and animals that depend on the rain and the seasons? If one sylph starts making its own decisions, that kind of thinking can spread through the whole gathering. Then the gathering won't be able to work together anymore."

"What you mean to say is that he isn't useful to fairies like you anymore. Why not just let lone sylphs live out their lives in peace and freedom?" said Alexa.

"Look, a sylph spends its whole life listening to the caller's commands and the voices of its thousands of gathering-mates," answered Eva. "It never knows the meanings of the words 'silence' or 'loneliness.' Without a gathering, a sylph cannot hear these voices. It falls into depression because it has lost its life's purpose."

"But I can take care of Arthur."

"Really? A lone sylph can survive two weeks at most without proper help. And if it survives that long, it will go insane, suffering a madness that tortures both mind and body without mercy."

Alexa gasped. She looked down at Arthur, who had buried his head in Alexa's arm. She wrapped her other arm around him protectively.

"How long since the gathering exiled it?" asked Eva.

"Seven, maybe eight days," said Alexa. Arthur nodded without raising his head.

"Have you noticed it losing its sense of direction or talking to itself or screaming for no reason?"

"Well, some screaming," admitted Alexa, "but only when something jumps out at him. Look, Eva, I think he's fine. He has a new purpose now — to help me with my task."

"I don't know," said Eva, glancing at the pitiful sylph. "It's against nature. It shouldn't even wish to live."

"Listen to yourself, Eva!" snapped Alexa. "Lone sylph or not, Arthur is my friend. I will not abandon my friend to die or make him live locked up with a bunch of demented freaks." Arthur gazed lovingly at Alexa.

For the first time, Eva spoke directly to Arthur. "Sylph, do you wish to live?" Eva rolled her eyes like she couldn't believe she was asking a sylph's opinion.

Arthur looked at the ground, but answered, "N-n-not at

first, but now we do."

"Let me take you to the Home for Ungathered Sylphs."

"Oh, no—n-never that place! I've heard the st-stories. Crazy sylphies all around, flying in circles and screaming. Absolutely. Not…really." Eva knelt down beside him and spoke in a calming voice.

"They take good care of all the ungathered there. They have arts and crafts time every day, and plenty of other great activities. They even give you a nice, new homing charm."

"I know what that's f-for. It's not a h-homing charm—it's so you can't escape!"

"Would you rather die of madness and loneliness?" Eva asked.

"I would. Absolutely. Or not. Maybe." Arthur said.

Eva studied the unusual sylph.

"Just for the record, Alexa, I don't think anything good can come of this. Daria will stay with you, though. When the sylph starts showing signs of insanity, she can help you decide what to do."

"No, Daria can't stay with me," Alexa said, shaking her head.

"You're crazier than your pet sylph," said Daria. "Do you really think you can do this on your own? Or are you so selfish that you have to keep all the glory to yourself?"

A new voice flew in. "And why should she want to share the glory with you?"

Mara floated down into the oasis and rested her hand on the hilt of her sword. The breeze tousled her fiery red hair, and the sunlight glinted off the sword's scabbard. Alexa thought Mara looked very fierce and felt proud of her friend.

The Fire Fairy tossed a bundle of nightshade berries to the ground. Daria confronted the newcomer without a trace of fear and said, "Well, Eva, now we know where Alexa gets her appalling taste in makeup." Mara's eyes narrowed.

Alexa knew she had better step in right away. "Eva and Daria, this is my friend Mara of the Fire. She has fought bravely for me. Mara, these are my sisters, Eva of the Lake and Daria of the Forest."

Mara lowered her wings a little to Eva but only nodded to Daria. Neither Eva nor Daria showed the slightest sign of lowering her wings.

"So let me make sure I understand this," said Daria. "You won't accept help from your own sister, but you welcome this…this stranger?"

"Mara saved me when Aerioth attacked. And you should see her fight! She makes our aerial defense teacher look like a spriteling."

The attacker's name transfixed Eva's attention. "Aerioth? The High Oth?"

The other three fairies stared at Eva in horror. Arthur hid behind a bush.

"Well, the council thinks she's the High Oth. No one knows for sure," said Eva.

Daria spoke up. "That settles it. I am not leaving you — you'll have to break my wings to stop me. You need protection, and I wouldn't trust this Flamey to brush Snarfle's tongue." Mara scowled back at Daria.

"Shut up, Daria!" Alexa yelled. "You weren't there when Aerioth tried to kill me!"

"Alexa!" said Eva. "Don't ever speak to Daria that way!

She is your sister! Blood is stronger than any other magic. How did you become so arrogant so quickly?" Mara tapped the hilt of her sword, her eyes still on Daria.

Alexa's eyes darted back and forth anxiously. She would have to tell the truth. "I just don't want either of you to die," she blurted.

"What? We have a lot more chance of surviving this than you do," said Daria.

"No, you don't. Someone is going to die," Alexa insisted. She told them about Ispirianza's Ring Dream and how the Great Oak had foreseen that someone on Alexa's journey would not survive. "I just couldn't bear it if you or Eva died because of me," she said. "And Ispirianza said if one of my sisters got killed, I probably would not have the will to complete the task."

Daria held the back of her head with her hands, thinking hard. "Okay, now this makes more sense," she said. "You were actually trying to protect your big sisters? Unbelievable."

Eva put her hand on Alexa's shoulder. "Whether or not I believe in Ispirianza's Ring Dreams, little sister, know that I would gladly sacrifice myself to save the life of either of my sisters." Mara rolled her eyes.

"Really?" asked Alexa, her lip trembling.

"Of course we would," said Daria. "Didn't you know that?" Tears began to pool in Alexa's eyes, but she fought them back.

Eva and Daria whispered for a minute out of Alexa and Mara's hearing. They decided that Daria would stay with Alexa. Eva would return to Kendlenook and try to discover how the Oths knew about Alexa's journey. She worried that a disguised Oth might be hiding in Kendlenook and reporting

Alexa's plans to Aerioth.

Eva's sylphs re-gathered overhead in a swirling mass. Then Eva whispered something in Daria's ear, hugged both her younger sisters and flew off in the midst of the gathering. The wind currents they created ruffled the meadow grass in a great waving circle and stirred up dust in all directions.

"What did she say to you?" Alexa asked Daria.

"She told me to keep an eye on it." Daria nodded her head toward Arthur.

"Arthur is not an 'it,'" said Alexa.

Daria turned to Mara, who still had her hand on her sword. "Now that I have things under control, you can take your big, bad sword and go back to your canyon—or wherever it is you start your little fires."

Mara looked to Alexa.

"Wait, Daria," Alexa said. "Mara is my friend and we need her. She knows this land and what plants we can eat. She can lead us to the Oth caves and has all kinds of ideas on how to get inside."

Daria thought about it while cracking her knuckles and finally admitted, "Well, I guess we can use her."

Mara spoke up. "Fairy of Protection or not, you're on my turf now, so you'd better listen up, Pinecone. We eat, we rest until dark and then we fly." She passed a nightshade berry to Daria, who reluctantly bit into it.

"Delicious, aren't they?" asked Alexa.

"I guess they're okay," said Daria. Mara's eyes narrowed.

TWENTY-NINE

How to Steal Candledark

L ate that afternoon, Alexa awoke with her fingers grasping the chain of Margaret's locket. Arthur was poking her in the cheek with his flipper. Alexa jabbed Daria, a big clump in the blanket next to her. The groggy blanket stirred and moaned, then went quiet again. How can she sleep so soundly out here and in the middle of the day, no less? Alexa wondered.

Mara was already up and packing. Alexa lost patience and kicked Daria into flight. "I'm up! I'm up!" Daria shouted as she spun sleepily in the air. They munched on the remains of the wild plants Mara had gathered the previous day. Mara sat on a branch and watched three Shadow Fairies darting after each other in the dappled sunlight. Just for fun, Mara tossed a small branch at the dark sprites. In an instant the Shadow Fairies whooshed hundreds of wingbeats away into the lengthening shadows of the hills.

Mara chuckled to herself and asked, "So you really think you can catch one of those things?"

"I have to," replied Alexa.

"Can I sell tickets?"

"Thanks for your confidence."

The group turned south, flying along the foothills of the White Mountains. The bristlecone pine trees there did not grow in dense forests like the trees near Kendlenook, but rather grew far apart in an open and mostly bare landscape. The harsh mountain winds twisted and gnarled the trees into shapes that looked more dead than alive, but the trees here lived longer than any others in the known world. Some had roots close to five thousand years old.

The dryads of the White Mountains were famed as some of the oldest and wisest in the world. Alexa had heard many stories of this place from Ispirianza, who had, of course, never traveled here but knew it only from Zymandria's descriptions. Alexa made a mental note to tell Ispirianza that the forest had not been cut off by the Scarring as she feared.

"Daria's really nice once you get to know her," Alexa whispered to Mara while Daria flew a little ahead. "Just don't get her started on food, falconry, council politics, weather patterns and, oh yeah, fashion—don't talk about that either. Oh, and forest creatures—she has strong opinions on that subject. And Romorians. Other than that you're pretty safe."

"Uh, huh," said Mara.

"What's with those dryads over there?" asked Daria. Despite the late hour and darkness of midnight, no less than five or six dryads were waving at the fairies from the tops of their trees.

"Blessings to you, Bright One," one called out.

"Remember the mark of the hourglass, Alexa of the Meadow," another shouted. More dryads emerged from their trees.

"Bright One?" asked Daria. "What are they talking about?

And how do they know your name?"

"I don't know," Alexa said, looking away from the dryads. By now some of the dryads were holding up spritelings and pointing to the three fairies.

"Would you give us a look at Margaret's locket? Just a quick peek?" a dryad begged. Alexa waved and kept flying. She acted embarrassed, but she secretly loved the attention.

"I feel like we're in a parade," Mara said, holding her head up and waving back at the dryads like she was the High Fairy. "Hope the Oths don't hear all the fuss they're makin'."

"Let's g-g-go," said Arthur. "Which way?"

"Yes, we need guidance, O Bright One," Daria said. Mara laughed. Alexa knew she wasn't going to live this down.

As they flew along the base of the White Mountains, the hairs on Alexa's neck and arms began to stand on end. Her eyes felt drawn to a narrow, dark canyon carved into the mountain. Alexa's mind grew numb as she turned toward the black chasm and beat her wings toward its mouth.

"Hey, Flowers," said Mara. "Evernaught is this way." She pointed south.

"No, no. This is the way," Alexa said with a blank stare.

"Uh, sorry. I've seen it before, remember?" said Mara, looking concerned. "You've never been here in your life. What's wrong with you?"

"This is the way!" snapped Alexa. "We fly through that canyon to the top of the mountain." She never even turned her head from her flight path.

"I think you should listen to Mara on this one," said Daria, darting toward Alexa. She clearly sensed something was wrong. Daria grabbed Alexa by the shoulder and whipped her around. Alexa's unfocused eyes just stared.

"Let me go!" Alexa shouted in a voice so deep it startled her sister. Daria held on tightly to her struggling sister's shoulders.

"Mara, come look in her eyes. She's in some kind of trance!"

"It's there! It's that way, I tell you!" Alexa insisted.

"What is?" Mara peered into the deep channel.

"The way! The way!" said Alexa. Then Alexa heard them: a thousand whispers on the wind coming together into one. The voices drifted from the canyon and grew louder.

"I feel you near…" the voice called. "Come to me.…"

"I…I…," Alexa stammered. "I will!"

"Alexa, who are you talking to?" asked Daria. "You will what?"

"There! We must go there!" Alexa struggled to pull away from Daria's grip.

Mara flew right up to Alexa and slapped her hard across the face. Then she slapped her again with the back of her hand. Alexa's hands rose to her stinging cheeks as her eyes focused. She looked surprised to see Mara and Daria.

"Alexa, snap out of it!" Mara cried. Daria caught Mara's arm before she struck again.

"Okay, I think we have our Alexa back now," said Daria. Alexa shook her head hard and blinked. She then looked toward the canyon like a monster was stalking her.

"Let's…let's get out of here," Alexa said, as she stared at the chasm's mouth.

"Music to my ears," Mara said, as she and Daria each took one of Alexa's arms and led her quickly away from the voice.

"What was that all about?" Daria asked.

"I don't know," Alexa said, still rubbing her tingling cheeks. She didn't want to worry her friends. "I haven't had much sleep lately. I just flipped out for a second. Thanks for bringing me back."

"You can count on me to slap you whenever you need it," Mara smirked. From then on, Daria flew with one eye on Alexa at all times.

They soon landed at a blackberry thicket to have a snack and discuss how to sneak into Evernaught.

"I hate to admit it, but the Oth disguise sounds like a great idea," said Daria.

"But what about the bumbleflies?" said Alexa.

"Bumbleflies?" asked Daria.

"They attack anything that doesn't smell like an Oth. Ow!" Alexa sucked on her finger where a blackberry thorn had pricked it.

"What does an Oth smell like?" asked Daria, looking at Mara.

"I don't have a habit of goin' around sniffin' Oths," said Mara.

"But you fought Aerioth," said Alexa. "How did she smell?"

Mara thought for a minute. "I was kinda busy at the time, but I guess she smelled like candledark."

"That's helpful," said Daria, rolling her eyes. "So we need to already have candledark in order to steal candledark?"

"Yep. So I guess this is your lucky day," said Mara.

"Oh, you're leaving and we'll never see you again?" said

Daria. "That is lucky!"

"Daria, behave," said Alexa. "Okay, Mara, why is this our lucky day?"

"'Cause of this." Mara reached her berry-stained hands into her satchel and tossed a stick-like object over Daria's head. Daria buzzed her wings, lunged upward, caught the object and then did a back flip down to the ground. Alexa clapped her wings in delight at Daria's move. Mara pretended to be unimpressed.

Daria studied the unusual stick in her hand. It was smooth, black and waxy with purple sparkles. It tingled with energy and hummed faintly. "Is this what I think it is?"

"You catch on fast, Pinecone," said Mara.

"Are you serious?" demanded Alexa. "You had candledark all this time and didn't tell me?"

"Ya can't catch a Shadow Fairy with just one stick," Mara said.

"How did you get it?"

"From some Canyon Fairies I know," said Mara.

"And where'd they get it?"

"A while back, these fairies found an Oth who'd blown into a thorn tree durin' a storm. Her dress got so tangled in the branches that she couldn't escape the thorns. Every time anyone came close, she screamed and hurled spells at 'em."

"What did they do?"

"Afraid the thing would attract more Oths or curse their whole canyon, they had to get rid of her. While they argued how to do it, the Oth took off, but her dress stayed behind. Can you imagine—a naked Oth flyin' around?

"In the dress pocket was this stick of candledark. The elder

Canyon Fairy kept it to study it. I thought it might come in handy, so yesterday when I went out to gather food, I stopped by that canyon. When the elder fairy wasn't lookin', I stuck the candledark stick under my dress."

"You *stole* it?"

"Don't looked so shocked. What do you think you're plannin' to do with the candledark in Evernaught?"

"Good point," replied Alexa. She thought for a second. "But somehow I don't think I'll enjoy it as much as you are."

"But how are we going to make the disguise?" Daria asked. "Oth dresses don't look anything like fairy dresses."

Arthur perked up, hoping this meant they'd cancel the plan.

Mara sighed. "You fairies have no faith in me at all. Do ya really think I'd steal the candledark stick without takin' the dress as well?" Mara pulled from her satchel a complete Oth outfit. Arthur darted away at the sight of it. The dress was black, purple, tattered and very evil looking — it was perfect!

"You are The Fairy!" Alexa praised, running her hand along the strange fabric.

"You may be devious, Mara," said Daria. "But you are pretty useful." Mara smiled smugly.

Arthur just went back to being worried.

"Now as the most wily of the bunch — and seein' that we only have one dress — I get to wear it and sneak into the cave," Mara declared.

"No!" cried Alexa. "Absolutely not! I will not have you risking your life for me."

"What do you think we've been doing, Alexa?" asked Daria. "And it's not just for you, remember?"

Chapter 29

"Ispirianza gave this task to me," Alexa said. "If I don't have faith in myself, then I have no business going into Timefulness and trying to stop the Scarring."

"Oh, so that's what you're up to," said Mara. "No offense, but you won't last ten seconds in Evernaught."

"You may see me as just a naïve little spriteling," Alexa said. "But the human appeared to me, I'm the one with the locket and I'm the one who is going into that Oth cave! It's my decision to make."

Daria raised her eyebrows. Mara smiled proudly and put her hand on Alexa's shoulder.

"I don't like this one bit, but I won't stop you," grumbled Daria. "If there is even a hint of trouble in that slimy old cave, you just give three whistles, and Mara and I will be there faster than a sylph."

Alexa sighed as reality set in. "I can't believe I'm going to sneak into a cave full of Oths."

"Cheer up," said Mara. "The bumbleflies'll probably kill you long before you even get ta the cave."

"Thanks," Alexa said. "I feel so much better."

THIRTY

Up in Smoke

L ater at their camp, Alexa went behind a sequoia tree to try on the Oth dress. As she slipped the silky black glove over her hand, an eerie feeling swept over her. The power of deception flowed through her as the cloth of the dress slid onto her bare skin. She wondered how long a fairy could imitate something without becoming what she was only pretending to be. The dress seemed to transform her feelings. Strange. As she fastened the choker around her neck, Alexa began to panic. She frantically unfastened the clasps and buttons.

"Get it off me! Get it off!" she cried. Mara and Daria scrambled to help the frightened Alexa take the dress off. Alexa let it fall to the ground and backed away.

"What's wrong?" Daria asked. "Was it awful? Did you hate how it felt?"

"No," said Alexa staring down at the dress. She rubbed her

neck where the choker had been. "I...I loved how it felt. It made me feel powerful. That's what scared me." Daria and Mara traded wide-eyed looks. Alexa looked down into the fire.

"Well, it seems like the dress is a little much for the Meadow Fairy," Mara said. "I'll just have ta put it on and steal the candledark myself, like I said in the first place."

"No!" Alexa said. "Nobody's putting that thing on."

"Mara, you're not the only one who can pull this off," said Daria. "I am totally capable of sneaking into that cave."

"Listen, Your Forestness," Mara snapped. "You are way outta your league here. If you even—" Suddenly Mara and Daria heard a violent popping coming from the fire behind them. They turned to see that Alexa had thrown the Oth dress into the flames.

"Alexa, what have you done?" Mara yelled. "That's our only way into Evernaught!"

Daria stared in disbelief at Alexa. Then a strange movement from within the fire captured all three fairies' gazes. The dress began to slowly writhe and twist on its own as it burned. Daria looked at Mara, then back into the fire.

A ghastly wail rose from the dress as it flared green and blue and smoked purple. The dress seemed to sit straight up, then cringe to the side as its screams turned into a high shrieking sound. With a bright white flash, the dress gasped and the fire died down to a flicker. The fairies stood stunned.

"Okay, I see what you mean now," said Daria. A faint whistling and popping still rose from the fire.

"Well that plan literally went up in smoke. Got any bright new ideas, Bright One?" Mara said with a raised eyebrow.

"Come on, Mara. You saw what that dress just did in the fire—it's like it was alive or something," Daria said.

Alexa cautiously poked at the smoldering dress with a long stick as if to make sure it wouldn't jump back out of the fire. Arthur watched from behind her shoulder.

"Maybe there's a back entrance into the caves," Alexa said.

"Yeah, sure. The secret one that only the really sneaky Oths take," Mara shot back.

"If only we could get in from below," Daria said.

Mara suddenly spun around. "Woblins!"

"Where?" a panicked Arthur squeaked as he jumped for a hole.

"Unbelievable," Mara said. "There's a swarm of Oths and bumbleflies right over that mountain, but the thought of a little ground woblin gets him all trembly."

"Woblins aren't little. They're b-b-bigger than you," Arthur defended himself.

"Exactly," smiled Mara. "The woblins have holes and tunnels all over this plain, right? We could travel underground through the woblin tunnels and right into the Oth cave." Alexa's eyes brightened at the idea.

"How would we find our way?" asked Daria.

"We just ask 'em," said Mara. "They have a language, right?"

"They do," said Daria. "Can you speak it?"

"Not me," said Mara. "You're Miss 'Look at Me I Talk to the Animals.'"

"I speak eight different animal languages, but we don't learn Woblinese in Kendlenook. There's no use for it," Daria said.

"Zhep keek, shirp!" said Alexa sadly, remembering the woblin chatter.

"Don't tell me to go away," Arthur replied. "It's terribly rude."

The three fairies stared at Arthur: Alexa with confusion, Mara with annoyance...and Daria with realization.

"Arthur, did you just translate what Alexa said?" Daria asked.

"What does t-t-translate mean?" said Arthur.

"Do you understand the woblin language?"

"Only tree woblin. The grammar is a bit d-different from ground woblin. Absolutely. Or not." said Arthur.

"Why didn't you tell us?" said Alexa.

"I didn't know it w-was important."

"You didn't know it was imp—" Mara looked like she might strangle Arthur. "Well, here's your chance to finally be useful. You can talk to the woblins for us."

"What? N-no! Ground w-w-woblins are creepy and crawly and want to eat us. I'll go into the Oth cave before f-f-facing one of those, those digging, scratchy things."

Daria asked, "How did you learn to speak woblin?"

"From the t-tree woblins back home," said Arthur. "The gatherings have to tell them about b-b-bad weather coming so they can warn all the less intelligent animals. But t-t-tree woblins have the s-sense to stay up high, unlike th-those around here, always p-popping their heads out of the ground and jumping out at other c-c-creatures." Arthur shuddered. "No ground woblins—absolutely no. Final no."

As Arthur continued talking to Daria, Mara tiptoed silently behind him, with her satchel raised in the air. With one swish and swoop, she snatched Arthur into the bag before Arthur could even stutter. Muffled screams came from inside the satchel.

"Okay, sylpho," Mara said. "Alexa needs you to translate for her and you're gonna do it, like it or not. Got it?" More muffled protests came from inside the bag. Daria sat back and smiled.

"Arthur," Alexa said to the satchel. "It's really important, and we'll protect you. Please." The bag got quieter, but Mara still wouldn't let him out.

"Let's go find us some woblins," said Mara.

The three fairies — and one jittery sylph in a bag — swept low over the plains near the White Mountains. They saw plenty of woblin holes, but no furry heads peeking out of any of them.

"Those creatures overrun the place like rats, but they all disappear as soon as you actually want to talk ta one," complained Mara.

"We need something to bargain with," Alexa said. "What do they like to eat?" asked Alexa.

"Slugs and g-grubs, mostly," said the bag.

"Ugh," said Alexa.

"Land next to that hole. Arthur, say something to them. Maybe a woblin will come out if it hears words it understands." Mara snatched Arthur out of the bag by his scruff and held him over a woblin hole.

"Queeechernch shep shep tiiiich chep," said Arthur with his eyes closed and nose in the air.

Sleepy woblins tumbled out of their holes so quickly that they fell all over each other. Arthur struggled to squirm out of Mara's grip, but Mara kept a firm hold.

"What did you say?" asked Daria as woblins swarmed around her.

"Slug stampede."

The woblins sniffed suspiciously at the fairies and twitched their whiskers in irritation.

"Tell them we need to talk to them about a life or death matter," said Alexa.

Arthur turned his head away from the ground as he spoke. "Shwrep cheech chiiiiich ke-ke-ke pneck knawk schwerpeeeeee." A particularly large woblin with long whiskers scampered toward them. Arthur tried again to fly for it. Mara tightened her grip.

"Oh, and introduce us, too," said Alexa, remembering her manners.

"The leader's name is Skrum," reported Arthur. "He says, 'May your tunnels have strong walls.'"

"Ask if their tunnels lead to the Oth caves," said Alexa.

After another exchange of noises, Arthur reported that the woblins never tunneled into the caves because they preferred not to become the main course of the Oths' dinner. All the woblins gathered around their leader were now chattering nervously with each other. Anytime an owl's shadow floated over the plain, the woblins vanished. Then a woblin chirped an "all clear" signal, and they appeared again.

Alexa thought for a moment about how to best explain the long and complicated story to the simple creatures. She started with the Scarring. The woblins understood immediately. They called the Scarring "The Great Hole Dug By No One" and sadly reported that no slugs or grubs lived in The Great Hole. They had lost an entire colony of ground woblins and twenty tree woblin pines to The Great Hole just this year.

Alexa explained that she needed to visit the human world to stop the digging of The Great Hole Dug By No One. The woblins knew nothing of humans. Alexa went on to explain that she must have the Oths' candledark to enter Timefulness. After her speech, Alexa asked again, "So, will you please help us? We need your gift of digging. By doing this you will save the entire race of fairies and restore balance to the land."

Skrum signaled that he understood. He paused thoughtfully, then finally replied, "Trk n'var kerzee."

Arthur translated: "No."

Before Alexa or the others could plead their case further, Skrum and the woblins skittered down their holes into darkness.

"That went well," said Mara.

THIRTY-ONE

The First Glimpse of Evernaught

The three fairies flew back to camp, discouraged. Arthur looked relieved. The task of stealing candledark seemed impossible. Two perfectly good plans had come to nothing.

They decided to scout the area around Evernaught for new ideas. Once the moon set and the stars brightened, they started on their way.

So near the Oths' lair, the fairies did not dare light any candles. As they fluttered in the blackness, a strange mixture of excitement and fear energized Alexa's spirit. She imagined she could feel the caves of Evernaught, which she knew lay only a thousand wingbeats or so away.

The mountains to the west loomed larger and larger as they flew onward. The peaks rose like jagged black knives against the starlit sky. Mara gestured for everyone to fly closer to the ground. Slowed by the need for caution, it took hours to travel the last short distance. The fairies hid in cracks in the rocks as glowing Oths glided like phantoms overhead.

"What are those green glowing balls they're holding?" whispered Daria.

"Lumastones," answered Mara. "That's how they see in their pitch black caves. They hate candlelight."

"Look at them patrolling the woods like ghosts," hissed Daria. "Pure evil."

Alexa shivered. Mara peeked out of the crack and slowly climbed out.

"Stay quiet and walk behind me," Mara finally said. "No more flying." She hiked along the back side of a hill and crept low up the slope. Alexa, Daria and Arthur followed her into a thick stand of trees at the crest of the hill.

Mara pulled back the brush. "Look!"

Alexa crowded in next to her and gasped in amazement. Daria stared over her shoulder and started cracking her knuckles nervously. The black entrance of the Oth lair opened up on the barren hillside like a gaping mouth ready to swallow any soul unlucky enough to fly too close. A gray mist cloaked the cave, masking their view of the evil within. Echoing voices and dark music rose out of the ground like an unquiet grave. So many Oths flew to and fro that Alexa couldn't count them. The glowing lumastones in each Oth's hands made them look like a swarm of ghastly fireflies.

Arthur covered his ears. "Make it stop! Make it stop!" he cried.

All three fairies turned to him at once. "Shhhh!"

"But it hurts," Arthur complained, but in a quieter voice.

"What hurts?" asked Daria.

Chapter 31

"That noise! Don't you hear it?" said Arthur.

The fairies stood silent for a moment, straining their ears. Alexa thought she heard a buzzing noise. Once she said so, Daria and Mara agreed with her.

"Yes, buzzing, that's right," moaned Arthur. "It b-b-bores holes in my poor head."

"Bumbleflies," said Mara. "See those dark things flying around in circles outside the cave?"

When Alexa had pictured the bumbleflies in her mind, she had thought of normal-sized bees or flies. "They're almost as big as the Oths!" she said.

"They are, but remember that Oths aren't any bigger than fairies," said Mara. "Look just above the cave and a little ta the left. Yes, the giant ball-looking thing. That's the bumblefly hive."

Alexa's skin crawled. "We'll be dead before we even get into the first cavern!" she cried.

Arthur started to screech at the buzzing once more. Daria tried to smother his face with her hand to keep him quiet. Arthur bit her finger, and Daria snapped her hand back, crying out in pain. She pushed Arthur to the ground and pinned him down with her foot. Alexa gaped in horror as three of the distant glowing lights stopped in mid-flight.

"Shush," Alexa whispered. "They can hear us!" Arthur continued to wail with his hands over his ears. The lights got slowly bigger. The Oths were definitely flying toward them.

"Get that fricketing sylpho away from here," snapped Mara. Alexa wrapped the hem of her dress around her hand and muffled Arthur's mouth with the cloth. The three fairies fled to the safety of the cracks in the rocks behind the

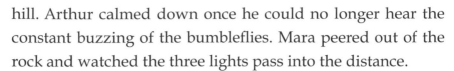

hill. Arthur calmed down once he could no longer hear the constant buzzing of the bumbleflies. Mara peered out of the rock and watched the three lights pass into the distance.

"I'm so glad you brought Arthur the Valiant with us ta fight the Oths," said Mara.

Alexa looked at Arthur and shook her head. "Okay, what are we gonna do?" she asked Mara and Daria.

"We rub the candledark all over ourselves ta fool the bumbleflies," said Mara, still looking out into the darkness. "They can't see very well, and they're a bit short on brains."

"But we'll never get past the Oths," said Alexa, rubbing the raw place on her neck where the Oth dress had burned her skin.

"We better get outta here before the sun comes up, or we're all bumblefly breakfast," said Mara.

"Stop. Listen," Alexa said to the others. Mara listened. Daria studied Alexa's face to make sure she wasn't zoned out like before.

"Pssssst!" The other fairies heard it as well. "Pssst…pssst!" The whispers came from a nearby hole. The fairies drew closer and saw the faint form of a small, light-brown woblin face in the darkness. The dark circles of fur around its eyes made it look like a masked raccoon. Another large woblin loomed behind the first.

"Pecheech cich snush ev-a-notche?" the woblin whispered.

"What did that thing say?" Mara asked Arthur.

"He's h-h-hard to understand, but I'm pretty sure he asked, 'You wanna get into Evernaught?'"

"Yes, yes! Can you get us in?" Alexa asked, excited.

"Shhh. Pipe down, Sparkles," the woblin said. The fairies

could understand him!

"You speak our language?" Alexa asked.

"Let's just say I get around," the smaller woblin answered. Daria and Alexa exchanged surprised glances. "Fairish comes in handy in my line of work. If you want to get into Evernaught, we can get you into Evernaught. But you can't tell Skrum or any other woblins, all right?"

"Why not?" whispered Alexa.

"That's for us to know," said the woblin. "Uh...but, we'll need a little something in return for our services." The woblins kept to the shadows.

"Let me handle this," Mara said, brushing Alexa aside. "What did ya have in mind, Fuzzy?"

"Not much," said the mystery woblin. "Just a trinket really. The kind that can only be found in Oth caves."

"Look, you tell me what it is ya want, and I'll tell you if we can get it for ya," said Mara. She acted as if she'd bargained a few times before.

"We'll get you in," the woblin's eyes peeked out of the hole, "for the price of one bumblefly egg."

"Why would you want one of those?" asked Alexa.

"You just let us worry about that, okay?" the small one said.

"Look," said Alexa. "Are you trying to hurt other woblins or something?"

"No, no. Nothin' like that. We'll keep that bumblefly safe and well fed, believe me."

Alexa looked at the woblin doubtfully.

The woblin sighed, "Honey brew, Sparkles. We can make amazing brew outta that honey."

"But you can make honey brew out of any bee's honey,"

said Mara.

"The kind we're talking about has...let's say...quite a kick to it, if you know what I mean," the woblin answered. "And if we're the only woblins to have one of those bad boys, everyone will have to come to us for the stuff. So we can set the price as high as we like."

"I assume this brew is not the healthiest thing in the world for woblins," Mara said.

"Oh, no, no, it's very good for the whiskers, and everyone will love it—believe me," whispered the woblin, peeking out of the hole and glancing around nervously.

"Let me get this straight," Mara said. "You want us to help you make extra-strong honey brew so you can have some black-market monopoly and get rich off the backs of other woblins? Is that what you're askin' us ta do?"

"Well, your choice of words lacks a certain polish, but yeah, that's pretty much it," said the woblin.

"Deal!" said Mara, shaking the woblin's paw.

"Wait, Mara," Alexa interrupted. "Should we be helping them do this?"

"You want to get your candledark, don't ya?"

"Yes, but..."

"And you heard what he said about it being good for the whiskers."

"I'm fine with it," Daria said. "They can make birthday cakes with the bumblefly honey for all I care."

"Excellent! The name is Snof, and it will be a pleasure doing business with fine fairies such as yourselves," the small one said. "And this is my partner, Nibs."

"Pleased to meet you," said Mara.

THIRTY-TWO

Through the Tunnels

As the sun rose, the fairies and Arthur retired to a hidden hollow to rest. They had hours until the sun set again, and they needed all the energy they could gather for the task ahead.

Alexa sighed and scratched at the bandage still wrapped around her leg. Four days had passed since her fight with Aerioth. Her leg felt better, but she decided to keep the bandage on another day just in case.

Alexa slept soundly but came fully awake as soon as Arthur landed on her arm. "Is it time?" she asked.

"The sun's almost down," said Arthur, sounding like he wished Alexa would bend time and slow the sun.

Alexa took a deep breath and let it out. "Okay, let's go." She nudged Daria and Mara awake.

"Before we go, we should paint ourselves," said Mara, pulling acorn shells full of paint from her bag.

"What for?" asked Daria.

"Anytime a fairy faces her enemy, she should change her spirit by changin' her appearance."

"But the Oths won't even see us — hopefully," said Alexa.

"It's not ta scare 'em," said Mara. "It's ta build courage in those who wear it." Daria and Alexa agreed to be painted.

It worked! Daria looked absolutely frightening when Mara had finished painting black swirls on her face and arms. Alexa felt more confident in a jagged purple design. Mara looked like an outright killer in red and black. Daria and Alexa were amazed at how different the paint made them feel.

"Want some, Arthur? I have a green that would go nicely with your, uh, flipper," said Mara. He squeaked and darted away.

The group met Nibs and Snof at a hole on the edge of the plain. Arthur asked to go back into a satchel before they entered the tunnels. He preferred seeing the inside of Alexa's bag to the feeling of packed earth enclosing him. The fairies watched the woblins scramble into the holes and gazed into the dark tunnel. Snof popped his head out again and gestured with his arm.

"Shall we, ladies?" he said, then scampered back into the tunnel.

Wordlessly the fairies took out lighting wands, lit candles and flew into the grave-like darkness.

The air felt cooler and damper the deeper they descended. The woblin diggers led their guests through a maze of dirt tubes that curved this way and that. The faint, lonely candlelight moving through the corridor was the only evidence that anything existed in that world of darkness. Sometimes an opening led to the ground above and let in fresh air and a little starlight.

The fairies had no trouble flying through the tunnels, but the nearness of the walls and lack of stars overhead took a toll on their courage. Alexa could have sworn the walls were tightening around her, and she began breathing faster and heavier. Not able to see but a few wingbeats in front of them, the world seemed very small and prison-like. For a long time Alexa could see nothing but candlelit woblin bottoms scampering forward and the earthen walls whizzing by. Occasionally they flew past burrows of woblins sleeping or preparing meals.

Alexa knew that woblins built their tunnels so well that they almost never collapsed, but the thought of being buried alive still hovered in the back of her mind.

The group flew for what seemed like hours.

Then Alexa suddenly crashed face first into Snof when the woblin stopped quickly.

"Here's where the tunnels closest to Evernaught end. We have to dig from here. Stay quiet."

Snof and Nibs dug furiously. Four other "packer" woblins that had been trailing behind the fairies now came forward and followed the diggers, using all four of their paws to press the loose dirt into the sides and floor of the tunnel.

Alexa couldn't believe how quickly the group moved. Digging slowed the woblins down some, but not nearly as much as Alexa expected. She wondered how they knew which direction to go without any landmarks or stars to guide them. Somehow they just knew.

The universe now seemed full of dirt—dirt walls

surrounding them and dirt flung all over them. As they flew along, Mara took the stick of candledark from her sash and bent it slightly. A smell like burnt cedar wood mixed with musty peat moss tickled Alexa's nostrils. A cloud of dark curled through Mara's candlelight.

"Just in case," said Mara. She rubbed the candledark on her bare arms and legs, then handed it to Daria, who did the same. Alexa then took the stick from Daria.

As they flew deeper, Alexa realized why the woblins made so many holes that opened to the outside. The air grew stuffier and mustier by the minute. She worried that the candles were burning all of the breathable air.

Nibs said that he didn't dare push through to the surface because they were so close to Evernaught. They couldn't chance the Oths spotting them.

Finally the four packer woblins stopped their frantic stomping and pressed their bodies to one side of the tunnel. Snof came back to inform the fairies that he and Nibs would soon break through into a cave.

"We will tunnel up into the cave wall," said Snof. "We think we're somewhere near the north side of Evernaught. Nibs and I will wait for you down the tunnel a ways so we can guide you out. But if the Oths see you, you're on your own."

Snof beckoned for Alexa and her friends to follow him to the front of the line. Nibs sat poised to dig the last few inches of earth out of the way. Alexa felt she was flying into her own funeral.

"Okay, here's what we do," whispered Mara. "Once the woblins open the hole, I'll stick my head in first and figure out where we are. Hopefully they dug into one of the storage rooms so that we won't have to face any Oths right away. Most of them should be out, but probably not all."

"Maybe we'll break right into the cave where they keep the candledark," Alexa said hopefully.

"Don't count on it. I hear Evernaught is almost as much of a maze as a woblin colony," said Mara. "Once we're inside, I'll lead. Arthur, you'll have ta fly outside of the satchel now. Daria, you have the bags ready? When we find candledark, we stuff the bags full and head straight back to this tunnel."

"Don't forget our bumblefly egg," said Nibs. "We did our part."

"Don't worry—you'll get your payment," assured Mara.

"Excellent."

Daria said, "Let's send Arthur back with the woblins. If we don't meet him above ground by dawn, he can fly to Kendlenook and tell Eva. He's too small to carry candledark anyway."

"Good idea," said Alexa. Arthur looked back and forth like he didn't know which was worse: the woblin tunnel or the Oth cave.

"Stay together, but remember the way back ta the tunnel in case we get separated," said Mara. "Ya don't want to get lost in there."

Alexa couldn't have agreed more.

"Ready?" asked Daria.

Mara nodded right away. Alexa closed her eyes for a second, then opened them and nodded. Daria took a deep breath and waved to Nibs.

THIRTY-THREE

Deep in the Caves

Nibs scratched carefully through the last layer of soil. Alexa's heart pounded as she brushed dirt out of her eyes and saw the wall open in front of her.

Mara inched forward on her stomach. Her head disappeared. After a few seconds, her arm beckoned to Daria and Alexa.

Alexa crawled behind Mara, and Daria followed Alexa. Alexa couldn't believe she was about to get her first glimpse inside a real Oth cave. The air was fresher than in the tunnel, but it had an odd smell. The cave into which Alexa emerged contained no Oths—a good first sign. Piles of all sorts of junk filled the room: cracked pots, torn bits of fabric and spoiling fruit.

Alexa pinched her nose shut.

"Perfect," said Daria. "Those woblins dug into the Oths' trash room."

"Actually, it is perfect," agreed Mara. "Anyone who comes

in'll just toss stuff in and leave without lookin' around."

"With this stink, who can blame them?" said Alexa.

"At least we can follow the smell to find our way back," said Daria.

Mara led the other two fairies into the next chamber and the next. Their candles shone against oozing wet walls as they moved through the caves. The rooms looked like empty sleeping chambers, but they saw no candledark.

As Alexa crept along, distant voices bounced off the black stone walls. A strange, exotic rhythm echoed from an unseen cavern. It sounded like ghostly chanting and primal drumming. The beautiful but terrible melody called to Alexa's deepest passions. "What's that?" she whispered.

"Sounds like some sort of ceremony. Guess they didn't all go out tonight after all," said Mara.

"Great," said Daria. "We had to come on Oth festival night."

The three fairies sneaked through several more empty caverns, each larger than the last. High over their heads, hundreds of stalactites hung from the ceilings like the teeth of giant predators. The stalagmites that grew from the floor were encrusted with jagged crystals that made the cave sparkle with a terrible beauty. The fairies walked over the spiky floor because Mara worried that the breeze from their wings might alert the Oths to their presence. They drew closer and closer to the noise of the ceremony.

Daria motioned and they put out their candles. A radiant light beamed from an opening far ahead. The firelight brightened into a dazzling blaze and shot shards of light through the stalagmites. Alexa's eyes had trouble adjusting after so long in the dimness of the woblin tunnel.

A cavern of Evernaught

The fairies began to crawl. They peeked out the opening of their tunnel into a huge cavernous lair where a bonfire burned with a strange blue light. Even larger stalactites clung to the ceiling, like swords jutting out of the stone. Ominous shapes flickered on stone walls that seemed to drip like toxic raindrops.

Around the blaze, an army of Oths leaped to the music, swinging their arms and flinging their hair up and down. Another group used mallets of woblin bone to beat stalagmites poking up from the floor. Alexa had never heard such reckless yet seductive music. The Oths were dancing themselves into a trance-like frenzy. There must have been hundreds of them. Black tattered robes flowed. Shadow Fairies leaped in and out of the fire like specters. Oth spritelings watched from the edges of the circle. It had never occurred to Alexa that Oths might have Shadow Fairies, too. And the idea of Oth spritelings just seemed unnatural.

The music and dancing dazed Alexa until Daria pinched her arm and motioned toward Mara. Mara pointed to the other side of the bonfire, where Alexa saw a pile of black sticks stacked unevenly. Candledark!

Then Mara started to mouth words and make gestures. Alexa had no idea what she was trying to say. Mara whispered in Alexa's ear, but she couldn't hear a word over the racket of the ceremony. Finally Mara had to yell in Alexa's ear to be heard. Alexa felt her eardrums would explode at the volume.

"Wait for the right moment, then we'll sneak around the edge of the ceremony," Mara shouted.

Alexa lifted her hands and mouthed, "But they'll see us!"

"We'll stay close together and hide in the cloud from my

candledark stick," Mara yelled. Just then they saw a blinding flash of blue light and heard a deafening crash. All three fairies ducked back into the tunnel. Had they been seen?

"Just part of the ceremony, I think," said Mara in a low voice. "Wait 'til they start dancing again." A hush fell over the Oths until Alexa could hear only the dull roar of the bonfire.

Alexa slowly lifted her head and peeked into the ceremony once more. A cloaked Oth with strange symbols painted on her forehead and white streaks down her jet black hair turned and looked in the fairies' direction. Alexa ducked down once more.

Then a booming voice rose from high above the flames. The three fairies looked to the ceiling, where an imposing Oth hovered and called down to the now kneeling crowd. The black and purple form was encircled by sharp and massive stalactites that flickered blue in the firelight.

"Aerioth!" Alexa mouthed to Daria, her eyes wide. Even Daria grew pale at the sight. Alexa studied the serpentine band covering Aerioth's ankle. She hated and feared Aerioth. But secretly—so secretly she herself did not know—she admired her.

"All fortunate enough to be in my presence should take pains to remember the words I speak to you tonight," Aerioth called out. Her words sounded like a battle cry, not at all warm and syrupy like when she'd spoken to Alexa. The crowd responded with wild wing-clacking and screams. Alexa and Daria covered their ears. Mara signaled for them to stay put.

Aerioth waved her arms, and the crowd hushed immediately. "I shall tell you the story of Her Holiness, the first High Oth, the mother of all who desire power, the very source of the spirit of the Oth." The lair erupted in chants and screeching. Aerioth did not even glance at the crowd, as if it were beneath her notice.

"Back in the Age of Ignorance, before the spirit of the Oth was born, fairies and dryads did not understand the nature of true power. The fairies of Faewick Forest performed the ceremony that would reveal their next queen, called the High Fairy. But they did not know the proper rituals and brought the wrong fairy to power, one called Llyranna. Another of the Fae had much more beauty and talent than this Llyranna, but the fairy council failed to give her the position she deserved.

"Llyranna ruled badly. She made laws that took rights away from other fairies. She and her followers decided that some things were evil and others good. But as we all know, everyone must decide for herself what is good and what is evil.

"Llyranna told other fairies how they should live and judged their behavior. This High Fairy wanted to make all other fairies just like her. But for the good of the world, the most beautiful, talented and powerful of all the Fae — Mother Oth herself — spoke up in rebellion!" The Oth brood squealed in delight.

Aerioth continued, "Mother Oth spoke the truth to Llyranna, that there is no right, no wrong, no black, no white — only beautiful shades of gray!" The crowd roared louder. "But the High Fairy would not listen to the truth. So our glorious mother had to devise lies that she used for the good of all fairies. She lied in order to reveal the truth. She told the fairies and dryads how the council had stolen the throne from her with the aid of a rebellious young dryad named Ispirianza."

Alexa gasped at hearing her friend's name.

"Mother Oth fought to overthrow the weak-minded Llyranna. Some brave fairies swore allegiance to Mother Oth and became the most powerful and mighty of the Fae.

"These events happened long ago. Many High Fairies have come and gone in the ages since and have refused to reverse their backward and selfish ways. But I promise you, all here tonight shall live to see the day when we strip the High Fairy of her power, the fairies' weakening magic will disappear from the earth and the Oth shall live forever."

Aerioth's passionate speech continued: "Listen carefully. I tell you that the Dark Prophecy rings true today! The three signs that herald the arrival of our Dark Redeemer will soon show themselves. I know it. I feel it. And we will soon meet the Dark Redeemer herself, who will finally free us from our bondage!"

Aerioth raised her arms, and a purple ball of flame rose from the bonfire with a loud roar. The group of Oths jumped to their feet, singing and dancing. Alexa and Daria exchanged looks of horror. Mara motioned that this was their opportunity to strike.

She took the candledark stick from her pocket, and a dark cloud enshrouded the three fairies.

"Daria, stay here," Mara shouted in the Forest Fairy's ear. "There's not enough darkness ta cover us all." Daria nodded in acceptance and threw Mara her empty bag.

"Let's go!" Alexa took a deep breath. The two fairies crept into the great cavern. The Oths were so entranced by their music that they paid no attention to the dark mass edging along the cave wall toward the candledark alcove. After what seemed like an eternity, Alexa and Mara finally inched all the way around to the other side. Alexa looked back and saw Daria's eyes peeking over the tunnel entrance from which they had come. How tiny she looked.

Mara and Alexa tumbled into the small alcove. Piles and piles of candledark cluttered the floor. They frantically stuffed two bags full. Alexa kept looking back into the cavern to make sure no one had noticed them. She shoved a few more sticks into the sash of her dress.

Alexa was startled by a poke in her side. Mara gestured with her head toward the back of the alcove. Alexa looked over to see another small room with rows and rows of neatly arranged white oval balls sticking out of nest-like holes. A circle of glowing lumastones surrounded and warmed them.

"Bumblefly eggs," Mara mouthed to Alexa. Alexa glided over, softly picked one up and tucked it into her sash. She nodded at Mara.

Suddenly another flash of light illuminated the cave, and they heard a loud bang and then a rumbling. Alexa didn't know whether to cover her eyes or ears first. "Let's get outta here," urged Mara.

When they entered the cavern once more, it had fallen silent. The Oths now knelt in some kind of unholy prayer. Alexa and Mara had to stay extra quiet now as they crept along the back wall. They had trouble feeling their way through the blackness of the candledark because the flash of light had partially blinded them. Alexa hoped the Oths were having the same problem. Alexa looked to where they had left Daria, but couldn't see her. She had a terrible feeling something was wrong.

Then Daria returned, waving her arms. She moved her hands around like a snake and then frantically gestured downward. Alexa and Mara looked at each other, confused, and then back at Daria. Dust and smoke rose out of the hallway from which Daria had come. The only noise was the crackling of the fire and a distant rumble.

Alexa's eyes widened as she figured out Daria's signals.

"Oh, no!" she whispered. "Those booms from the fire collapsed the woblin tunnel." Alexa stood motionless against the wall, not knowing whether to go forward or turn back.

"What should we do?" Mara asked. So even Mara was out of ideas? They looked around the cavern and saw no fewer than five tunnels leading out of the giant room, not counting the one in the ceiling near where Aerioth stood.

"I think we should go back to the garbage room and see if we can dig our way back into the woblin tunnel," Alexa said. "Maybe it only collapsed a little." She hoped Arthur hadn't been buried.

Just then, Mara and Alexa heard a sputtering sound very close, almost on top of them. Alexa looked around but could not find the source. Then the darkness around her started to flicker. With a sudden snap, their candledark stick went out. The cloud of darkness protecting them dimmed into a little point of nothingness.

The two brightly colored fairies now stood completely exposed in the middle of a crowd of Oths in the depths of the Evernaught caves. At first Alexa and Mara just stood there like dangling Oth bait. None of the kneeling Oths had seen them yet. The bag of candledark sticks felt heavy around Alexa's neck and started to choke her.

"Light another one," Mara hissed softly.

"I'll try," breathed Alexa.

Mara started slowly scooting along the wall. Alexa followed, trying desperately not to make any noise. She reached into her sash to grab a stick of candledark. As Alexa scraped along the wall, a tiny rock broke away from the cave wall and crumbled to the ground with a crackle. Alexa froze and just stared down at the rock, not wanting to look toward the Oths. She told herself that no one else heard the rock fall. She slowly lifted her head and looked at Mara. Mara just stood with her back pressed against the wall, her eyes wide and staring at the crowd of Oths.

Alexa followed Mara's gaze and saw a little spriteling Oth looking back at her. The spriteling looked confused, but said nothing. Mara lifted her finger to her mouth, smiled and gave a "shh" expression to the spriteling.

"Ooooh, look at the pretty fairies," the spriteling shouted.

The spriteling's mother, and fifty or so kneeling Oths, turned to stare. Only the sound of the crackling fire filled the cave. Alexa smiled and tried to look natural—whatever that meant.

"Fairy spies!" a booming voice echoed from above. Alexa looked up to see Aerioth pointing directly at them. Hundreds of black eyes now fastened on Alexa and her friend.

"Fly for it!" Mara yelled.

An Oth in the caves of Evernaught

THIRTY-FOUR

Chase Through the Caves

Mara leaped toward the tunnel at the center of the cavern. Alexa's wings pumped faster than they ever had before. She passed Mara, not daring to look back.

Aerioth raced after them with her lumastone in one hand. Alexa made it to the pitch-black tunnel first, with Mara directly behind. If it weren't for the faint light of Aerioth's lumastone, Alexa would not have been able to see a thing. They buzzed right past three confused Oths traveling in the other direction. Alexa felt the weight of her satchel of candledark cutting into her shoulder.

Suddenly a fork in the tunnel loomed in front of Alexa. She had no idea which way to choose, so she swung toward the larger opening on the right.

"No!" Mara shouted. "The other one! Fresh air." Alexa swooped around and doubled back toward the other tunnel. Now Mara was in the lead. Angry Oth shrieks echoed through the caves. The light from Aerioth's lumastone grew brighter and brighter. Alexa glanced back to see Aerioth drawing closer and scores of Oths teeming not far behind, each clutching a lumastone. The satchel weighed Alexa down and slowed her flight. Within seconds, Aerioth overtook Alexa and grabbed her sagging bag. Alexa buzzed her wings in panic.

"Hello again, my dear child," Aerioth said sweetly to Alexa. The Oth wasn't even winded. "You really shouldn't leave so soon. It wounds my feelings. Don't you like my humble home? I'll arrange for you to stay…forever."

Fear choked Alexa. In desperation, she swung the satchel off her shoulder and let Aerioth have it. Her sudden lightness made Alexa lunge forward. Aerioth let the bag fall away and gripped Alexa by the hem of her dress.

"You know, I really don't need all that candledark, my dear," Aerioth said. "But I appreciate the thought, really I do."

Alexa looked back just in time to see another satchel streak from above, hit Aerioth squarely in the face and send her shrieking backward into the swarm of other Oths. Alexa thanked the Great Song for Mara's good aim. Now free, Alexa beat her wings and whizzed past Mara.

In a desperate effort to shed weight, Mara unsheathed her sword and hurled it into the swarm of Oths. Screams rose as the crowd parted and Mara's sword flew end over end, past the chasers and into the darkness.

The light from the Oths' lumastones now looked dim compared to a brighter light straight ahead. Alexa hoped it wasn't more Oths.

No, the light came from outside, where the sun was beginning to rise. Alexa's heart soared at the sight of the sun.

Chapter 34

Freedom, warmth, protection. But then she saw several dark shapes drifting back and forth at the cave entrance.

"Bumbleflies!" Alexa shouted to Mara. "What do we do? We don't have any more candledark." Alexa's instinct was to stop, but she knew the Oths would overtake her.

"Just fly straight through the swarm," yelled Mara. "Surprise them." Alexa figured it was all they could do. The giant fairy killers grew bigger and bigger as Alexa barreled toward the entrance. Up close, the evil insects looked even more fierce, especially the massive stingers sticking out of their back ends.

Alexa closed her eyes, trying to still her mind and concentrate. She pictured the bumbleflies flying slower and slower. She focused all of her energy until time around her seemed to crawl.

Alexa broke into daylight. She had bent time with so much force that the bumbleflies probably only saw a green and pink streak flash past them.

The swarm hummed louder but still flew in circles. By the time they figured out that a fairy had flown past them, Alexa was a hundred wingbeats away from the entrance. Exhausted from the time bending, she summoned her deepest strength.

She glanced over her shoulder. To Alexa's horror, she saw two Oths pulling a struggling Mara back into the cave. Alexa panicked, not knowing what to do. Then an even more horrible thought made Alexa's mouth go dry.

"Daria!" In their haste to save themselves, she and Mara had left Daria deep in the Oth cave. She had to go back. She turned around just in time to see a wall of Oths racing toward her with a swarm of bumbleflies close behind. Aerioth led the charge.

On second thought, maybe flying straight into certain death wouldn't help Daria that much. Alexa veered east, hoping against hope that Daria had stayed hidden and could find her own way out of the lair.

Alexa's body and mind were so exhausted that she knew she could not stay ahead of Aerioth for long. Aerioth and the lead bumblefly raced ahead of the others. Alexa didn't think Aerioth had any candledark, so she flew straight into the sun. This seemed to slow Aerioth down. But then a small cloud crept in front of the sun, casting a shadow over the land. Would luck never shine on Alexa? Aerioth and the gigantic bumblefly closed in on their prey.

Alexa could see the flowing waters of the Black River below. An idea flew into her head. She worked her way up and up until the air became so thin that her wings barely held her. With Aerioth no more than three wingbeats away, Alexa veered to the west and stalled one wing. She plunged into a spiraling dive just like the one she had performed in advanced aerodynamics class. To Alexa's surprise, Aerioth stalled and spiraled after her. The two careened down toward the river. The confused bumblefly remained in the air far above them.

Alexa's brain pushed back against her skull as the world became a blurry circle and the river loomed closer and closer. Alexa hoped Aerioth was still spinning above her.

About twenty wingbeats above the surface of the flowing water, Alexa reversed her wing angle and tucked her arms into her body. Her Maple Seed Stop rapidly slowed her descent just as it had before.

As Alexa jolted to a halt in mid-air, she saw Aerioth spin

out of control. Alexa's feet gently dipped into the water, but Aerioth's body slammed into the river with a violent splash. The current sucked Aerioth down the rapids. Alexa watched as Aerioth struggled in vain against the angry current. The rapids pulled Aerioth under the foaming water. "You don't look so scary now!" she shouted. She could see Aerioth's body churning in the bubbles as the stream carried her enemy farther and farther away. Alexa's victory thrilled her and scared her. All she had ever wanted in life was to become a mother. But she was becoming a fighter, a killer.

Alexa darted upstream. Aerioth had probably survived the fall, but the Oth's soaked wings would keep her out of the air long enough for Alexa to flee. Aerioth would never catch Alexa now. Alexa flew for the cover of the trees, proud of herself for outflying the meanest Oth known to fairies.

Then sharp claws pierced into Alexa's sides. The air around her seemed to flutter in turmoil. A sudden pain stabbed through her spine. Aerioth's bumblefly minion grasped Alexa's arms, weighing her down. Its six thin legs scraped against her skin. Alexa struggled as the bumblefly curled its body and aimed its needle like stinger straight at her heart

Alexa dipped sharply downward because she could do nothing else. The stinger swung away from her body, but the bumblefly held on—barely. Its front claws scrabbled for a better hold. Suddenly she heard a ripping sound from her right wing. She gasped and risked a quick look.

Part of Alexa's wing hung in tatters. The insect's claw had stabbed the wing and then torn right through to the edge. Alexa tucked into a somersault and careened toward a boulder next to the stream. She angled her wings to slam the bumblefly into the boulder. Her head reeled back as they both hit the giant rock. She heard a loud crack as the bumblefly's thorax split open and green slime oozed out of its back. Still, it managed to hold on.

Alexa folded her wings and arms while plunging downward. The bumblefly was forced to let go as Alexa knifed through the water's surface. She held her breath for as long as she could. The swift current pulled her downstream into bubbling chaos. She bumped around a sunken log and several boulders and finally grabbed onto some reeds hanging into the water at the river's edge.

When she felt her lungs would burst, she surfaced and took a deep, frantic breath. She saw the wounded bumblefly sway and land upside down in the water. Its wings buzzed helplessly. The writhing bumblefly floated past her, slowly drowning. Victory again.

But only half a victory. At the start of her quest, Alexa had hoped that she could defeat violence with peace. But now she had learned that, all too often, only violence could defeat violence. She hated that knowledge.

Alexa crawled out of the water and collapsed on the ground. "I can do this," she said to herself. And at that instant it was true. Each test, each trial she faced made Alexa a little harder, a little more callous—and a little more of what she never wanted to become.

THIRTY-FIVE

Three Soggy Sticks

lexa clawed her way to the shelter of a currant bush, startling a quail into flight. Alexa barely noticed. After that, she either slept or fainted — she was not sure which.

Alexa woke, coughing violently from the dryness in her throat. Her whole body ached. She turned back to the river and drank deeply, lying on her stomach in the shade. She found the energy to wash her filthy arms and face and watched the dirt dissolve and float away. She stretched out her wings to let the warm sun dry them. Alexa wasn't sure if she could fly at all, but that wasn't what concerned her most.

"Daria, please be okay," she whispered. "Please." Her thoughts then turned to Mara, captured by Oths. She remembered Ispirianza's warning that someone would die. Her nightmare deepened.

After a short rest, Alexa started out for the place where

she was to meet her friends, flying slowly and low to the ground, in case her torn wing refused to hold her up. Though she kept a sharp lookout, she saw no one—friend or enemy. Alexa feared what she might find—or might not find—when she arrived at the meeting place. Was there any chance Daria might be there? Would Mara? Had Arthur already left for Kendlenook to tell Eva that they were all dead?

By midday, the sun shone hot overhead. Not a single cloud marred the sky, and not a breath of wind stirred the air. Alexa touched down limply on the flat expanse of the Great Woblin Plain, near where she and her friends had first spoken with the woblins less than two days before.

A chorus of chirps and squeaks erupted from behind Alexa. She turned to see Nibs and Snof and several other woblins sitting up on their back legs. No sign of Daria or Mara.

"Where's Arthur?" she asked them in a raspy voice.

"Gone," Nibs said. "He took off right after you went into the caves."

"We dug ourselves out after the tunnel collapsed," said Snof.

While fighting for her life, Alexa had no time to think about anything else. Now she remembered that she'd lost her satchel of candledark—the only reason they had gone into the caves in the first place. Then she remembered the few sticks she had stuck in her sash.

She reached down and pulled out a stick. The woblins sniffed at it curiously. Alexa bent it, but nothing happened. She tried harder and frowned. It was soaking wet. Would it work if she let it dry out? And even if it worked, she only had three sticks—how could that be enough to catch a Shadow

Fairy? Daria and Mara had sacrificed themselves for nothing.

"We're sorry you can't find your friends," said Nibs. "But there's that matter of our payment." Alexa snapped out of her daze.

"Oh, yes. Of course," she said softly, her voice cracking. She reached into her sash and pulled out a bright white bumblefly egg. The woblins' eyes lit up, and Snof made a "gimme" gesture with his hands. Alexa handed it over, and the rejoicing woblins scampered into their hole amidst mischievous laughter.

Alexa now stood alone in an empty wilderness. Collapsing to the ground, she let her failure wash over her. She wished the earth would swallow her up. She had no energy, no plan, no direction and no will. She thought of the daughters of Kendlenook, barely alive in their chrysalises. She thought of Ispirianza and her Ring Dreams. The grass ruffled around her as something landed nearby. Probably an Oth, but Alexa didn't even care.

"Hey, lazy wings," the voice of Mara said.

Alexa sat up. "Mara, you're here!" she shouted.

"Wow, you're getting better at spottin' things." Mara flopped down on the prairie grass next to Alexa. "I could sleep for a week."

"But how...how did you...?"

"Ya really didn't think a couple of cave-dwelling truth benders could hold me for long, did ya?" asked Mara.

"But how did you escape? Two of them had your arms," said Alexa.

"Ah, right, that's when you didn't come rescue me."

"But the other Oths were chasing me and—"

"I'm just jokin'," said Mara. "The day I need rescuin' is the day I clip my wings. And I definitely wouldn't have come after you if you'd been in the same fix."

"Thanks...I guess," said Alexa.

"Anyway, they had my arms pinned, right?" Mara sounded excited. "So I shoved a couple of candlesticks into their sashes when they were busy watchin' the bumbleflies swarm. Then I pulled out my lighting wand and lit 'em up. I'll tell you, when the bumbleflies saw those two Oths glowin' in candlelight like fairies, they attacked like woblins on grubs. While the bumbleflies were busy, I flew right through the swarm. No problem."

"Nice move!" Alexa said. "I never would have thought of that."

"What happened to you? You look like a drowned butterfly."

"Thanks a lot. This is what happens when you outfly the High Oth and get attacked by the nastiest bumblefly in the hive. That thing sliced my arms up and ripped my wing to shreds."

"Ow," cringed Mara. "That looks bad. Can you still fly?"

"Not as fast as usual, but I can still outfly you."

Mara laughed. "I'm glad to see the bumblefly didn't mess with your confidence," she said. "I can sew that up with some yucca thread until it heals."

Alexa's face turned grave. Since Mara had escaped without a scratch, Alexa had a sinking feeling that Daria wouldn't come back. Ever. A stone grew in her stomach.

"Daria hasn't come," said Alexa, white with worry. "She's probably still in the cave if she's not already...you know." Alexa couldn't say it, or even think it. Her breathing sped up.

"I wanted to go back to get her, but there were so many Oths and —"

Mara gripped Alexa's shoulders and looked right into her eyes. "Alexa, there's nothin' you could have done," she said. "Daria knew the risks."

"What do you know about it?" said Alexa. "I failed her. I've failed everyone."

"Whether she's dead or alive, you dishonor Daria by talkin' like that," replied Mara. "And you'll fail if ya give up. This is about saving those little fairies in their chrysalises, remember? Maybe about saving all of us! Rest, eat and get your strength back. Then you and I will find a way ta catch your Shadow Fairy and keep goin'."

"You don't have a sister, so you don't understand," Alexa said. "And I didn't tell you about my best friend, Kandra." Alexa lay down on her back and stared at the empty sky. "The Scarring destroyed her house the day before I left Kendlenook. She and her mother are both gone, and now Daria. What am I doing out here? I never doubted Ispirianza's word, but maybe I should have. Who am I but a plain old Meadow Fairy?"

"I'm gonna tell ya what you told Daria and me," said Mara, staring straight into Alexa's eyes. "It was you who the human appeared to, you who have the locket, you who were called to do this task. The fairy world needs savin', and you are the only one who can do it. Daria can't. Eva can't. Neither of 'em could ever understand your special calling. I can already imagine the stories they'll tell about you around the festival bonfires." Mara struck a dramatic pose and spoke in a deep voice:

"In those days, when all hope was lost, fearless Alexa of the Meadow, also known as the Bright One, set forth from

273

Kendlenook on a perilous quest to save the world." Alexa almost smiled. Her heart felt a shade lighter.

"You're a good friend, Mara. And I know you're right," she said. "But, Daria..." Mara put her arm around Alexa. Alexa didn't know what she would do without Mara's support. Mara might be rough or even mean-spirited at times, but Alexa could always rely on her for the most valuable of things — the truth. At times like this, the truth was what Alexa needed most of all.

"You know what?" continued Alexa. "Maybe Daria dug back through the woblin tunnel." She didn't even believe her own words as she said them. If Daria had dug through, she would be with them right now. Snof and Nibs would have brought her.

And now that the Oths had seen fairies in their own lair, they would be doubly watchful. There's no way Alexa could sneak back into the caves now.

"Please tell me you have the candledark," Alexa said.

"I had to throw it at Aerioth, remember?"

"So we have nothing but these three soggy sticks. Now I couldn't go through the Glass Corridor if my life depended on it, which it kind of does."

"The Glass what?" asked Mara.

"Well, that's the big secret. I didn't exactly tell you everything," Alexa admitted. "The Glass Corridor is the doorway to the human world. I think I told you that the humans cause the Scarring, right? Well, I have a human friend who can help me fix it."

"You have a human friend? No way!"

"Not like I can go to see her now," Alexa said.

"Don't you worry. We'll find a way ta get more candledark," Mara said.

Alexa looked at Mara in amazement. "I've never met anyone more confident than you, Mara. You really inspire me."

"Oh, shut up. I just make stuff up as I go along," said Mara. "So where's Arthur? Did he leave us for dead and fly back to hide behind Eva?"

"I doubt it," said Alexa. "The only thing that scares Arthur more than woblins is sylph herders. He's probably hiding in a hole right now, watching us until we fly away from the woblins. Let's go sleep. I can't think anymore."

As the two fairies took flight, Alexa winced in pain. Her shoulder muscles were so knotted she could barely fly. Her torn wing stung every time she flapped. She didn't try to resist the pain, because it kept her from thinking about Daria.

Sure enough, as soon as they passed the last of the woblin holes, Arthur popped out from behind a tree.

"Where have you been?" asked Alexa.

"H-hiding."

"From who?" asked Mara.

"Everyone," said Arthur.

"Why didn't you have the woblins re-dig the tunnel once it collapsed?," demanded Alexa. "We had to escape out the front cave entrance. Look what a bumblefly did to my wing!"

"The tunnel collapsed? We knew it! Burrowing under the g-g-ground just isn't right—or natural."

"You didn't see it collapse?"

"I just c-couldn't stand being with w-w-woblins underground any longer. I went away."

Alexa felt anger brimming over into her spirit, and she couldn't control it. "You coward! Daria's dead because of you!" Her harsh words stung Arthur like a whip. He shrank back and then began to cry loudly.

"Don't try to get sympathy from me, sylph," Alexa said. "Eva said you would lose your mind, and this is the craziest thing you could do. You deserted your friends. You don't even have any idea what it means to be a friend."

At this, Arthur squeaked out an "I'm sorry" and flew away. His pitiful cries became weaker as he disappeared into the woods.

Mara watched as he flittered away. "Look, I'm no fan of sylphs, Alexa, but that was awfully harsh."

"I don't have time to babysit a sylph who jumps at the sight of his own shadow," said Alexa.

Mara and Alexa could still hear Arthur sniffling in the distance. He followed just out of sight. "He doesn't have anywhere else ta go," said Mara.

"Eva warned me what would happen if I gave a sylph an unnatural purpose. He doesn't even have the will to die anymore." The sniffling behind them turned into a wail.

"I think he heard you," said Mara.

"Good."

When they got back to camp, Alexa didn't have the strength to redress the leg wound from her first meeting with Aerioth. The bandage was dirty and caked with dried blood, but her leg didn't hurt anymore—at least not compared to her wing.

Mara and Alexa slept and slept. The next time Alexa opened her eyes, the stars were out. She tried to lift her head. Mara was still out cold. After turning over, sleep forced Alexa's eyelids shut again.

In her dreams, Alexa heard something like rocks falling to the ground, but what woke her was the smell. Her eyes squinted in the sunlight. She wondered how long she had slept. What day was it? Once the green and purple spots faded away from her eyes and she could see clearly again, she thought she must still be dreaming. Because what she saw could not be true.

In front of her lay two satchels bulging with candledark! Alexa pulled out a few sticks and stared at them in disbelief. Just then, two feet caked with dried mud landed in front of her. Above the two feet was a dirty orange and green dress. Above the dress was the tired but smiling face of Daria.

Alexa jumped up and hugged her sister like she would never let go. Alexa's shoulder muscles burned as Daria squeezed back, but she didn't mind.

"Wow, you look worse than I do!" said Daria, pulling back and checking out Alexa's torn wing.

"So what?" said a joyous Alexa. "You're here, you're actually here. I thought that you—that the Oths—"

"Nope," said Daria. "You're showing some signs of growing up, but you still need me to protect you and get you out of trouble." Daria's legs were covered in a nameless muck, and she wavered as if she were about to collapse. She ran her fingers through her tangled and limp golden hair.

"Sit down, Daria," said Alexa. "No, lie down."

"Yes, Mother."

All the noise woke Mara. "Okay," said Mara. "Not even I can guess how you got out of that one."

"Oh, that part was easy," said Daria. "You two cleared the

whole cave of Oths when you bolted. I just flew right out." Alexa and Mara looked amazed. "Oh, by the way, did you two drop something? I happened across these two satchels and thought they might be yours."

"But what about the bumbleflies?" asked Mara.

"No problem," said Daria. "You're one stick short because I had to light one up and play Oth to get past them."

"If you had such an easy time, why do ya look like a falcon's dinner leftovers?" asked Mara.

"You try flying with those two bags. They weigh more than I do! I didn't want to chance having to go back in there, so I hauled both bags out. I couldn't even get off the ground, so I had to drag them for miles."

"You walked?" said Mara.

"It's not so bad," said Alexa. "Just slow."

"And there were Oths and bumbleflies everywhere looking for you," Daria continued, "or else I would have just flown one bag over and come back for the other one later. Walking takes forever. I don't know how Romorians and Cobbletons ever get anything done." Daria got a good look at Alexa's wing. "That's a nasty rip."

"Bumblefly," said Alexa.

"Where's Arthur?" asked Daria.

"Far from here, I hope," said Alexa. A sobbing wail rose from the edge of the camp. "Apparently not, though."

"Why, what did he do?" asked Daria.

"He almost got you killed because he lets his fear run his life!" said Alexa.

"He can't help it. Plus, I'm okay. He's been pretty loyal, Alexa."

"I can't trust him anymore. He's unreliable and getting worse."

"But now that he's lost the will to die, his mind will torture him," said Daria. "You're responsible for him now."

"I've got bigger issues to think about than a sylph's mental health," said Alexa. Then, because she was too happy to see her sister alive to want to argue: "Thank you for coming back alive, Daria. I don't know what I would have done without you."

Mara looked down and saw something familiar attached to Daria's golden sash.

"Hey, that's my sword!" Mara said.

"Sure is," Daria replied with a grin on her face.

"Look, just because I dropped it and you picked it up doesn't give you the right ta keep it," Mara demanded.

"Relax," said Daria. "I was planning on giving it back."

"Yeah, right," Mara said as she yanked the sword from Daria's sash.

"Watch it! You could hurt someone, Flamey," snapped Daria. "I don't know what your problem is, but it's time you consider who's on your side."

"I'm on my side, Pineneedles," Mara said. "I got no loyalty to you."

"Just stop it," said Alexa. "Mara, you lost your sword and now you have it back. Isn't that enough?" Mara unsheathed it and looked it over.

"There you are, Clarissa," Mara said quietly to the sword as she buffed it with her dress. "Been kinda lonely without ya."

"She named her sword," Daria said in disgust. "You've made friends with a total psycho!" Mara scowled at Daria.

Daria slept for several hours. Alexa used the time to think and came to a decision—a hard decision, but one she knew was right. Alexa knew Daria would not accept it, so she summoned the strength not to care.

When Daria awoke, Alexa told her, "Now that I know you're okay, you're going straight back to Kendlenook."

"Oh, really?" Daria said. "And who made you the High Fairy?"

"Daria, this is my journey and I don't need your help anymore. Besides, I can't worry about you all the time. Now go home!" Alexa hated to order her sister around, but she just couldn't handle the idea that Daria could die helping her. Ispirianza was right. She couldn't have been more right.

"You worry about me?" said Daria. "That's a laugh. You wouldn't even have any candledark if it weren't for me. You're in over your head and you're too full of yourself to admit it, O Bright One. But you don't seem so bright now. I'll tie you up and catch the Shadow Fairies myself if I have to."

The fear of losing Daria was undermining the mission. So Alexa did what any loving sister would do. She grabbed her sister by the shoulders and threw her against a tree.

"Look, I don't care what you think about me," said Alexa through her teeth. "I'm stronger than you think and you're going home." Daria grabbed Alexa's hand and twisted it. Alexa winced in pain.

"Who's going to make me, little sis?"

Alexa felt like they were little spritelings again play-fighting, and that Grandmother would break up their spat any time now.

"Fine. I'll just go on my own. You certainly couldn't catch me," said Alexa.

"With your ragged little wing? Alexa, now you listen to me!" Daria said right in her face. "I don't care what Ispirianza says about you alone being chosen. You need me, and I'm going to follow you like a flitter dragon until you're safely back home."

Just then, the golden blade of a sword brushed Daria's neck. Daria held dead still. She moved her eyes sideways and saw Mara holding the other end of the sword.

THIRTY-SIX

Watch Your Back, Flamey!

"Well, Pinecone," Mara said. "Looks like you need ta learn to follow orders. Alexa's got a job to do, and I'm here to see that it gets done." Alexa could see Daria's face turning red with anger.

"Mara, it's okay," said Alexa. "Let her go."

"Not until she promises ta do what you say." Daria stayed silent. "I can't hear you," said Mara, pressing the blade harder against Daria's skin.

"Mara, please," Alexa begged.

"Will you go home?" asked Mara. More seconds passed.

"Fine, I'll leave," said Daria, but Alexa didn't think she meant it. Mara calmly pulled the sword back and stepped away. Daria glared at Mara, then looked back at Alexa.

"Alexa, look at yourself," said Daria. "You've changed."

"Of course I have. I'm still afraid, but I don't let my fear rule me anymore. I've learned to think for myself and think of others first. I'm glad I've changed!"

"Guard yourself," Daria warned. "Fairies stronger than you would bend and break under the burden you bear. I see what you're becoming, and it chills my spirit."

"You are free to hate me," said Alexa, "as long as you go." She hated herself for having to say this to her sister.

Daria sighed. "If you will not accept my help, I won't force it on you." She looked straight at Mara. "Watch your back, Flamey!" Daria dumped the candledark out of her bag and flew toward home without even a goodbye. As her glittering gold shape got smaller and smaller on the horizon, Alexa longed to call her back, but she knew she had to keep going without Daria. She knew now how it felt to believe her sister dead, and it was much worse than she'd imagined. Sending Daria away was the only way Alexa could protect her, even if it meant Daria never spoke to her again.

"Now, what's your plan to catch this Shadow Fairy?" Mara asked.

"You shouldn't have threatened her like that," said Alexa.

"She was gettin' in your way, and you know it," Mara snapped.

"You're too reckless."

"I can't believe this," said Mara, throwing up her hands. "How many times have I saved you?"

Alexa didn't say anything.

"See? You can't even count that high." Mara picked up her satchel. "I'm gonna get some food."

Alexa felt her mind tearing in two and flying in different directions. A low sobbing continued to echo through the camp. "Arthur, stop it!" Alexa shouted to the air. The sobbing stopped.

The woods were now quiet. Alexa floated down to the creek to wash her leg and put a new bandage on the wound.

"Nobody in the entire forest understands how difficult this has been for me," she said to herself as she landed at the stream's edge. "Everyone has turned against me." A light breeze stirred the leaves of the aspen trees that huddled around the stream.

Alexa sank her feet into the cold water and carefully unwrapped the soiled and sagging gray bandage. So much time had passed that she expected the cut to be either healed or infected. The dried blood and pus pulled at the skin as she removed the last layer. Her leg breathed in fresh air with relief. The wound had some dirt in it, so Alexa washed it off, along with the dried blood. The flowing water felt good on her leg. Then Alexa's heart almost stopped.

She washed and washed her ankle, but nothing changed. She took a wild cucumber fruit from the nearest plant, wet it and scrubbed her leg even harder. The wound burned with pain. Fear and confusion poured over her. Alexa could not believe her eyes.

On her ankle she saw an angry red scar. A scar shaped like an hourglass.

"And on my journey I found I was weak. In my weakness I found humility. That was my true journey."

~Alexa of the Meadow

Part V:
The Unraveling

THIRTY-SEVEN

The Wearer of the Mark

lexa gripped the back of her neck as a thousand thoughts jammed into her brain. She forced herself to calm down. What exactly had Ispirianza said? The one with the hourglass scar would be the journey's greatest obstacle. Her motives were not to be trusted.

"It's me? I'm the journey's greatest obstacle? Should I be afraid of myself?" thought Alexa. "What if Ispirianza's Great Oak was mistaken?" Alexa rubbed at the scar. "And if its Ring Dreams were wrong about the scar, what about everything else Ispirianza told me?"

Alexa rocked back and forth in a daze. If Ispirianza had known that Alexa would bear the hourglass mark, would she have sent her on this quest in the first place? Alexa began to pace back and forth, feeling like she wouldn't be able to remember her name if someone asked her. She took flight, not knowing where to go.

She landed and lay face down on the roots of an oak tree. She pressed her cheek against the cool moss and stared blankly at blurry nothingness.

"What is happening to me?" she whimpered. "What am I going to do? Please help me."

A small hand touched her shoulder.

"Don't w-w-worry, Alexa," she heard Arthur's voice say. "You're going to b-be okay, I just know it." Alexa looked at Arthur through her blurred vision. His eyes were as bloodshot as hers from his constant crying.

"But I can't do this alone, and I've driven everyone away."

"I'm st-still here."

Alexa seemed not to hear him. "I just discovered that I'm my own worst enemy. How can I fight against myself?"

"You'll think of the r-right thing to do."

"But I fail no matter what I do. The Great Song has left my spirit. It plays its great melody against me."

A new voice broke in from above: "You mustn't say such things, child."

Alexa and Arthur looked up to find an old dryad covered in bark from head to toe. The dryad fluttered her wings and lighted beside Alexa. Arthur bolted to hide under the nearest rock.

"Who are you?" asked Alexa.

"Someone who knows your troubles well," the dryad replied. "My name is Wendrothia. I have learned much about your journey. Six hundred and fifty years ago, an acorn fell from the Great Oak. A raven carried the acorn to this place, which gave life to my own beloved tree. So in many ways the Great Oak is my mother. She speaks to my tree, who then gives me dreams."

"Then you know Ispirianza has given me a task I cannot do," cried Alexa. "And so many lives depend on it. I try so hard, but at every turn the Great Song plays against me."

"Nonsense, child!" scolded Wendrothia. "The Great Song gives life and joy to all who will receive its perfect melody. Only the harmonies we choose can play against it. It is up to us to move in tune with the Great Song."

"But how do I know how to move? I cannot hear the Great Song through all the noise of my life. And when I do hear something, I can't understand it."

"You must find time to stand still. You've journeyed for many days."

"It seems like forever," agreed Alexa.

"And how often have you called upon the dryads' wisdom to guide you?

Suddenly embarrassed, Alexa hesitated before answering. "I asked for directions once but never for wisdom."

"But Ispirianza promised the help of her dryad sisters, while the Great Oak foresaw the aid of others, yes?"

Alexa's eyes grew wide. "Yes, she did. Can your tree send a message to Ispirianza for me? Ask her what I should do next!" Alexa couldn't believe she hadn't thought of this before.

But Wendrothia shook her head sadly. "A younger tree has not the roots to speak to an older tree."

Alexa couldn't hide her disappointment.

"So you felt you had enough wisdom and strength to complete this entire journey on your own?" Alexa didn't answer, but just looked at the ground. "It seems you have not made use of the gifts given to you. My child, the truly wise know when to seek wise counsel, and the truly strong will accept that help. Even a fool may succeed if she listens to wise advice." Wendrothia smiled. "Of course, the problem is that you first have to be wise enough to know who has enough wisdom to give you wise advice." Alexa giggled in spite of herself.

"I'm not wise or strong," said Alexa. "I'm pushing away everyone."

"You are not pushing me away. And what of your sylph friend? He is still here, just hiding."

Alexa breathed deeply before admitting, "Words come out of my mouth that I don't plan to say."

"Sometimes our true motives hide themselves from us. The heart and mind are often strangers in the same body."

"How can I keep going if I can't trust myself?" asked Alexa.

"I cannot tell you what lies at the end for you. Learn to hear the Great Song, and dance only to its melody. All other movement gets you nowhere."

"The task weighs too much," Alexa said. "I can't carry it any longer."

"Then share the burden. Do not push away those who wish you well. You may think yourself noble and brave, taking the problems of the world onto your small shoulders, but I call it pride." Alexa started to understand. She had grown so much during the journey—but mostly just physically. She was so busy fighting and dodging the Oths that she paid no attention to the real war that was raging.

"Thank you," said Alexa at last. "I will accept what I've been given." Almost immediately, she felt better.

As Arthur and Alexa flew back to camp, Alexa looked down

at her scar. After talking to Wendrothia, Alexa was confident that Ispirianza's Ring Dreams were correct. Alexa herself was the greatest threat to the mission. And, in a sense, she had pushed Wendrothia away, as she did not share the truth about who wore the hourglass mark. She could not trust herself. The giant mess she had created made the truth so obvious. Despite the dryad's words, fresh fear blew into her spirit like a storm. She could do only one thing.

When Arthur and Alexa got back to camp, Mara was cooking a meal. The scent of boiling watercress, nightshade and mustard filled the camp. Mara had even cut some yucca thread to sew up Alexa's wing.

"It's about time you showed up," said Mara. "Just can't seem to get rid of that sylph, huh?" Arthur didn't respond to the insult. He was just happy to be back in Alexa's presence.

"Mara, I'm sorry," Alexa said. "Thanks for your help. I've tried to carry the world by myself, but not anymore."

"Don't get sappy on me now," said Mara. "You're soundin' like an old dryad. I'm only here to stave off boredom."

"You're a true friend to me."

"Yeah, yeah. Well, to tell ya the truth, Alexa," said Mara. "You're the only friend I've ever had. Most fairies think I'm too...bossy." Alexa flew over to give Mara a hug. Mara held out her arm to stop her.

"I told you, don't get mushy." Mara glanced down and noticed Alexa's ankle scar. Her eyes bulged.

"Alexa, is there something you'd like to share with the rest of the class?"

"I know, I know," said Alexa. "I have the mark of the enemy."

"But I thought that Aerioth had the mark under that ankle band."

"Me, too."

"Maybe it's just a coincidence," Mara said. "Yeah, maybe the real enemy has one, too, and you just happened to get a cut in a funny shape."

"Mara, look at it. It's a perfect hourglass. And it just happens to be on my ankle. That didn't happen by accident."

"So what? This means you have to do the opposite of whatever ya think is right?" Mara's voice reeked of sarcasm. "Okay, here's a test. Let's fly straight back to Evernaught, hover outside the Oths' cave and yell, 'Aerioth sucks slime' at the top of our voices. What do ya think?"

"That's the dumbest idea I've ever heard."

"Then I guess we should do it since you're the enemy and everything you say leads us to destruction."

"Be serious, Mara. I know exactly what to do. Ispirianza could only see part of the truth. Trees just give their dryads little glimpses, not the whole picture. If Ispirianza had known about this scar, she would have sent someone else."

"What are ya sayin', Alexa?" Alexa put her hand on Mara's shoulder.

"I want you to go into Timefulness in my place."

"Me? No way! Arthur's the one who's supposed to be going crazy."

"Mara, you're stronger, smarter and more talented than I could ever be. We didn't meet by accident. The Great Song knew."

"To tell ya the truth, I was never really into this 'Great Song' or 'Big Woo' or whatever ya call it. I don't know anything about Timefulness or humans. I don't even know your human friend's name."

"Elsie," said Arthur. The fairies both looked at him. "Just t-t-trying to help," he added.

"I'll stay around to help you, don't worry," Alexa said. "But once I get you on your way, I'll head back home and you'll have to finish the rest. I'll teach you everything I know, which isn't much. We'll catch both your Shadow Fairy and mine. I'll go through the Glass Corridor with you and introduce you to Elsie."

Mara sighed. "I'll do whatever it takes, but this—this is nuts. While we wait for your senses ta come back, let's just go catch us some Shadow Fairies. Although you never told me why we have to have this pixie silk that only Shadow Fairies can make. I guess 'cause you're the enemy."

"Not funny," said Alexa. "See, a fairy's wings beat slower in Timefulness. That's why we can't fly there without help. In fact, the magic of the Glass Corridor won't even let a fairy through without pixie silk. You have to use the pixie silk to connect yourself to your Shadow Fairy so that you can actually fly down there in Timefulness. Your Shadow Fairy stays above time but in the same place as you are in Timefulness. It's like you're flying in one realm and casting a shadow in the other realm."

"Sorry I asked," Mara said.

"At least it d-doesn't sound d-dangerous," said Arthur. "Can we catch the Shadow Fairies here or d-do we have to go somewhere else?"

"We need a big fire," said Alexa.

"We should get at least a day's travel between us and

Evernaught then," urged Mara.

Alexa would have loved to rest for a few days. Her whole body cried out for it, but she knew they had to keep pushing forward until the Scarring stopped and the Bridge of Trees was restored.

Mara sewed up Alexa's wing with the strong yucca thread. It took a long time and it pinched something awful. As soon as Mara bit off the end of the thread, Alexa laid her head down on a bed of cattail fluff and slept a deep, dreamless sleep.

THIRTY-EIGHT

How to Catch a Shadow

The sun sank behind the western plains. The fairies and sylph flew northeast along the bristlecone pines of the White Mountains.

Alexa wanted to find the tree of Ispirianza's friend Zymandria, but she had no way of identifying it within the vast landscape. They searched for a sheltered place to make a fire and planned exactly how they would use the candledark to catch the Shadow Fairies.

Alexa's leg itched, but she tried her best to ignore it. Instead, she concentrated on not flying lopsided, since the yucca thread on her injured wing threw her off balance.

"How long does it take to catch a Shadow Fairy?" asked Mara.

"No idea," said Alexa. "Never tried before."

"Then how do you know this will work?"

"Because Ispirianza said so. She explained all about Shadow

Fairies, like how they talk with their hands and that they only weave pixie silk if they feel they must," said Alexa. "They lose some of their lightness and freedom when they give of their spirits."

"Do we have to talk with our hands, too?" asked Mara.

"No," Arthur said, flying in circles around Alexa. "They can hear just f-f-fine, but they won't listen to anyone unless we hold them still."

"You've been paying attention, Arthur," said Alexa. "Ispirianza says Shadow Fairies don't think we fairies ever have anything wise to say, so they don't bother trying to talk or listen to us."

"And here I thought they were the dumb ones," said Mara.

"Also, we have to catch our own Shadow Fairies. The challenge is how to tell which ones are ours."

"No problem," said Mara. "There'll only be two of them dancing in the fire tonight."

"How do you know?" asked Alexa, who remembered seeing hundreds at a time during the festivals in Kendlenook.

"Did you forget we're in the middle of nowhere? You don't see any other fairies around here, do you?" Mara replied.

"And since we've got different wing shapes, it should be easy to pick out whose is whose," said Alexa.

"Now you're catchin' on," Mara said. "Let's turn up into the mountains for a while. We can hide the fire better up there."

"Yes, hiding is good," said Arthur.

The little group veered to the left and flew on in silence until Mara pointed out a hollow below.

"That won't work," said Alexa. "Too many trees. Ispirianza said we need a big clearing so that the Shadow Fairies can't just escape out of the firelight and into the shade of the trees — or up the trunk of a tree, for that matter."

They flew farther into the hills. "Okay, how about there?" Mara pointed down at a little grassy meadow surrounded by hills on three sides, all except the north.

Alexa nodded. It looked good to her. While Mara whipped up a fire, Alexa looked around the dark meadow. Though small, it made her feel at peace and at home. She never took much pride in being a Meadow Fairy because all the other kinds seemed more glamorous, but the spirit of the meadow definitely flowed in her blood.

Mara seemed entranced by the bonfire she had created and by the ghostly image of her Shadow Fairy dancing in the light of the flames. Of course she would, thought Alexa. Mara must feel the same way about fire that Alexa felt about the meadow. Daria had always preferred the cover of trees.

The sight of the flickering flames made Alexa suddenly homesick. She imagined familiar faces around the fire listening to Ispirianza's human tales. For a happy minute, Alexa and Mara just sat and stared into the fire like two friends on a camping trip. Then the weight of her task bore down on Alexa once more, and home felt farther away than ever. Alexa felt she might never see Kendlenook again.

"Okay, let's give it a try," sighed Alexa. "I thought of an idea while we were flying earlier. We have to trap the Shadow Fairy in a circle of candledark, right?"

"If you say so," said Mara. "Wait, don't we have ta make a dome of candledark so they don't fly out of the top?"

"No," said Alexa. "They can't fly. Haven't you ever noticed how a shadow always moves along the ground? A Shadow

Fairy always has to touch something real. The air doesn't count."

Mara tapped her lighting wand on her chin. "But if we start turning on candledark sticks, the Shadow Fairies won't come near 'em. We have to turn 'em on all at once."

"But we only have two pairs of hands," said Alexa.

"I have hands," offered Arthur timidly.

Alexa turned back to Mara. "That's where the leaves come in," said Alexa, grinning.

"Okay, I get it," said Mara. "We ignite all the candledark sticks, put 'em in a circle around the fire, then cover 'em with leaves. The shadows come ta dance in the fire, we uncover the candledark, and there ya go."

Alexa and Mara watch for Shadow Fairies

"Exactly," Alexa said. She then glanced at Arthur and back to Mara. "But how could we possibly uncover them all at the same time?" she asked in exaggerated tones.

Alexa waited for Arthur to think of the answer so it would seem like his idea. Mara's eyes lit up, but Alexa put her finger over her mouth for the Fire Fairy to stay quiet until Arthur figured it out.

They waited and waited. "Hmmm," Alexa continued. "How could we ever uncover all of the candledark at the same time? It's almost like we would need a burst of air to blow them away." Arthur just hovered silently. "Too bad we don't know when or where a strong wind will blow."

"Yeah, t-too bad," said Arthur. Then he sprang into the air. "Oh, oh, I know! I can b-blow them off for you, no problem. I can blow thousands of leaves all by myself."

"Wow," said Alexa. "What a great idea! What would we ever do without you, Arthur?" Mara just shook her head.

"Wait," said Mara. "Problem. If the Shadow Fairies can hear us, ya just told 'em our whole plan."

"You listen about as well as a Shadow Fairy," said Alexa. "I just said that Shadow Fairies never listen to us because they don't think we have anything to say. Think about it. Do you ever listen to sylphs?"

"Of course not," said Mara. "'Cause they're totally stup— ah, I see your point."

Mara and Alexa laughed, although Alexa felt bad about it.

"Hey!" said Arthur. "I'm not stupid. I know what you w-w-were going to say."

"Oh, Arthur," said Alexa. "We're not laughing at you, we're

laughing with you."

"But I'm not laughing," he said.

Alexa and Mara glanced at each other, then burst out laughing harder. Arthur just looked at them.

"Okay," said Mara, wiping tears from her eyes. "What about when we start igniting the candledark? That will get the Shadow Fairies' attention. They might hide, and we won't know how long it will take for them ta come back out again."

Everyone sat in silent thought. Only the crackling of the fire broke the stillness of the night.

"Maybe I can do it," said Arthur. "Although I don't know h-how someone as dumb as me could possibly help fairies as smart as you two." He explained his idea.

"Good, Arthur," said Alexa. "And of course I don't think you're stupid—only Mara thinks that."

The three arranged twenty sticks of unlit candledark in a circle surrounding the fire. Alexa and Mara flew several hills away into a deep valley, so that they could not see the fire. They knew that their unseen Shadow Fairies were somewhere near them. While they hid—and kept their Shadow Fairies from seeing what Arthur was doing—Arthur ignited each candledark stick and covered it with a pile of leaves.

When he finished his job, Arthur searched out the fairies and told them they could return to the fire.

"This had better work," said Alexa. "We don't have enough candledark to try again." She shuddered at the memory of fleeing through the bleakness of Evernaught.

The two fairies sat close to the fire, acting as though they were just warming themselves. Arthur hid in the darkness, waiting for Alexa's signal to start the wind.

Before long, a Shadow Fairy slipped into the firelight and began to move among the flames. No Shadow Fairy could resist a chance to dance in a midnight fire. Its graceful movements mesmerized the two watching fairies. Alexa smiled at Mara — the plan was working! Mara pointed out a tear in the Shadow Fairy's wing, so it must be Alexa's.

A few moments later a second Shadow Fairy appeared in the firelight. The two fairies watched them circle and play like two ghostly dancing partners. Alexa watched how they acted toward each other. They could definitely communicate, either through the dance or by reading each other's minds.

Ispirianza had called them the wisest of fairies, even wiser than the dryads. "True wisdom brings joy and a sense of humor," Alexa had heard Ispirianza say. "The wiser you become, the less you want to debate or show off. That is why the Shadow Fairies refuse to speak, because truth is beyond words. The intelligent argue; the wise dance."

Alexa began to raise her arm to give Arthur the signal.

"Wait!" whispered Mara. "What is that?" She pointed at the fire. Cold chills poured down Alexa's spine. Another Shadow Fairy suddenly appeared in the flames. And another!

Mara grabbed Alexa's arm. More Shadow Fairies meant that others were close by.

But who?

THIRTY-NINE

The Shadows of Ghosts

Mara stood up and peered around the edge of the firelight. Nothing. Just darkness. Alexa strained to hear any movement. Nothing. Where could the others be hiding? Why didn't they show themselves?

"Do you see anything?" whispered Alexa. Mara shook her head as she slowly drew her sword.

Alexa poked Mara's shoulder and pointed frantically to the flames. In the fire now danced six Shadow Fairies.

"Oh, this is getting spooky," Alexa said. "Who could be watching us? There are no trees out here, so they can't be dryads." Alexa didn't know what to do. There was nowhere she could hide in the dark, moonless night.

"Stay here," said Mara. "I'll check out the area for fairies or you-know-whats."

Alexa's wings shuddered as Mara flittered away.

Now Alexa stood alone in a sea of darkness with a fire and

six dancing black specters. She dared not look at the Shadow Fairies, but stared instead into the abyss of darkness. She couldn't see Arthur and didn't want to wave at him anyway, because he might blow the leaves too soon. Alexa did not want to trap four strange Shadow Fairies along with her own and Mara's.

Suddenly a blinding light flared in the night sky, and Alexa could see Mara's orange dress high above her. Alexa looked around the dim landscape now illuminated with a pale orange light. Mara had used her lighting wand to cast a flare into the sky, but Alexa saw no one else. The flare soon flickered out, and once again eerie darkness descended outside the circle of flickering firelight. Alexa then heard a drumming of wings close to the edge of the darkness. She crept toward the sound.

"Hello? Who's out there?" she said in a quivering voice. A hand reached out and grabbed Alexa's shoulder.

Alexa screamed as she reeled around.

The hand belonged to Mara. "I found Arthur and told him to stay hidden until the signal," she whispered.

"Who's out there?" Alexa said.

"I couldn't see a soul," Mara said, looking into the fire. "It's like they're the Shadow Fairies of ghosts."

"Let's get out of here."

"But the candledark sticks are already lit! We have to spring the trap now."

"Wait, look at that Shadow Fairy," Alexa said, pointing to one of the dark dancers. "Does the pointy shape of her wings look familiar?" Mara stared at the form.

"Aerioth!" cried Mara. "It looks like Aerioth's wings!" Alexa froze with fear. She had hoped Mara would say the

Shadow Fairy couldn't possibly be Aerioth's.

Alexa and Mara had been trying to trap the Shadow Fairies, but now it looked like they were the ones being trapped. Mara lifted her sword to the darkness.

An ear-piercing cracking noise split through the night, followed by a loud shout. Numerous strange points of light appeared across the sky. A choir of blood-curdling screams filled the air, followed by total silence. The lights then drifted toward the ground and went out. What on earth could be happening?

Mara fired another flare, and she and Alexa darted skyward to get a view of the whole meadow. Alexa picked out Arthur's tiny body cowering behind a rock. Out of the corner of her eye, Alexa saw three dark forms streaking away into the night.

"Oths," Alexa cried. "But look, they're flying away!"

"It's now or never. Come on!" The two fairies dove back to the fire.

"Do you have any idea what just happened?" asked a dazed Alexa.

"No, but we gotta do this now! The candledark'll go out soon."

When Alexa and Mara looked again at the fire, they saw only two Shadow Fairies. One of them had a torn wing. Wait. Now there was a third! But who—?

"Okay, Flamey, let's spring the trap," a voice said. Alexa and Mara turned to see Daria swoop into the light.

"Daria! But... How did you get here?"

"I never left, you know," Daria said. "I've been trailing you the whole time. Actually I was following three Oths who were following you." Daria sounded casual, but Alexa thought she heard her sister's voice tremble a little.

"You never listen to me, do you?" Alexa said. "Right now I'm kinda glad about that."

"What just happened?" Mara asked.

"Later. Right now let's catch these Shadow Fairies."

"I'll keep watch," Mara said, her sword still drawn. Daria and Alexa studied the fire. Just one Shadow Fairy danced in the firelight now, and it did not have the torn wing. The two others soon joined in.

"Now!" Daria commanded. Alexa waved to Arthur. Almost immediately a streak swirled around the bonfire. A strong breeze rushed in and made the fire grow bigger. The fairies' faces lit up, and the Shadow Fairies began to flitter nervously. In an instant, Arthur picked up speed and blew the leaf piles completely away. A dark cloud swirled upward from each stick of candledark, creating a circular barrier of darkness through which the Shadow Fairies could not pass.

Alexa stepped through the cloudy ring and appeared next to the fire. The three Shadow Fairies flipped and dived through the flames, much faster than before. They bounced off the wall of darkness created by the candledark.

"Okay, they're trapped," said Daria, standing next to Alexa.

The dark fairy figures hovered.

"Listen up, Shadows!" yelled Mara from Alexa's other side. "And do what we say!"

The figures responded by trying to escape more frantically than ever.

"Be calm," Alexa told Mara with a frustrated sigh. "I'm about to ask a huge favor."

"Lower your wings," suggested Daria.

Alexa stepped forward and did so, using her gentlest voice to say, "Please forgive me for bothering you like this, noble Shadow Fairies. I would not dare to do so unless my need were very great. I greet you in the name of Ispirianza, dryad of the Great Oak, and beg that you would listen to my request."

The Shadow Fairies slowed to a graceful side-to-side movement. Alexa hoped that meant they were listening. She spoke especially to the Shadow Fairy who had the same wing shape as her own. "You have shadowed me all my life, but we have never spoken. Please nod if you understand me."

The three Shadow Fairies nodded their heads. Alexa was overcome with awe that she was actually communicating with them. She took a deep breath and explained all about the Scarring, the Bridge of Trees and the bramble nectar. The shadows remained dead still when Alexa explained that if the Scarring weren't stopped, it would mean the end of the fairies of Faewick, including the Shadow Fairies.

"I must go to the human world of Timefulness in order to restore the Bridge of Trees. Do you know of the humans and the Glass Corridors that connect our realm to theirs?"

Alexa's Shadow Fairy nodded again. "And the Great Shift when the fairies bent time and created our realm, Slightly Above Time?"

The Shadow Fairies indicated that they understood. Daria couldn't believe it. "They remember more of our history than we do," she said.

Alexa's Shadow Fairy gestured for her to continue. Alexa knew this part would be the most difficult. "Here is what I must ask of you. To travel into Timefulness, I need the pixie silk that only you can weave." She turned to Mara's Shadow

Fairy. "We need pixie silk for my friend Mara as well. I understand this involves a great sacrifice for you, but please consider my request. We, too, have risked and will risk much more on this journey."

"Why do you need pixie silk for Mara?" interrupted Daria.

"Long story. Later," said Alexa.

In the silence that followed Alexa's speech, nothing moved except the flames. An owl hooted somewhere overhead, then the sound faded away. Alexa chewed on her lower lip and waited.

Finally her Shadow Fairy began to gesture with her hands. She pointed first to Daria's Shadow Fairy and then to a tree outside the smoky circle of candledark. Alexa leaned forward, trying to understand.

"I think she wants you to release my Shadow Fairy," said Daria.

"But we can't," said Mara. "What if we open a place in the circle and all three run away?"

"Open the circle," said Alexa, staring at her own Shadow Fairy. "It's a gesture of faith. Mine won't run. If she does, she wouldn't have granted my request anyway."

Mara reluctantly picked up three smoking sticks of candledark and tossed them aside. The air brightened where the sticks used to be.

Daria's Shadow Fairy touched the others briefly, then fled swiftly along the ground, out of the firelight and into the shadow of the trees at the meadow's edge. Alexa and Mara's Shadow Fairies stayed in the fire.

"What's happening?" shouted Arthur from the darkness.

"Shush," said Daria.

Chapter 39

Mara started to put the three candledark sticks back in place. Alexa caught Mara's eye and shook her head. Mara shrugged and held onto the sticks.

"Thank you for staying," said Alexa to the Shadow Fairies. "Will you help me?"

Alexa's Shadow Fairy crouched down and bent her head forward. She stayed in this position for several long minutes. Then she beckoned for Alexa to come closer.

Alexa stood so close to the fire that it almost singed her dress and hair. Its intense heat radiated on her face and dried out her skin. The wind changed, and the smoke blew directly in Alexa's eyes. She did not move. After the smoke blew in the other direction once more, Alexa saw the Shadow Fairy raise her flat palm above her shoulder.

"What does that mean?" Alexa asked. The Shadow Fairy beckoned her closer.

"I can't," Alexa said. "The fire will burn me."

Daria spoke softly, "Reach out your hand to her. I think she wants you to touch her."

Alexa glanced at the Shadow Fairy, who nodded. Alexa raised her palm in a reflection of the Shadow Fairy's position and slowly extended her arm into the heat of the fire. Her fingers touched something cool and smooth right where the Shadow Fairy's hand would be. Alexa held her palm against the Shadow Fairy's for as long as she could. She closed her eyes. She pulled back when the fire began to burn her fingers.

"What does she feel like?" asked Daria.

"You can't touch a Shadow Fairy," said Mara.

"Yes, you can," said Alexa, gazing at her hand. "I felt connected. At peace." Alexa looked back at the Shadow Fairy.

"Will you help me?"

In answer, the Shadow Fairy began to spin her body around and around. She twisted faster and faster.

A light, almost invisible thread spiraled upward from the Shadow Fairy's hands. The breeze blew it one way and then another. The thread grew longer and longer.

"It's pixie silk!" said Mara. The Fire Fairy snatched up an ordinary stick from the ground, swiftly scraped off the remaining scraps of bark and jumped into the air. "Help me," she said. "If this stuff gets tangled, we'll never get the knots out."

Alexa and Daria jumped into the air to join Mara. "Arthur," Alexa called. "Try to calm this wind for us."

"Okay, Alexa," piped the sylph's high voice.

"Handle it carefully," warned Daria. Her hands darted everywhere but hesitated to touch the delicate-looking strands.

"I think it's stronger than it looks," said Alexa, touching the waving pixie silk.

"Here's the end," said Mara from above. "I'll start coiling it." She began wrapping the silk around and around her smooth stick. Alexa and Daria worked together to keep the uncoiled part from tangling.

The Shadow Fairy kept weaving, and the single strand stretched higher into the air. A sudden gust of wind almost yanked the coiled part out of Mara's hands.

"Arthur!" Alexa yelled.

"Sorry," he called back. The wind died down.

Finally, the Shadow Fairy slowed her spinning to a stop. She knelt down, sat on her feet and didn't move.

The end of the pixie silk tore free of the Shadow Fairy's hands and floated into the air. Daria grabbed it. Mara kept winding until Daria's end reached her stick.

"Here you go." Mara offered the coiled pixie silk to Alexa. She took it in both hands and slowly sank to the ground.

Daria collected the candledark sticks in a pile and left them to smoke themselves down to nothing. The air cleared, and the stars glittered overhead.

"We did it," Alexa whispered. "I can't believe we actually did it." She turned to the exhausted-looking Shadow Fairy. "Thank you." The Shadow Fairy raised her head for a moment and then let it fall back down. Now they turned to look for Mara's Shadow Fairy, but she had escaped into the darkness. Alexa looked distressed, but Daria just laughed.

"Mara, that's just what I would expect from your Shadow Fairy," Daria taunted. Alexa circled the fire in desperation.

"Oh, she's long gone by now," Daria said.

"Shut up, Daria," said Mara. "Now how am I gonna go into Timefulness?"

"Why do you want to go into Timefulness anyway?" Daria asked. The candledark started to sputter.

"Daria, I can't be trusted to do this." Alexa glanced at her ankle and remembered that her sister didn't know about the hourglass scar yet. "I gave the task to Mara."

"Mara?" gasped Daria. "You've got to be kidding me." Two of the candledark sticks went completely out. "All this talk about how you alone were chosen for this quest, and you just hand it off to some stranger?"

"She's not a stranger," Alexa said. Another three sticks died.

"Well, it looks like you're the only one going now, little sister."

Alexa's heart sank into her stomach.

FORTY

The Crazy Thing About Sylphs

Alexa rolled over and stretched in the makeshift bed they'd thrown together the night before. The afternoon sun warmed her closed eyelids. Two sides of her spirit argued with each other. Should she be excited at finally getting the pixie silk, or fearful of the unknowns that lay in wait for her?

Fear won out.

Alexa opened her eyes. Daria slept beside her, Arthur faithfully watched for danger, and Mara was nowhere to be seen.

Alexa noticed her Shadow Fairy hovering close by.

"Hello? Miss Shadow? Do you have a name? It feels rude just calling you 'Shadow Fairy.'"

The Shadow Fairy put a finger in her mouth, then beckoned to Alexa. She led Alexa to a poisonous plant adorned with sprays of little white flowers and pointed to it.

"Poison hemlock? That's your name?"

The Shadow Fairy gestured "no" but that Alexa should keep thinking and guessing. She waved her hand toward another plant growing nearby — one with bright flowers that Alexa recognized right away. "Camellias!"

After the Shadow Fairy had pointed back and forth between the two plants several times, Alexa guessed: "Poisonamelia? Hemlocamelia?"

The Shadow Fairy shook her head hard.

"Sorry I'm so dumb," said Alexa. "Thank you for trying to talk to me. I know it must be boring for you."

The Shadow Fairy sat on the grass next to Alexa, with their hands touching. Alexa could feel peace radiating from the Shadow Fairy and calming her.

Still, the hourglass scar weighed heavily on Alexa's mind. "What if I'm doing this so that Grandmother will love me as much as she loves Eva?" she wondered. "What if Elsie can't help fix the Scarring?"

Mara soared into the shade of their resting spot, a full bag dangling from her shoulder.

Alexa nudged Daria. "Time to eat," she said.

"Mm, hm," said Daria, opening one eye.

"What's another name for poison hemlock?" asked Alexa.

"Queen Anne's Lace," said Mara promptly. "Why?"

"Annamelia!" exclaimed Alexa. Mara and Daria looked at her strangely, but the Shadow Fairy, who now had a name, reached over and patted the bottom of Alexa's foot.

Alexa grinned at her new friend. "Pleased to meet you, Annamelia."

When the group set out to the north in the late afternoon, Alexa still was not sure how to proceed. They traveled quickly, with Arthur darting out in front and behind to scout the area. Twice he came hurtling back, shrieking that he'd seen fairy-eating falcons. The first time it turned out to be only a swallow. The second time it was absolutely nothing. Arthur's stuttering increased as well.

Eager to keep the topic away from Arthur's worsening state, Alexa said to her sister: "Stop holding out on us. How did you get rid of those Oths?"

Daria smiled. "I took on three Oths with nothing but owls."

"Owls? Oths wouldn't be afraid of owls," said Mara.

"No, but they might be worried if they thought they were way outnumbered by fairies. I noticed a group of great horned owls in the bristlecone pines as we flew to the meadow. I asked them — in Owlish, of course — to gather as many friends as possible. Then I gave them all lighted candles to dangle on yucca twine from their talons. When I gave the signal and shouted, the owls uncovered their candles, and to the Oths it must have looked like a small army of fairies was closing in."

"Pretty brilliant," said Mara, only half committed to the compliment. Alexa wondered why she could never think of such great plans herself. Daria and Mara both did it all the time.

Daria and the owls with candlelight

Desperate for a rest, the fairies decided to stop in some vacant woblin holes they found nearby. Arthur did not join them. Alexa leaned back against the cool dirt wall and drifted off to sleep, thinking of her bed in the Kendlenook tree house and how Grandmother always took such good care of her. She had once thought Grandmother's nagging was the worst thing anyone could endure. Now that seemed like comfort itself.

She awoke about an hour later, the back of her head heavy with worries. Untroubled sleep had become a stranger to Alexa. She worried that the Oths were still following them. She worried about whether she had enough pixie silk. She worried about worrying too much.

That evening, Alexa and her friends took off for the Black Canyon Pass. Alexa hadn't enjoyed going through it on the way to Evernaught, and she didn't look forward to doing it again. Up so high in the mountains, the air was frigid and thin, so flying took more energy than usual. The friends spoke little because the high altitude left them short of breath.

In their haste to get back to Kendlenook, the fairies no longer stopped to prepare hot meals. They just ate raw miner's lettuce they collected along the way. Alexa had eaten so much miner's lettuce, she began to gag at the thought of it.

When the sun burned its way into the eastern sky, Arthur returned from scouting ahead and guided the fairies down to the hiding place he had found. Alexa carefully stowed her bag, which contained the coiled pixie silk and the locket, between two large rocks, where no one would accidentally step on it. Alexa would sometimes open the locket to look at Margaret's picture and wonder about the human realm.

"Bumbleflies!" cried Arthur from his lookout in the pine tree. All three fairies plus Annamelia dove for cover.

"Where?" they cried. Arthur stared into the valley.

"There!" He was pointing to a pile of black rocks.

"Arthur, those are rocks," said Alexa.

"Rocks don't move like that. It's a swarm of bumbleflies!"

"I swear I'm gonna kill you, sylpho," Mara said, hand on sword.

"Arthur, you have the best eyes of any of us. Look closely," said a concerned Daria, studying the sylph. "Can't you see there's nothing moving?"

"They're c-c-c-coming to eat us!" he insisted. Alexa looked at Daria, who shook her head. Even Annamelia crossed her arms in impatience. Alexa grabbed the trembling Arthur, flew him up to the rocks and made him touch one.

"See, Arthur? Nothing," she said. Arthur looked closely. Then he flew ahead in embarrassment.

When it was time to rest, Alexa collapsed into a patch of grass. They didn't bother preparing their sleeping areas much anymore. She closed her eyes. Time passed. Arthur's voice rang in Alexa's ear. "That's a-a-all wrong," he said.

"What?" Alexa sat up confused. She looked to Arthur sitting a few wingbeats away, but he wasn't looking at her.

"This whole th-thing is wr-wrong," he said to himself. Alexa studied Arthur, trying to understand his mumbling. "Sylphs can g-g-go but fairies c-c-can't." He stuttered badly now, even when he was only talking to himself. "Too many eyes—too m-m-m-many eyes watching. N-n-n-need more sylphs. Wait f-f-for the night t-t-to cover us."

"Arthur, what in Kendlenook are you saying?" asked

Alexa, startling him.

"N-n-n-n-n-n-nothing."

"You're starting to freak me out. Now go to sleep."

"Sylphs d-d-d-don't sleep."

"But I do—at least I used to," said Alexa, as she lay back down. Alexa worried Eva may have been right about Arthur. She closed her eyes again. Time passed.

"Alexa!" Arthur whispered her out of sleep again.

"What now?"

"Oths! I heard s-s-some Oths."

"Arthur, look at Mara standing guard over there. There are no Oths."

"No, no. I was c-c-catching gnats by the river when I overheard Oths t-t-t-talking about you. They know where you are. They're s-s-s-setting a trap for you, Alexa! Don't g-g-g-g-go to the Glass Corridor."

"Arthur, stop it," Alexa said, rolling away from him. "Of course I have to go to the Glass Corridor. Rocks aren't bumbleflies, either."

"The Oths w-w-w-w-w-were r-r-r-r-real, I know it," Arthur pleaded. "Talking about how to t-t-t-trap my friend Alexa."

"That doesn't make any sense. If they know where I am, why don't they just capture me or kill me. Why would they just follow me around?"

"I will go t-t-try to f-f-f-f-find them again. Hear more."

"Arthur, you're really starting to worry me. Mara will make sure we're safe. Relax." Alexa closed her eyes yet again. Time passed.

The late afternoon sky grew strangely dark. The clouds were heavy with rain about to fall. Supper was raw miner's lettuce, again — yum. Alexa ate less and less with each meal. The hunger and lack of sleep made her gaunt and pale. Her flying became slower, her thinking cloudy.

"Alexa, you've really got to start eating more," Daria said. "You're getting as thin as a sapling."

"I'm okay," Alexa said. "I just need a few weeks of sleep."

The three fairies and sylph prepared to take weary flight once again. Alexa stashed her extra dress in her satchel. As she rummaged through her satchel, she began to panic.

"It's gone!" shouted Alexa. "It can't be, I was so careful." She frantically searched the area around where she had slept.

"What's gone?" asked Mara.

"My object from Timefulness — the locket," yelled Alexa. "It's not here!"

FORTY-ONE

The Voice in the Darkness

"I can't get through the Glass Corridor without it," cried Alexa.

"Calm down, calm down," said Mara. "When was the last time you saw it?"

"Right before I went to sleep. I was looking at Margaret's picture."

"Did you get up at all durin' the day?" asked Mara. "Maybe to, uh, use the forest facilities?"

"Not once."

"Doesn't Ispirianza have more objects you can take?" asked practical Daria. "Just get another one when we pass back through Kendlenook."

"It's not that simple, Daria. She said that particular object chose me, so I need it to stop the Scarring. An Oth couldn't have taken it. Mara and Arthur were..." Alexa looked up at Arthur who was darting back and forth with his eyes downward. Alexa closed her eyes as anger filled her body and flowed to the top of her head.

"Mara, could you help me look for it by the river?" Alexa asked calmly through her teeth.

"But you said ya had it up here when —"

"I know what I said — just come!" Alexa snapped.

Once they fluttered out of Arthur's earshot, Alexa whispered, "Listen, Arthur's gone completely gaga. I'm sure he's taken the locket so I won't go to the Glass Corridor."

"What?" whispered Mara. "I know he's a few locusts short of a plague, but he'd never betray you like that."

"You know he's been seeing things that aren't really there," said Alexa. "He thinks he's saving me from Oths."

"That deranged little swampsnake!" said Mara. "Gimme a few minutes alone with him. I'll make 'im squeak."

Alexa sighed. "I should have listened to Eva. She knows about these things, I don't."

After deciding on a plan, Alexa flew up the hill, while Mara edged around a stand of trees where Arthur couldn't see her. Daria was still combing the camp for the locket.

"Arthur, do you think those cumulonimbus clouds are a sign that the storm might pass us up and blow north?" Alexa asked. Arthur became excited.

"Well that k-k-kind of cloud usually means that there's a southwesterly d-d-depression. But since there is a wind coming from..." Whumph! Arthur disappeared in a flash of fabric. The bag frantically jumped from side to side in Mara's grip.

"Arthur, how could you!" Alexa demanded. "Where did you put it?"

"The O-O-O-O-O-Oths. They're plotting. Don't go to the p-p-portal!" mumbled the bag.

"Let me handle the portal. That's not your decision. Where did you hide the locket?"

"You'll n-n-n-never find the r-r-right tree!" Arthur said defiantly.

"So it's in a tree, huh?" Mara said.

"I listened to m-m-m-more Oth plans, I know who... hmmmph!" Mara squeezed the bag. Alexa felt terrible about treating Arthur like this, but she desperately needed the location of the locket.

"Listen up, Valiant," said Mara between clenched teeth. "I saw you put it in that pine tree hole, so come clean." She let up the pressure on the bag.

"P-p-p-pine tree? You d-d-don't know a cedar t-t-t-tree when you see one. And you call me d-d-d-dumb," the bag said.

"Thank you very much," said Mara smugly, flying to the only cedar tree in sight. In a few seconds, she spotted the hole. In a few more seconds, Mara was back. She passed the heavy locket into Alexa's open arms. Alexa breathed a sigh of relief.

The brooding clouds that had been gathering finally gave way. A hard rain started to fall on them. Not noticing the downpour, Alexa eyed the sylph in the bag.

"Arthur, you've put us all in danger—again," Alexa said gravely. "I simply can't trust you anymore. You can't stay with us."

"B-b-b-b-b-b-b-b-b-b-b-b-b-b-but l-l-l-listen to m-m-m-me. I know who—" Mara choked the bag quiet again.

"I've been wrong before, and I've made you suffer," said a

now-soaking Alexa. "If I cause you more pain by doing this, I'll have to live with it. But what comes next is bigger than all of us." She took a deep breath, not wanting to say the next sentence. "Mara will fly you away in the satchel to the tree woblins. She will instruct them to let you go after a day. Then you're on your own." The bag started writhing even harder and squeaking louder and louder. Alexa looked away. "I'm sorry, Arthur." Then she nodded to Mara.

"See ya in a few hours," Mara said. She took wing toward the woblin forest.

The sound of Arthur's stuttered pleadings faded into the rain. Alexa tried not to let Daria see the pain in her face.

Daria touched Alexa's shoulder. "He was losing his mind," she said. "You had to do it."

"Everything I've done has gone wrong," Alexa said quietly as sheets of rain washed over them. "I wear the scar well."

The sorrow in Daria's face was like looking into a mirror for Alexa.

"I wish I had never seen that human," Alexa continued. "I wish the Scarring had swallowed me up that night."

"Don't say that."

"What? Don't tell the truth?" said Alexa.

Daria just said, "Let's find shelter until Mara gets back."

Despair giving way to exhaustion, Alexa climbed into a hole in the trunk of a giant pine. Annamelia dimly hovered around the opening, preferring to stay in the cloudy light. Daria stood watch under an umbrella of thick bromeliad leaves so her sister could rest inside. The hole opened into a large hollow chamber sheltered from the rain. Alexa rested her head on a burly knot inside the ancient tree.

The wooden hollow flashed and flickered. Then Alexa heard a distant thunder. The inner tree chamber fell dark again. The sound of the beating rain outside soothed her ears. She tried to think of nothing.

Suddenly a fluttering from high above in the dark chamber startled Alexa from her rest. "Who's there?" she cried.

The unknown stranger did not answer. The fluttering grew stronger. The air seemed alive with some secret magic. "Are you a dryad?" Alexa asked of the darkness. "I'm sorry, I didn't mean to disturb your tree."

"I'm not a dryad," a soft voice echoed. Its comforting tone sounded strangely familiar to Alexa. She felt at peace in its presence. It was nothing like the dark whisper.

"Do I know you? I feel that I do," said Alexa.

"You have never seen me, but you have felt me and heard me," the beautiful voice said. Alexa's neck and arms tingled.

"Show me your face, I beg you." Alexa saw the spark of a lighting wand over a candlestick high in the chamber. The light grew into a flickering flame. A magnificent Cloud Fairy appeared out of the darkness. Indeed, Alexa did feel that she knew her. The Cloud Fairy was even more beautiful than Eva, but older. Her gray-streaked silver-blue hair flowed over her shoulders, and her wings sparkled in the candlelight. Alexa stood speechless at the sight.

"Do you know who I am?" asked the Cloud Fairy.

"I think I do," Alexa said, almost choking on the words. A single tear ran down her cheek.

"Do you know what must be done next?"

"I'll do whatever you tell me, Mother."

FORTY-TWO

The Pain of Birth

"**I**f you would do whatever I tell you, then first I tell you not to fear." Alexa's mother, Ciriana, spoke with the authority of love. Alexa stared at her, taking in every detail.

"How could I fear if you are with me?"

"I have always been with you, yet you have been afraid," said Ciriana.

"Why have you not shown yourself to me before, Mother?" Another tear trickled down Alexa's face.

"Tell me, Alexa, do you know what is happening to you?"

"I think so, but I don't dare say it, because I don't want it to be true. I've dreamed of you my entire life, and I don't want you to go away."

"Saying something does not make it true, my daughter. Consider the Oths."

"How is this possible? I know I'm not sleeping."

"And yet you are not fully awake, are you?"

"But I am not a dryad," said Alexa. "I didn't know fairies could have Ring Dreams."

"I have known no other fairy to have Ring Dreams, but your gift has brought you to me. The birth elements that have caused you so much shame are the very source of your magic," said Ciriana. "Since I could not find a flower petal for your chrysalis, I put in a pine needle. Because of this, you have a close connection with the trees. The granite also roots you in the earth."

"But my magic has done me no good," cried Alexa.

"You have not learned how to use it, my child."

"I have had no one to teach me," pleaded Alexa.

"This journey is your teacher. Listen to her well."

"But she tests me before the lesson. I fail before I can learn."

"A lesson spoken has no power. A pure heart in action learns what no book can teach. Do not fear your failure. Do not fear death itself. Now, you can either use what you have learned, or give up and waste your hard-earned knowledge. Consider these tree rings." Her mother turned to the rings.

But as Ciriana turned, Alexa did not see the back of her mother's head. Instead, the face of Aerioth revealed itself. Likewise, the Cloud Fairy's clothing had transformed into the tattered black lace of an Oth. Alexa gasped in terror.

"Fear not, my child," Aerioth laughed. "You knew your mother could not stay forever. Or were you unaware that she and I are not so different than you think? You see," Aerioth said, fingering the hem of her dress. "We were both cut from the same cloth."

Alexa's confusion turned to anger. "You are nothing like

my mother!"

Aerioth flew closer, but Alexa did not back away. "Your mother and I were as close as two fairies could possibly be." Aerioth's face grew serious. Alexa feared she was telling the truth.

"You know," Aerioth continued, "we have so little control over what happens to us in this life. But what amazes me is the power of that small amount of control we do have. Tiny decisions we make seem so unimportant, but, all together, they make us who we are. That is where the real magic lies."

"What do you know about real magic?" Alexa asked.

"Oh, you'll find I know a great deal, my sweet Alexa." The gentle tones in which Aerioth spoke were more frightening to Alexa than if the Oth had screamed. It was as though she could see both what people hated and loved most about themselves. Then she would flatter what they loved and torture them with what they hated. "Your mother and I started out exactly the same, yet my small decisions led me to power, while her small decisions led her to death."

"Leave me alone. Get out of my sight!" Alexa shouted.

To her surprise, Aerioth obeyed and turned away. As she did, the image of Alexa's mother appeared again on the same body.

Alexa fell to her knees. "Mother, what's going on?" she cried. "Please don't leave me again with that, that liar!" Ciriana looked down at Alexa with loving concern. Her hand reached out to her daughter, but never quite touched her.

"This time she tells the truth, Alexa. We grew up together in Kendlenook. I loved her deeply."

Alexa was now unsure whether she was listening to her

mother or another of Aerioth's lies. But the sight of her beloved mother broke her heart so completely that she was powerless to doubt any words the Cloud Fairy spoke.

"You and Aerioth were friends?" Alexa struggled with this idea.

"Back then, before she became an Oth, I called her by her true name: Aeria."

"Why didn't Grandmother keep her away from you?"

"Oh, my daughter. A mother cannot live her child's life. Besides, it was because of my mother that Aeria came into my life."

"Why is everything so confusing? Why must it be so hard?"

"Life tends to be much harder for those who have great gifts," said Ciriana.

"Mother, this journey is ripping out my heart piece by piece! I cannot succeed, but I cannot give up, either."

"Alexa, listen to me." Her mother paused to make sure she did. "What you feel is merely the pain of great transformation—a change of vast significance."

"What kind of change, Mother?"

"An Awakening. The becoming of what was once lost."

"But if this Awakening is so important, why use me? I can't even trust my own heart. Ispirianza didn't know I would bear the mark of the hourglass."

"Of course she knew." The words shocked Alexa to her bones. "Search your spirit, Alexa."

Alexa's eyes stung, but she would not blink for fear of her mother returning to the form of Aerioth. "What good will it do me to search my spirit if I can't trust what I find in it?"

Ciriana looked into her daughter's eyes and smiled. "If your heart is pure and untroubled, follow it. But if it is fractured and in turmoil, then change it. Questioning your own motives is a sign of maturity. This is a gift, not a curse. The Great Song will guide you to know the difference."

Alexa finally found the courage to say the words she had hidden from herself.

"I feel a powerful evil growing inside me, Mother. I fear I will become like Aerioth."

"Use that fear, daughter. Keep it close to you. It's as if each of us has two wild dogs fighting inside us—one of fear and greed, the other of faith and selfless love. They fight fiercely within you now."

"I know it. I can feel it," said Alexa. "But which will win?"

"That's simple. Whichever one you feed the most, Alexa."

Alexa let the words sink into her. She thought of the road ahead into Timefulness. She thought of Elsie and her Speaking Stone. She thought of the hundreds of chrysalises still unopened.

"What should I do next, Mother? Please guide me."

"My mother could not live my life, and I cannot live yours." Her voice grew in urgency. "Our time together will end soon. Listen closely. You have become more powerful. You have also become more dangerous. Greater power means the ability to do greater good or greater evil. The difference lies not in what you say—not even in what you do—but in what you desire. Weigh your emotions. Meditate and pray. Seek wise counsel. Know that my spirit stays with you always."

Ciriana turned away. Alexa reached out in vain to stop her. Aerioth again stood before Alexa.

"Always do what is best for you, my child," Aerioth said.

Alexa pulled back her hand. "Your nature is, at its heart, good. Doubt not your emotions."

"Mother, help me!" cried Alexa.

"Mother, help me!" mimicked Aerioth.

Alexa clenched her teeth. "Do not mock me. I have the strength of my mother in me."

"Oh, yes, the strength that got her killed?" Aerioth jabbed. "Like mother, like daughter."

A glint caught Alexa's eye. She looked down to see that Mara's golden sword had appeared under her own sash. The power of violence once again surged through Alexa's veins. She wrapped her fingers around the handle of the sword and felt its strength.

Without a word, Alexa drew the sword and raised it to strike Aerioth down. Aerioth stood still, tapping her fingers along the hilt of her sheathed dagger, daring Alexa to continue. As Alexa drew back the sword to strike, a wave of understanding stopped her.

She realized she couldn't risk striking the beauty of her mother, even to kill Aerioth. To keep the goodness of her mother alive, she had to let the evil of Aerioth live. She lowered the sword, and it disappeared. With a cruel laugh, Aerioth flew high into the chamber and snuffed out the candle that illuminated her. Darkness once again overtook the flickering light and covered the lone fairy.

"Alexa?" a voice from the rain shouted into the tree.

"Yes, Daria?" Alexa was surprised that she did not have to struggle to focus her thoughts.

"Mara's coming. And Arthur's not with her."

FORTY-THREE

Mara Meets Dagger

"What's our next move?" Mara asked. "Should we wait out this storm?" Alexa emerged into the rain with newfound energy. Daria commented on how rested she suddenly looked. Mara said her color was coming back.

"I think we should shelter for the night," Daria said. "If we start at dawn, we can reach Coldwater Camp by tomorrow evening."

"No," replied Alexa with authority. "No more delays. What do I need to enter Timefulness?"

"You know the answer to that: Margaret's locket and pixie silk," Daria said.

"And I have both of those things, right?"

"Yes."

"Then what are we waiting for?" Alexa said. "I say we fly as fast and as far as we've ever flown in a night and keep flying until we reach Kendlenook. We'll arrive by tomorrow afternoon. I'm tired of sitting around, waiting for Oths and bumbleflies to catch us."

"What's gotten into you?" Daria asked. Alexa didn't even bother telling Daria about the Ring Dream. She wouldn't have understood.

"I know what I have to do, so I'm going to do it. I'm going down that corridor, and I'm going to reverse the Scarring with Elsie's help."

"Sounds like a plan to me. Let's go!" Mara said. Annamelia flittered around in excitement. Alexa grabbed her satchel and sprang into the air, her Shadow Fairy following below. Mara and Daria looked at each other, shrugged, then scrambled to keep up.

Alexa flew as if a shark were chasing her, the driving rain needling into her eyes. Mara and Daria fell far behind.

"Alexa, hold up!" Daria shouted. But Alexa did not slow down.

They flew all through the night, stopping only to drink. The rain ceased just before sunrise. As the landscape brightened, Faewick Forest lay before them in the distance through a morning haze. Kendlenook was only hours away now. What used to be Alexa's entire world now seemed strangely small. As they traveled southward, Daria looked more and more serious. Alexa thought she even saw a tear on her sister's cheek.

"What's wrong?" asked Alexa. Daria glanced to the west, and Alexa followed her eyes. At the barren foothills of the Dragontooth Mountains, Alexa could make out dozens of small and isolated forms moving about on the exposed rock.

"What are those fairies doing over there?" asked Mara.

"That's the birthing grounds of Kendlenook," replied a solemn Daria. "That's why we're out here. If we fail, none of those chrysalises will ever hatch."

"Why are the fairies bendin' down like that?"

"The mothers are whispering to their daughters, of course," said Alexa.

"Why would they do that?" asked Mara.

Alexa looked at Mara inquisitively. "You know how fairy mothers whisper to their spritelings while they sleep, to inspire them to grow and become all they are meant to become? Mothers do that for us before we come out of our chrysalises, too."

Mara just stared at the distant figures in the vast landscape. "I don't think my mother ever whispered anything to me," she said. "I've never heard of a mother doing that."

"Really?" said Alexa, in shock. "I didn't think fairies could grow without the constant inspiration of their mothers—or at least grandmothers." At that moment, Alexa could clearly picture her own mother, sitting alone in the desolate birthing grounds, without food or water. Her tears offered life to the small chrysalis while she, Alexa's mother, was slowly dying. She wondered what words her mother had whispered to her. What had she intended that Alexa should become?

Thirteen years was Alexa's entire life so far, but somehow it didn't seem that long ago that Grandmother had left little Eva and Daria and gone to search for her beloved daughter, Ciriana, who should have already returned from the birthing grounds. Grandmother had warned her daughter not to try for a child in the year of the Great Drought. She was proven right.

Instead of bringing Ciriana back to Kendlenook, Grandmother arrived home with a tiny new granddaughter that she'd found struggling for life on the rocks next to Ciriana's lifeless form. Alexa had always tried to block this picture from her mind, but now the image was as vivid as if it were happening that very minute.

"Look, it's Jayna!" shouted Daria, pointing to the western sky. "That's a great sign!" Mara followed Daria's gaze and saw no fairy — just a dazzling burst of color that seemed to cut the Dragontooth Mountains in two.

"All I see is a double rainbow," said Mara.

"That's Jayna — the only Rainbow Fairy in all of Faewick. I've even talked to her," bragged Daria. "She's the most important of all the Cloud Fairies, and the only fairy gifted as the Fairy of Hope. Do you think she saw us?"

"Nah," said Mara. "She's a good thousand wingbeats away."

"It's still a good sign, though," Daria said. Indeed, all three fairies' spirits lifted as they passed the rainbow.

Now that they were so close to Kendlenook, Alexa made sure to stay hidden so no one would delay her. The familiar clatter of fairy wings and grasshoppers echoed through the forest. The three fairies flew from tree to tree to maintain their cover, but stayed clear of any dryad trees. She didn't want to stop to talk to anyone.

Alexa noticed that Mara looked nervous. "What's the matter?" she asked.

"There are so many fairies around Kendlenook. Crowds just don't agree with me," said Mara, glancing around her as if a swarm of mosquitoes were about to surround her.

Alexa couldn't believe that fearless Mara was actually afraid of something. But then she remembered what a solitary life Mara had led.

"Don't worry. All my friends from home will love you. Besides we aren't actually going into Kendlenook. If we did, we would have to spend so much time answering questions and explaining things that I'd never get to the human world in time to do any good. We'll just sneak around the edge."

"Look out!" yelled Mara as she drew her sword.

From high above, a magnificent peregrine falcon dove toward the fairies. Mara flew to meet it with her sword raised. The falcon flared its majestic wings and veered around her to land on the top branch of a dead pine tree.

Daria gave a cry of delight and flew up to the giant bird. She gently stroked its hooked beak as it nuzzled against her, its striped feathers rustling in the breeze. Mara stared in amazement.

"Mara, meet Dagger," Daria said. "He's the keenest-eyed falcon in Faewick and a friend of mine. So sheathe your sword and tell him you're sorry." Dagger tilted his head expectantly.

"I'm sorry…I…I've never seen a falcon and a fairy together before, at least not outside of mealtime," Mara stuttered. "They're fairy killers!"

"Not around here," Daria said. "Did you think Forest Fairies just sit around all day hugging trees? We keep balance among the woodland creatures and warn them about threats to their homes and families—like fires, for example."

"Just keep it away from me," Mara said.

Daria echoed Mara's previous boasts. "Out in the wilderness you might have been High Fairy, but you're in my territory now, and you'll do as I say."

Mara, still wary of the falcon, just nodded. "Still…a falcon with a name?" Mara asked. "That's just weird."

"Says she who named her sword," Daria laughed. "Let's get some news."

Daria spoke gently to Dagger in a language unknown to Alexa or Mara. She mostly clicked and whistled softly through her teeth. Dagger responded happily with a series of high screeches that echoed through the forest. Alexa and Mara had to cover their ears, but Daria listened intently.

"It seems word of your adventures has reached Kendlenook," Daria told Alexa. "Dagger says you're quite famous."

"Famous for what?" Alexa asked.

"Being brave and daring," answered Daria. "Boring stuff like that."

"They really like me?" asked Alexa.

"I didn't say that," Daria corrected. "Some are pretty upset, especially since Grandmother seems to have turned Kendlenook into a war zone. "

"What?" asked Alexa.

"Seems Eva knew she couldn't keep hiding the reason you were missing. She broke down and told Grandmother that you were on a quest to save Kendlenook. Grandmother, of course, guessed who was at the bottom of this. She went straight to Ispirianza and threatened to kill her if she didn't say where you were." At this point, Daria burst out laughing. "And do you know what Ispirianza did? She just looked Grandmother in the eye and said, 'No!'"

Alexa was so stunned she could only laugh nervously.

Daria continued to translate.

"So Grandmother stormed off to the council and got them to send all these search parties out to look for you. Then she tried to put Ispirianza on trial and have her imprisoned as criminally insane. Since Ispirianza's the most senior member of the council, aside from the High Fairy, no one knew what to do. The council split into two sides, and they've been fighting with each other ever since."

"All this because of me?" asked Alexa. "They don't know all about the quest, do they? Like about the humans?"

"No, that's why most fairies think you're stupid or dead."

"That's a relief."

"At least the Cobbletons are rooting for you," said Daria. "But all the Romorians think you're eagle meat."

"With everyone in Faewick lookin' for Alexa, it'll take forever to get past Kendlenook," Mara worried. "We'll be dodgin' fairies the whole way,"

"No problem," said Daria. Alexa smiled, knowing what her sister had in mind. Daria clacked some words to Dagger. He threw back his head and bounced on his perch amid rapid screeches. Daria beckoned to Mara.

"Oh, no," Mara said, backing up against the tree trunk. "You're not getting me to ride that thing."

"Oh, come on, Miss 'I'm-so-tough-'cause-I-have-a-sword,'" Daria said. "Don't be such an Arthur."

"He'll take us high above the trees, so nobody will see us," Alexa promised. "They'll just see the underside of a falcon. We'll be there in no time."

"Fairies on a falcon? It's just not natural," Mara sighed.

"Come on," said Daria, already on Dagger's back. "Hold

onto this set of feathers here. Alexa, you ride in back. Remember, keep your wings folded." Mara closed her eyes and grabbed a handful of feathers. With a couple of clicks from Daria, the bird whooshed its mighty wings, and they shot into the air high above the forest.

Mara screamed. The wind blew at them so strongly with every stroke of the falcon's powerful wings that the fairies could barely keep their grip on the feathers. The falcon felt like one big flexing, flapping muscle. Alexa and Daria just smiled and enjoyed the ride. Mara screamed again. Once they had reached a certain height, the falcon trimmed its wings and began to soar, circling ever higher on a thermal air current. Mara screamed again.

"Not too high," shouted Alexa. Daria clacked and whistled at Dagger. "We're not falcons — we can't breathe if the air gets too thin." Dagger leveled off, and Mara shot a thankful look at Alexa.

As they soared above the forest, Alexa peered over Dagger's shoulder and could see all of Kendlenook spread out below her. When she spotted the Great Oak glowing in the early morning sun, she thought longingly of Ispirianza. She would love to see her once more before diving into Timefulness, but she had no time to spare.

Alexa recognized a clearing next to a fast-flowing creek. "There," she yelled, pointing east. Daria passed on Alexa's directions to the falcon.

"Should we have some fun with Mara?" Daria asked Alexa.

"I don't see any fairies around here. Why not?" said Alexa.

"No!" shouted Mara with eyes bulging. "I don't want any fun! I'm fine, really." Alexa smiled and nodded at Daria.

Dagger the falcon gives the fairies a ride

"I just wanted to point out that you are riding the fastest animal in the known world," Daria yelled to Mara.

"No way," said Mara. "No bird can fly as fast as a sylph, or even a fairy bending time."

"Who said anything about flying?" Daria yelled. Alexa laughed.

"What do you mean?" asked Mara nervously.

"I mean you had better hold on!" Daria shouted.

"I am holding on!" Mara responded.

"Not tight enough!" yelled Alexa, who buried her head behind Mara's shoulders and tightened her grip on Dagger's feathers. Daria gave three quick clicks. Dagger banked sharply up and faded to the side.

Mara realized what was about to happen. "No, no, don't!" she begged.

The falcon suddenly nosed down, folded his wings tightly to his sides and dove straight for the ground. Alexa's stomach rose to her throat. All three fairies screamed at the top of their lungs as the wind howled past them. Faster and faster they fell. The ground rushed at them like it wanted to kill them. Mara's eyes grew larger as they whizzed past the tops of the trees, and Daria glanced over to revel in Mara's terror. At the last moment, Dagger flared his wings and swooped up so quickly that all the fairies' blood rushed to their feet. He stretched out his talons and landed softly on a tree stump. Immediately the world fell still and silent. Dagger casually ruffled his shoulder feathers.

Mara's face was as white as a Snow Fairy's. Alexa and Daria started laughing hysterically. Then Mara joined in.

"And I thought life in Kendlenook was boring!" said the

Fire Fairy.

Daria rubbed Dagger's head. The fairies climbed off the falcon's sleek back, so dizzy they could barely fly. They sat together on the stump to get their wits back. Annamelia danced around the moss that skirted the stump.

"Mara, let me show you something," Alexa said. She grabbed Mara's hand and flew her to the mossy maple tree where she'd hid the Speaking Stone. The stack of rocks with which she'd marked the tree still stood.

Alexa pushed away a curtain of ferns to reveal the hollow beneath the tree where she had stashed the phone. She shoved aside the mucky litter of dirt and damp leaves until she spotted the shiny purple smoothness of Elsie's phone. It had acquired a few stray leaves and a pile of mouse droppings, but otherwise looked safe and undamaged. Alexa breathed a sigh of relief.

An amazed Mara studied the weird and beautiful object from all sides. Practical Daria stood guard. "Wait until you see what it does," Alexa told Mara.

She stepped on the symbols in the order she remembered from before. The phone beeped in exactly the same way. Elsie answered. Mara gasped.

"Alexa, is that you? Please be you!" said Elsie's voice.

"Of course I'm me," Alexa said.

"Where have you been?" Elsie demanded. Mara just stared at the phone.

"Do you have any idea how long it takes to fly to Evernaught and back? That's all the way past the White Mountains, where the oldest trees live," said Alexa.

"Old trees? You mean up near Blackstone Peak?" said Elsie.

Waves of shock tingled over Alexa. The dryad had translated the mysterious whisper 'Uchaf Du Maen' as 'Highest Darkest Stone.' Could it be the same thing? "What is Blackstone Peak?" Alexa asked.

"Oh, it's an ancient burial ground up near the bristlecone pines," said Elsie. "Everyone says it's haunted. All the older kids dare each other to go there at night. We can check it out when you're here if you want—but not at night."

"No," said Alexa. "I don't want to go there." Her skin crawled.

"Is Daria with you?"

Alexa snapped back to the task at hand. "Yes, but she's watching for Oths."

"Are those anything like the flying sharks?"

"Worse. Hey, my friend Mara is here, too. Mara, say hello to Elsie."

"Um…hello," stammered Mara.

"Hi, Mara. Nice to meet you," said Elsie. "Okay, Alexa, what's the plan?"

"I have everything I need to come into your world. Can you come to the place where you lost your Speaking Stone—I mean 'phone'?"

"I can be there in a few minutes."

"Okay," said Alexa. "I can't wait to see you again!"

"I can't wait to see you for the first time," said Elsie.

"Stay on the phone. I'll tell you when I'm about to go through the portal. But first I need to get my pixie silk ready, so you might not hear from me for a few minutes." Alexa grabbed her satchel and took out the spool of pixie silk. "Can one of you hold the end while I unravel this?" Alexa asked.

No one answered.

"Come on," said Alexa. "I need help."

Still no answer. She looked up, but Mara was no longer behind her. Annoyed, Alexa parted the ferns and peeked out at the forest. She saw no one.

"Fine, I'll do it myself," Alexa muttered. Annamelia darted back and forth along the ground outside the tree trunk. The Shadow Fairy moved so quickly that Alexa had a hard time tethering the silk to her. Daria and Mara were still nowhere to be seen.

"Annamelia, please stay still," said Alexa, chasing after her shadow. The Shadow Fairy did not slow her frantic pacing.

"What's wrong?" Alexa asked her. The Shadow Fairy made a rapid series of signs. "Slow down, slow down. Oh, how I wish you could talk." She couldn't understand any of the gestures, but she felt Annamelia was trying to tell her something important. "What is it? Where's Daria?" The Shadow Fairy motioned to something behind Alexa.

Aerioth spoke.

FORTY-FOUR

War of the Wind

"Thank you ever so much for your help," said Aerioth. "I simply couldn't have found it without you."

The sound of Aerioth's voice whirled Alexa around as if by magic. A flood of panic shot through Alexa's back to her fingers and toes. Aerioth stood on top of a broken tree trunk, a warrior ready for battle. She held a glowing lumastone in one hand, even though plenty of sunlight filtered down through the trees.

On a twisted branch below Aerioth stood Daria, her wingtips held securely by the pale hands of another Oth in a terrifying mask. Daria struggled, but the Oth bent her wings back painfully. Daria couldn't speak because the Oth had tied a black sash around her mouth. Mara was nowhere to be seen.

"Pardon the intrusion, dear. Were you going somewhere?" Aerioth said with false sincerity. "We appreciate your leading us to the last portal. Now we can destroy it more...

permanently."

Alexa's breath left her as she realized the Oths knew about Timefulness. They must have been the ones who had destroyed the other entrances. But why? Didn't they also suffer from the Scarring?

Alexa glanced toward the hidden stone circle but quickly looked back at Aerioth so as not to reveal the portal's exact location. "What portal?" she said.

"You're so adorable I could just eat you," cooed Aerioth. "But here's a lesson about how to properly lie: Never dart your eyes back and forth like that. And never look toward the ground—it just screams of insincerity. Instead, look the other fairy straight in the eye to build trust in the mind of the listener."

Alexa kept her hands behind her back and tied the end of the pixie silk to the back of her sash. She might have a chance to fly for the portal and jump through. But if Aerioth then destroyed the portal, she wouldn't be able to return. And she couldn't just leave Daria in the hands of the Oths. Three young dryads heard the talking and stepped out of their trees to watch the argument like concerned neighbors. "Do you really think I'm just gonna show you where the portal is?" Alexa said. "Well, I won't. And you'll never find the exact place. It's too well hidden."

"My dear child," Aerioth said, every part of her face smiling except her eyes. "What makes you think I need to know exactly where it is to destroy it?"

Aerioth raised the glowing orb above her head, and a bright red light burst forth from it. A shadow moved across the forest. Above the Oth's head, dark clouds formed, swirling into a haunting vortex that covered the sky. The forest's calm breeze whipped into a wind so strong that Alexa's bronze hair snapped back and tangled.

Dead leaves and dust swarmed and danced in the violent wind. Alexa pushed the hair from her eyes and looked to the dark spinning clouds. A giant, light blue mass circled over the forest. Around the circling blob flew two black forms, dancing complicated arm movements with long, black signaling silks flowing behind them.

Through eyes squinted almost shut, Alexa saw several sylphs whip past — or at least she thought she did. Then another sylph appeared, and another and another, until a whole gathering filled the hillside, flying together in flowing patterns. Alexa's blood ran cold. The blue mass was a sylph gathering, herded by two former Lake Fairies who had turned Oth.

Sylphs would never hurt or kill anyone of their own free will, but they would follow the directions of any skilled fairy with the proper homing charm. The wind grew stronger and stronger. The three dryads flew for cover as their young trees bent in the wind. A funnel cloud formed overhead. The moss, sticks and leaves covering the stone circle blew away and exposed the portal. The carved stone pieces started to shake loose from each other. Alexa heard a voice coming from the Speaking Stone.

"Alexa! What's going on?" Elsie shouted over the phone. "It's getting windy like a tornado, but we don't have tornadoes here!"

"Take cover, Elsie!" Alexa screamed and flew as hard as she could to the portal entrance.

Aerioth summons a storm

A wall of dust and dry leaves slammed her back. Alexa concentrated and began to bend time. The leaves and dust started to slow, but not nearly enough for her to reach the portal. She clung to a tree branch to keep from being blown away. She could do nothing to stop Aerioth, so she just held on. Then Alexa saw Aerioth moving toward her. The Oth somehow had more than enough strength to walk against the wind unaided.

Aerioth arrived at Alexa's side and looked down at her. "Oh, little Meadow Fairy," she called through the wind, "what would your mother say if she could see you now? Maybe she would admit that my way turned out to be the best way. The only way." Aerioth smiled, but her eyes stayed hard. "Everyone loved your mother. All of Kendlenook cried when she died protecting your chrysalis. Do you think you were worth her sacrifice? I'm sure they don't."

Aerioth whipped the dagger out of her sash and sliced through the air. A single sylph lay impaled on the tip of the knife, killed instantly. Its tiny homing charm flickered and then went out.

Aerioth flipped the dead sylph off the dagger and onto the ground, then she turned the weapon toward Alexa.

Suddenly Alexa saw a flash of red and Aerioth spinning around to meet it.

Mara pulled up sharply to face Aerioth, her eyes blazing with fire and her hands grasping the golden sword. Aerioth laughed as Mara lunged at her throat. The Oth easily pushed Mara back.

Mara swung her sword again, but Aerioth grabbed her arm, broke her grip on the sword and sent it flying into the wind. Alexa knew she had to help somehow.

But suddenly, large rocks began flying through the air. Mara, Alexa and even Aerioth ducked into sheltered spots. Alexa peered up the hill and saw two sections of carved stone break away from the archway that led to the Glass Corridor. The pieces tumbled down the hill toward her. She crouched behind a tree and held on tightly.

The Glass Corridor entrance—the last portal to Timefulness—had broken.

FORTY-FIVE

The Truth

Alexa eyed Aerioth with hatred. But instead of victory in Aerioth's eyes, Alexa saw frustration. Aerioth shrieked at the sky in anger. Breath by breath, the wind died down. From the west, another massive swarm of sylphs began to circle in the opposite direction of the Oth storm. The counter-spinning slowed the wind and shrank the tornado's funnel cloud into nothingness. Urged on by their herders, the two sylph gatherings battled for control of the wind. A mighty war now raged in the stormy sky.

Alexa watched the new sylph herd that swooped ever lower as the storm died down. She caught a glimpse of a shiny blue fairy herding the new sylphs with her red homing charm and colorful signaling silks twirling behind her. As the sylph herder swooped lower, Alexa couldn't believe her eyes—Eva!

Eva danced and spun so expertly that even two Oth herders couldn't handle the wind she created. But how? How could she have known?

The confused wind swirled and struggled as the competing sylph gatherings fought for control of the weather. The two Oth sylph herders frantically waved their flowing black signaling silks to keep their storm raging, but Eva's gathering proved too skillful.

Eva guided the sylphs in such a way as to isolate the two Oth herders and blow them head first into the creek. As the drenched Oths swam for the shore, Eva swooped down like a hawk, snatched the Oths' charms from around their necks and put them on herself. Almost instantly the two sylph herds joined into one massive gathering that followed only Eva's instructions. Alexa squealed with delight.

The young dryads popped their heads out of their trees.

Aerioth screamed in frustration and took flight. But she got less than a tree's height away before the three young dryads pulled her down. Young dryads are as strong and flexible as their trees, and these sisters couldn't have been more than twenty years old. Two held Aerioth's arms and the other pinned her wings together. They flew their prisoner before Alexa.

"We deliver the fate of this destroyer into your hands, Bright One," the dryads said as they held Aerioth. Eva swooped down out of the sky. Alexa flew up to Eva and wrapped her arms around her sister's neck.

"I think we have everything under control now," Eva said.

"Eva! How did you know to come?"

Eva explained, "That crazy Arthur showed up, babbling about Oths setting a trap for you—and sylph herds and lockets and traitors."

Chapter 45

"And you believed him?" asked Alexa.

"I didn't know what to believe," said Eva. "So I took him to the only Fairy of Truth I know."

"The High Fairy!" Alexa gasped. "You took Arthur to the High Fairy?"

"I sure did."

"And?" asked Alexa.

"The High Fairy believed every word of it," said Eva. "She called up a sylph herd for me, but said that, to engage in a sylph battle, I would need a special caller who could think for itself. Sorry, himself. I said that the only sylph I know who could think for himself was hovering in front of her."

Eva glanced up to the sky. Descending toward the fairies was a smiling Arthur, wearing a red homing charm.

"You made Arthur the head caller?" Alexa couldn't believe her eyes.

"The High Fairy herself gave Arthur his new homing charm," said Eva.

"Yeah," said Arthur. "She's r-r-really nice."

"It looks very handsome on you, Arthur," Alexa said. The little sylph straightened his shoulders and puffed out his chest.

"As soon as we saw the storm clouds come in from nowhere, I knew exactly where to go," said Eva.

"Did you see? Did you s-see, Alexa? Creating a counter-wind was m-my idea!" Arthur said, flying in circles.

"I saw," Alexa beamed. "That was brilliant! You saved me, Arthur."

"It was n-nothing really, said Arthur, trying to hide a prideful grin.

In all the excitement, Alexa had almost forgotten someone, but now she remembered with a jolt.

"Where's Daria?" she said in a panic. No one had seen Daria or the Oth holding her since the winds started. Arthur spotted a pile of leaves and pine needles stirring on the forest floor. An arm reached out and pushed through the pile. A bright orange dress emerged behind it—the dress of a Fire Fairy.

A disheveled and swordless Mara approached Alexa, with her head hung low and tears falling from her eyes. She knelt before Alexa and said, "I'm sorry. I let you down."

"Don't be ridiculous, Mara," said Alexa, truly astonished. "You fought with great courage. I'm proud to call you my friend. Do you know why the Oths want to destroy the Glass Corridor entrance so much?"

"They don't want any fairies going into Timefulness and meeting humans," Mara explained. "For many years, the High Oth has sought power over all of the Fae. If fairies were to go into Timefulness, they would find out—"

"Quiet!" screamed Aerioth, still held firmly by the dryads.

Just then an Oth appeared from behind the hollow trunk on which Alexa had last seen Daria. Her mouth was gagged and her wings tied with the same Oth sash that had bound Daria before the storm. Following her out of the log was a stern Daria, with a scary Oth mask stuck in her sash. She shoved the Oth to the ground.

"Daria, you're okay!" cried Alexa and Eva.

Daria didn't answer. She wasn't even smiling. In fact, she had a look of angry determination in her eyes. Without a word to her relieved sisters, Daria broke a heavy branch from the dead tree, walked straight to Mara, kicked her to the ground and swung the wooden weapon at her. With two crushing blows, Daria broke both of Mara's wings. Mara shrieked in pain and begged Daria to stop. The way the Fire Fairy's wings lay limp and crumpled, Alexa doubted that Mara would ever fly again.

"Daria, have you gone mad!" shouted Alexa. Eva screamed in disbelief. Instead of replying, Daria grabbed the shrieking and sobbing Mara by her hair and dragged her toward the creek. "Stop! What have you done? Mara is our friend!"

"Mara is no friend," Daria said in fury. She turned to the terrified Fire Fairy. "Or should I call you Maroth?"

"No, Daria!" Alexa said. "You're crazy!"

"Think about it, Alexa," said Daria. "A fairy younger than you manages to fight off the most powerful Oth?"

"I helped," Alexa pointed out.

"Uh huh. Then she insists on joining you. And suddenly the Oths know your every move, showing up everywhere you go. Why do you think she took so long to gather food each day? Why did she always want to travel at night, avoiding the sunlight? Why didn't the Scarring destroy her? How do you think she knew her way around Evernaught so well?"

"Those things don't make her an Oth!" Alexa insisted.

"Maybe not, but having an Oth for a mother does," said Daria. She shoved a distraught Mara's head into the cold running water of the creek. The orange-red color of Mara's hair began to run onto her arms and dress, revealing jet-black hair underneath. The golden color washed away from her black fingernails. The healthy glow in her skin paled. The image of Alexa's new best friend washed down the river, revealing a total stranger.

FORTY-SIX

Like Mother, Like Daughter

lexa stared at Mara in disbelief. Mara stared at the ground, breathing hard. She wouldn't look at Alexa.

The pain behind Alexa's eyes mounted as she accepted the truth. She felt as if her heart had been ripped out of her chest.

"How did you know?" Alexa asked Daria in a raspy whisper.

"The Oths who captured me were talking about what a great job this 'Maroth' had done, getting you to trust her enough to lead her to the Glass Corridor. 'Her mother must be proud,' they said."

Two tears made their way down Alexa's cheeks. She looked toward the sky and swayed as though about to faint. She spoke quietly now. "What is that you said about her mother, Daria?" she asked. Alexa heard the familiar laugh of Aerioth coming from behind her.

"You did well, my daughter," the captured Aerioth said to Mara. "All the way up to your last attack on me. Even I started to believe your act." Alexa closed her eyes, her face still skyward. The tears that had welled up in her lower eyelids grew into a stream. Aerioth continued, "You have, however, failed to release me from these leafheads here."

The weight of her friend's betrayal crushed Alexa's spirit. So many questions crowded her already confused mind. She grasped for some kind of hope. She opened her mouth and forced words out.

"But Mara's not even old enough to be a full Oth," Alexa said. "Ispirianza told me that a young Oth has to complete a test of deception to become fully darkened."

Aerioth's voice crackled with delight. "My dear Alexa, that's the beauty of it all. You were her test." The words burned Alexa like fire. "I haven't quite decided whether she passed or not, though."

Mara looked into Alexa's eyes and watched her heart break through them. Alexa crumpled to her knees, numb to all feeling. Mara began to bawl. Alexa just stared at the one who, a moment ago, she had thought of as her best friend. Grief slowly replaced her numbness. No one had told Alexa that grief felt so much like fear.

"Well, Maroth," Alexa said, her voice cracking. "Congratulations." At those words, Maroth threw herself at Alexa's feet, sobbing and broken. Alexa could not even look down at her.

"You could have made this less complicated," Alexa said. "Why go with me into the Oth cave and pretend to be chased? Why not just give me the candledark?"

Chapter 46

Aerioth interrupted. "If she had done that, my dear, would you have really trusted her enough to tell her your entire plan and show her the portal?"

"Alexa, please understand," Maroth sobbed. "It started out as a test of deception, but I learned a better way of life because of you. I learned what friendship and family should mean. I've never had friends. I've never had sisters. I want to turn away from the life of an Oth. I throw myself at your mercy."

"Enough, my daughter," Aerioth said to Maroth. "No need to continue your convincing little act. You've passed the test. You're a full Oth now."

"No, Mother. I have long since abandoned my test." She turned to Alexa. "I am truly your friend. I swear it, Alexa. Please forgive me."

Arthur and Eva looked to Alexa. Even the dryads were moved. Alexa wearily rose to her feet and turned away from Maroth. She walked up to a weeping Arthur.

In a low and gentle voice she said to the sylph, "Arthur, I'm sorry for not trusting you. I was wrong to send you away. If you have any feeling for me left in you at all, I would like you to do something for me."

"Anything, Alexa. You're the one who gave m-m-me a reason to live."

"Thank you, my friend." Alexa looked back at Maroth. "I want you to take your sylph herd and carry this flightless Oth to the Desolate Islands to live in exile for the rest of her life." Gasps arose from the other fairies.

"But, Alexa," Arthur said. "She can't fly. You could be s-s-sending her to her death."

"She would send all the fairies of Kendlenook to their

deaths," Alexa said.

"Alexa," Eva interrupted. "Listen to yourself. Maroth has asked for forgiveness. Such a thing has never happened before. It is your duty as a compassionate fairy to forgive all who ask."

"My duty is to the fairies of Kendlenook," Alexa said.

"She seems truly sorry," Eva insisted.

"Lies, lies, lies!" shouted an enraged Alexa. "She created a world of lies for me to live in, and I fell for it all. Now she will say anything to escape exile."

"Even if she's still lying, you need to forgive her," Eva said. "If not for her, for your own heart. You'll be no better than the Oths if you live in such bitterness. Ispirianza says the only thing that could turn an Oth back into a fairy is the power of forgiveness. You now have this power. If she's lying, she'll remain an Oth—there's nothing to lose but your own hatred."

"Eva," Alexa said, looking her in the eyes. "Even if I should forgive her, I cannot. And even if I could," she looked back at Maroth's pain-filled eyes, "I will not!"

"Alexa, think of what you are saying," Eva cried. She turned to Daria, who had stayed silent the entire time. "Daria, help me."

"You weren't there, Eva," said Daria, in complete control of her emotions. "She deceived me just as completely as Alexa. She's a skilled Oth now. I can't find the strength to forgive her, either."

"Alexa, please listen," Maroth said. "I wanted—

"Quiet, Oth!" Alexa cried. "I shared secrets with you! I told you everything about myself. You were my best friend! And you just turned around and repeated everything to my worst enemies. You would have let them kill me, too."

"No!" Maroth sat up straight. "You don't understand. Partway through the journey—I don't know exactly when—I changed. All my life, I've lived with Oths and heard about what weak and shallow creatures fairies are, but you're not like that at all. More than anything else, I want to live in your world instead of mine. You have no idea what it's like at Evernaught—no one ever does anything for anyone else. Just to survive, you have to watch your back every second. I didn't know there was a better way to live until you taught me, Alexa."

"Enough," said Alexa. She turned to Arthur. "Maroth took you away when I asked her to, even though she knew you told the truth. I'm asking you to take her now." Arthur gulped hard and tapped his homing charm. The massive sylph herd swooped in from above the trees and lifted Maroth off the ground with the wind it created. Eva did nothing to stop the herd, leaving the decision to Alexa. The mournful sounds of Maroth's crying died in the distance. Alexa wept.

"That was a brave and noble thing you just did, young one," Aerioth said. "You have more spirit than I thought. I'm very proud of you." The dryads tightened their grip on her arms.

"You praise me for what I've done to your own daughter? I've never known such a monster." Alexa's cheeks were still wet with tears. She strode up to Aerioth and studied her face. She then reached down and took the crooked dagger from Aerioth's sash and raised it to the sky. A faint look of fear entered Aerioth's eyes. "Except myself," Alexa said. Eva gasped.

Alexa grabbed a lock of her own hair and sliced it off. Then another and another. Clumps of bronze hair drifted to the ground. Eva cried at the sight of Alexa mourning the loss of a friend who never was. In the breeze, the shiny strands of hair danced along the mud and then blew away. Alexa sheathed Aerioth's dagger in her own tattered pink sash and looked again to the Oth. She turned her hot anger into cold anger so she could use it and not be consumed by it.

"Thank you, Aerioth," Alexa said. "You have taught me to hide my fear and push away my pain. I need that more than ever now." Aerioth said nothing. At that moment Alexa realized that if you want to learn about yourself, the best teacher is your enemy. "It seems your fate now rests in my power as well." To Alexa's surprise, Aerioth just smiled.

"Oh, dear child," she sang. "A little Meadow Fairy like you could never have power over someone like me. I merely stayed to see the look on your face when you found out about my daughter." Aerioth let out a long screech.

At once, six sticks of candledark fell from the trees and bounced on the ground, covering the earth in a haze of darkness. Then two masked Oths dove down from high in the canopy with a deafening shriek. The fairies on the ground ducked and covered their ears. The two Oths snatched Aerioth from the hands of the surprised dryads and flew her away in a black cloud of candledark.

Alexa didn't even watch as Aerioth disappeared. She didn't really care anymore. She wondered if she would ever be able to trust anyone again. The lack of forgiveness in her heart terrified her, but she couldn't deny it. Deep down, she feared that she herself might make a wonderful Oth.

But all Alexa could do now was help the others as they tried to repair the portal for her to continue on to Timefulness. If she could succeed there — even though she might lose herself to the darkness — at least she could give the fairies the gift of their daughters.

As Eva threw the sticks of candledark into the river, Alexa quietly began to prepare her pixie silk once more. Annamelia floated on nearby fern leaves. Daria and the dryads combed the forest floor for the pieces of stone blown from the ring. They called to one another as they found each piece and hauled them up to the portal. Alexa washed in the creek and changed into a brand-new dress that Eva had brought for her. A spare dress in a new satchel waited on the creek's shore.

Daria fitted the last piece in to complete the stone ring once again. "All fixed," she said, trying to encourage Alexa. "Now get down there and reverse that Scarring so I can get my sister back. Then we'll throw you the biggest party —"

"Daria, stop it. Can't you see what's happening?"

"What do you mean?"

"I've already prepared myself for the fact that I may never return," said Alexa. "Mother sacrificed herself for me, and I feel I may need to do the same for the daughters of Kendlenook. When Ispirianza's Ring Dream predicted the death of someone on my journey, she may have been preparing me for my own fate."

On hearing this, even tough Daria began to tear up. Eva's cheeks already glistened with tears.

"You stop it," Eva told Alexa through her sobbing. "You will return in less than two weeks. That's how long you have. My youngest sister always does what she sets out to do. She's the most capable fairy I know."

Alexa had always wanted Eva to be proud of her. She wanted the compliment to make her feel better. It didn't.

A hush grew over the forest. The wind ceased even to whisper. The three sisters looked up to see the three dryads on their knees. Indeed the trees themselves were all bending in the same direction. When they looked toward the west, they saw the High Fairy herself approaching with two regal fairies at each side. Her hair looked like Alexa's, cut short from when she had mourned those lost to the Scarring.

The three sisters lowered their wings and bowed their heads. The scent of rosemary filled the air. Alexa felt a fresh magic flow through her in the High Fairy's presence.

"Alexa of the Meadow," the High Fairy spoke. "Rise." Alexa relaxed her wings but kept her head down, not feeling worthy to look at Her Majesty. "Show your face, young one." Alexa lifted her head.

"I have heard many amazing things from a little friend of yours. I have also consulted with Ispirianza, wisest of all dryads after Zymandria herself. You have accepted a heavy burden upon your shoulders.

"As a Fairy of Truth and the revealer of the gifts of the Fae, I hereby announce your calling. You, just as your mother before you, shall be a Fairy of Inspiration." The High Fairy reached out and touched the top of Alexa's head.

Daria and Eva looked at each other and smiled with their heads still bowed. Alexa's heart swelled with emotion. She felt her mother's spirit near and remembered her words, "If you would do what I tell you, then I will tell you not to fear."

"Thank you, Your Majesty," Alexa said. "I will try my best

to live up to your faith in me."

Just then the Speaking Stone rang.

The High Fairy looked in amazement at the vibrating and blinking purple object.

Alexa smiled meekly at her. "I kind of need to take care of that," she said, before jumping on the green button.

"Hello, Elsie," Alexa said.

"Oh, Alexa, thank God. I was sure that wild tornado blew you away. Are you okay?"

"I'm fine, and ready to finally meet you," said an excited Alexa. The High Fairy looked on in wonder.

"Is that the voice of…is that what I think it is?" she gasped.

"Yes, Your Majesty. That's a human."

"Well, I never!"

"I'm ready," Alexa said to Elsie. "I have my locket, the pixie silk and my Shadow Fairy. Wait there just another few minutes."

"I will," said Elsie's voice. The High Fairy walked up to Alexa and whispered something into her ear. She whispered so quietly that no one else could possibly hear.

"I will remember," replied Alexa.

She carefully stowed Margaret's locket in her new satchel and tested the pixie silk's attachment to both her sash and Annamelia's. They flew together to the stone circle. Alexa looked through it and saw only dirt. Then she reached her hand through the circle. The dirt vanished.

Every imaginable color glittered and spun together into the most dazzling patterns Alexa had ever seen. The light curved around to create the walls of a long, braided tunnel. Eva, Daria, the three dryads and the High Fairy herself all gasped at its beauty. The Glass Corridor had opened.

"Stay safe," Eva said. "We will guard the portal so that you can return."

"I wish I could go with you," said Daria.

"I'll have Elsie," Alexa assured Daria. "She's a giant, you know."

Daria took a deep breath and slapped Alexa on the back. "Say hello to the humans for me."

Alexa threw herself into her sisters' arms. Now everyone was crying. Alexa wiped her eyes on Daria's dress, gave each sister one more hug and backed up toward the swirling depths of the Glass Corridor. Alexa turned to Annamelia and slowly reached down to touch her outstretched hand.

"Thank you for sacrificing so much for me," Alexa said. "Thank you for keeping me connected to my home. I will soon set you free once more." Annamelia nodded gently.

"Blessings on you, child," the High Fairy said. "Move with the Great Song."

"I'm coming, Elsie," Alexa called. "Hold on, little daughter fairies," she thought. "I'll be right back." She closed her eyes, leaned backward and fell.

FORTY-SEVEN

Descent into Timefulness

When Alexa next opened her eyes, she was floating in a glistening light. Her spirit felt as free as a falcon as she flew without even flapping her wings. In a few moments, her movement slowed, and the light dimmed. Alexa felt time itself slowing. Before her in the tunnel lay a formless void. The darkness sucked all joy from Alexa as it engulfed her.

As she sank deeper into despair, she felt as if time had stopped and she would remain forever in that state of emptiness, without light, sound or movement. She began to lose all sense of herself. Finally, distant voices began to fill the void. She heard Eva, Daria, Grandmother, Ispirianza—and even Kandra.

These voices soon joined into one voice, echoing through the darkness. Alexa recognized it as Elsie's. Alexa felt her wings and dress flutter. She was being pulled by an unseen force. Her spirits lifted as she moved toward a distant light. Colors began to swirl again. She picked up speed. The light and movement became haunting, beautiful music.

As the brightness surrounded her, Alexa started to make out forms that looked like the trees and moss of Faewick Forest. She saw a barrier of what looked like bubbling water between her and the forest. Almost at once she broke through and passed through another stone circle. She collapsed onto the mossy earth.

In the forest waited the gigantic and friendly face Alexa had seen once before on that fateful day. The enormous girl had a look of enraptured wonder in her eyes. Wow. She was a lot bigger than Alexa remembered.

Elsie's hand reached out to the tiny Alexa. The sight of the giant's hand closing in on her made Alexa's heart beat harder. For a second, she thought of jumping back into the corridor from which she'd just emerged. Instead, Alexa squeezed her eyes shut and felt Elsie's gentle hands scoop her off the ground and lift her up and up and up.

Alexa opened her eyes and gulped as she gazed into Elsie's enormous eyes. The Meadow Fairy drew in a deep breath and smiled at her new friend and protector. She tried to speak, but words escaped her. Finally Alexa forced out a broken sentence:

"Hello, Elsie. I'm Alexa of the Meadow. Pleased to finally meet you."

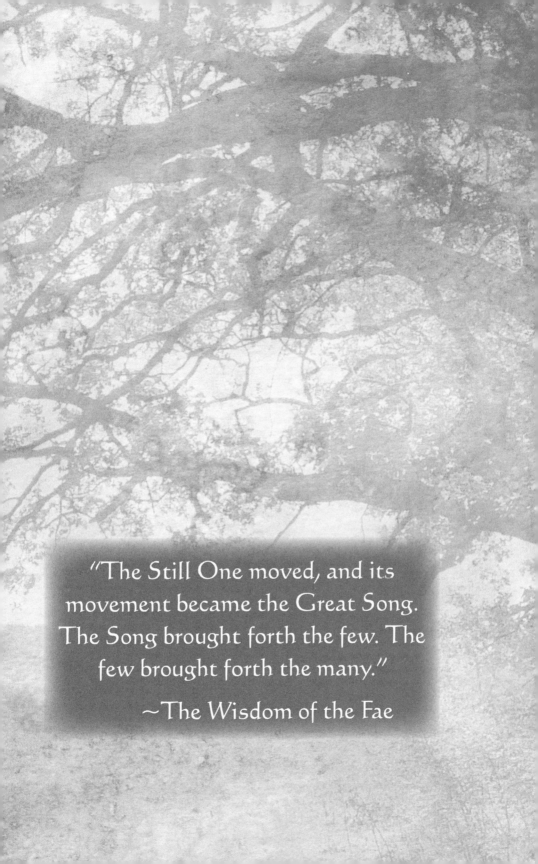

"The Still One moved, and its movement became the Great Song. The Song brought forth the few. The few brought forth the many."

~The Wisdom of the Fae

~ Acknowledgments ~

We would like to thank Brant Miller, Kimberly Hauser, Elsie Hauser, Andrea Zabel, Bill & Martha Forti, Ariel Abdallah, Meredith Dodds, Mel & Shirley Durocher and Mrs. Barnhart's junior high students at Western Christian School for giving such helpful input on drafts of this book.

Thank you to Blake English for his expert advice on aerodynamics and various other plot issues.

We are grateful to our editors, Susan Wampler and Stan Wedeking, for helping us polish and refine our story.

Finally, a special thanks to Scottish storyteller Alastair McIver for allowing us to adapt his story "Witch's Wood" for the festival scene.